AIYVEN MBAWA

Land of The Nurogons

The Zest for Quest

Printed and bound in Great Britain by Book Empire, 7, Lotherton Way, Garforth, Leeds, LS25 2JY

First edition

ISBN: 978-0-244-50220-1

Editing by James Taylor-Loftus

Proofreading by James Taylor-Loftus

Cover art by Goran J Tomic

Illustration by Olena Vecchia Pittura

Dedication

To Grandpa Tatani, for passing on this love for reading, and Kirsten, my sister, who experienced this journey with me.

Acknowledgements

Writing a book is not what I expected it to be – I'm not going to lie to you. There were moments when I felt that all was lost and I couldn't change a thing because it was too late; those were the worst moments. Soon enough I realised there was no point going about matters like I couldn't change anything and recover – that was an absolute lie. It's an experience that seemed toxic at the time, but I am now able to look back and smile.

I must start by thanking my parents for helping me persist with this project, even when my will and confidence were flagging. From sense-checking my manuscript and asking difficult questions, typesetting for sample printing, and finding the right materials and people to help publish my book, there was no chance that I could have achieved success without the support of my parents and many others.

To Kaitlyn, I thank you for being a good and feisty little sister and for coping with all the fuss about my book!

To Nana Juju, for encouraging me and my sister Kirsten to enter the BBC 500 Words competition, thereby getting the ideas for mine and Kirsten's books started. When we entered the writing contest, we didn't expect such an outcome. Although we did not ultimately receive the favourable reply we wanted, we remain eternally grateful.

My wider family helped tremendously. Grandparents, aunties, uncles, cousins and friends, were amazing in their prayers and support of my dream to publish my debut novel — especially during the Kickstarter campaign. I was overwhelmed by the amount of support, so thank you once again. To all backers and supporters of the Kickstarter campaign, I express heartfelt gratitude. That you had so much belief in me and Kirsten that you backed us and shared the word about our campaign is very humbling. Now our books are in print and it's all down to you. THANK YOU! THANK YOU! God bless you.

My book and Kirsten's *Sagas of Anya* would probably still be incomplete if it hadn't been for

v

James Taylor-Loftus our editor (Taylor-Loftus Publishing), Olena Vecchia Pittura our illustrator,

and Goran J Tomic, our cover designer. Kirsten and I would like to thank all three of you — James, for having to read and reread our manuscripts many times without complaint, and Olena and Goran, for implementing our illustration and cover design ideas so quickly and perfectly.

It would be absurd of me to imagine an interest in writing if my teachers had not been there to support me. All of those times where I got extra credits for my writing work — or when a teacher laughed loudly at what I had written — encouraged me more and more. I especially thank my Class 3 fellow-students; although highly embarrassing, it was wonderful to see you all so happy about my book. I must say, calling me 'famous' produced some uncontrollable antics as a 'bad' side effect.

Brooke, especially, needs a mention, for being the first actual reader (apart from my family) of my manuscript. Thank you for also handling the task of juggling two books at once, and managing to finish mine before the other in an incredibly short space of time!

The publication journey of this book coincided with the outbreak of the COVID-19 pandemic. I give special thanks and acknowledgement to all health workers who have selflessly put themselves and their families on the line by tirelessly caring for those with the Corona Virus. Special thanks also go to all essential workers who have kept life ticking over in so many different ways.

Finally, I cannot finish this acknowledgements section without giving God a mention. If you read back through what I have written above, you might well see the blessings and hand of God at work.

Contents

One

Is There Anything More to Expect?

Wake up, Smiths!' Mum yelled, ringing *"The Bell"*. It was *so* annoying. Every morning she'd get the famous bell Gramps had given her some years back and shake it like mad till we all woke up. It was slightly corroded as *"The Bell"* dated back centuries. Gramps had got it from *his* grandad. It had a wooden handle, newly polished so as not to give the holder splinters. However, as much as we tried, Mum wouldn't allow us polish the bell's body. She said it was a symbol of how long it had sustained.

Gramps told us *"The Bell"* had come from the times where there were maids in every house worthy of note, and the master or mistress used some sort of bell to summon them. Apparently, our bell was one of the few that remained. Mum kept it in a secret place, so I wouldn't be able to tell you or "lose" it. No one apart from her knows where the sacred bell is hidden. Not even Dad. I could hear Canada groan all the way from her room opposite mine. Mum shunned my sister and carried on ringing the bell.

I opened my bedroom door to see Dad walk out of his and Mum's room, stretching with an indignant look on his face wearing the tight pyjamas that he'd got seven Christmases ago.

'Dear, I do understand that you want us to be a — how should I say it — a *morning* family, but that. bell needs to go. There's a car boot next Saturday and I'm doing a load of...'

Mum stared at Dad, and he knew not to say anything else. 'This bell is staying no matter how much it pesters you. Canada's been having fewer detentions because of this bell. She used to wake up at blooming half eight!'

I raised my hand, and Mum nodded. She'd created all these bothersome actions for the mornings, raising our hands to ask to shower first, waving if we wanted someone else to shower, blah blah blah.

'Good boy, Hayden,' Mum stated, 'Let's try to be more like Hayden, eh?' She shot Dad a look, and Dad shrugged as if saying *"fair enough."*

I changed into my uniform and ran downstairs just as Mum finished making breakfast: pancakes with extra Cool Whip whipped cream and strawberries.

'Why such a fancy breakfast?' I asked, putting a fiver in my backpack for school lunch.

'What, you don't like it?' Mum asked. She was carrying four plates at once, some on her arm as well. My Mum used to be a waitress, a fabulous one who worked at a two-star Michelin restaurant. Everyone would give her tips, and because everyone who came was rich and posh, she ended up having at least £150 in the tip jar. Unfortunately, seventy per cent of it went to the managers.

'No, no, I love the way you've set it out and everything, but we only ever have pancakes at weekends. You did mention about the keep-fit program you do at school. Didn't you say you wanted to do it at home as well?'

She was a PE teacher at a primary school fifteen minutes away from our house. She'd asked the headteacher of the school to let her set up a health club. Every Wednesday, Mum would do stretches and all sorts of exercises out on the field, like an extra P.E. lesson.

Mum smiled. I knew that smile, and I didn't like it. It was the *"you'll-love-this"* smile, and then I always end up hating it.

'Let's wait till Canada and your father are done,' she explained, leaving me hollow and suspicious.

Finally, after half an hour or so, everyone in the Smith household was ready. We were tucking into our pancakes, enjoying every nanosecond, when Mum winked at Dad and cleared her throat rather pointedly.

Canada looked up from the pancake she was holding like a hungry dog. 'You guys...'

Dad grinned from ear to ear. 'We have some important news.'

Canada frowned, 'Well, spit it out, then!' She took a huge bite out of her near-done pancake.

'We've made a decision,' Dad started. 'This is our last meal as omnivores!'

Canada spat out her chewed-up pancake in shock. Me, being the most civilised child, didn't do anything but choke on my food.

My sister passed me a half-drunk glass of orange juice and I gulped the rest of it down.

4

'Ha-ha, we're not dinosaurs, Dad!' I chuckled after searching for any drops left of my drink.

Canada followed with an uneasy, slow laugh as well. 'Ha, ha, ha?' The last 'ha' sounded more like a *"you're not joking, are you?"* sort of ha, not a *"very funny"* sort of ha.

Mum swallowed her food and stared at Dad for a second. 'You don't get it. We're vegans after this meal.'

Canada took another slow bite of her pancake. Luckily, she didn't spit it out this time, but she did react quickly. 'What, you think we're fat? That's a cruel message to pass on to your own children!'

'Aw, dear.' Mum laid her hand on Canada's. 'It's hard to take in once you've first been told. I was the same when...'

Canada slipped her hand away from Mum's and shook it as if it were covered top to bottom with germs. 'When have *you* been vegan? You lived on a farm so you must've eaten pig for breakfast! Leave me alone, I'm not listening! I think the same goes for Hayden.' And with that, she stormed to her room.

Dad sighed and cut up more pancake. 'She's a teenager. Don't worry, Hayden, it'll be your time soon.'

'For what?'

5

'Teenage phases,' Dad dramatically explained. 'They're horrible. Especially for us parents. Canada gets stressed about an untied shoelace, Hayden. It'll be the same for you someday.'

Standing up from my seat, I said, 'I think I'm already having them.'

'Explain,' Mum implored, without looking up from her watch.

'Football's driving me crazy. Coach keeps on putting me as a defender, but I'm awesome as a striker!'

I imitated a move I'd seen from Cristiano Ronaldo and ended up bashing the bin.

'I know, I'll have to speak to your coach.' Dad sighed. 'Also, I know you're very much into being a footballer, so you need to keep fit. At least consider being vegan.'

I shook my head. 'Lionel Messi isn't vegan. He's only vegetarian during football seasons.'

'Stop it,' Mum commanded. 'Enough rubbish football talk and let's go to school.'

* * *

Grisworth Academy was my school. It was an alright school, never mind its horrible sounding name. Not as good as Ridge Meadows School for Boys that was on the opposite side of town, though. They had the whole lot: an equestrian club, a croquet club, and even a welly-wanging club! It was one of the best private schools near where we lived. Apparently, they had dormitories if anyone wanted to board at the school, *and* pyjama uniforms. Not gonna lie, the school sounds a bit snobbish. If I attended there and any of my out-of-school friends found out, I'd be named Snob-Nose for life.

Anyways, I was a Helper at my school, so I was put up on the big notice board in the corridor. There was bubble writing at the top done by Sienna Blackwood, the school's artist who was also on the board. The bubble writing read 'OUR SCHOOL MONITORS.'

My job was to help out with any substitute teachers and new kids, as well as with my best friend, Darren. We got substitute teachers *all* the time, so if they needed to know where things were, we'd have to help. Sometimes, I wish that I hadn't chosen to sign up for it. You had to be a monitor for at least a month before you could resign, and I'd only been a helper for a week. Some silly rule that the head teacher — Mr Stan — had made.

I was staring up at everyone on the Monitor Board when Darren came over.

"Cloakroom Monitor job now OPEN!" he read. 'Even better, look.' He pointed to Cathy Richards. 'She's the Chair of Councils, Cathy is. I'm not surprised. Her mum's a teacher! You do know Mrs Richards?'

I nodded. 'She's *so* annoying!'

'Like mother like daughter,' Darren observed.

'Tell me about it.' Then I suddenly thought the funniest thing. 'Remember that time when Cathy had her earphones on but forgot to plug the wire into her phone?'

Darren's eyes grew wider. 'Oh yeah! And we heard her listening to Freddie Mercury! And then she played The Beatles, didn't she? That was awesome.'

It was all going fine; we were having a good laugh, until the worst possible person turned up...

'I do know I'm beautiful, but would you stop staring at my picture?' It scared the life out of Darren and me.

'What?' said Darren nearly choking. 'Oh, c'mon, Cathy, get up to date! We were looking at — erm — Joseph!' He pointed to Joseph's picture to the left of Cathy's.

She blew a strand of hair out of her face as if she wasn't convinced. *That* freak? Nobody actually *wants* to be a homework monitor except for him. He thinks the teachers adore him because of that

8

small job. Huh, everyone knows who the teachers love most.'

I kind of felt sorry for the poor guy. Sometimes people teased him because of his mop of ginger hair and massive round glasses. But no doubt, Cathy was right about who the teacher's love most.

'Brush off, Cathy,' I spat, 'Go listen to some Queen or something.'

Darren spluttered with laughter, and Cathy's jaw dropped. Within seconds, she turned bright pink with embarrassment.

She leaned in and whispered, 'How did you know I listen to them?'

This just made us laugh harder, which triggered Cathy's *"fume"* button. She became redder, more with anger than embarrassment.

I nudged Darren as a sign to inform her of our findings and he seemed pretty fine with it. Anything to annoy a girl, especially Cathy, was fine with him.

'Well, the thing is, we...' Darren broke out in laughter before finishing his sentence.

Cathy became impatient. 'Spit it out, moppet!'

'You might not wanna hear this, but there was a time once when you forgot to plug your earphones into your phone.'

She seemed OK with it. *'So?'*

9

Ah, that's why she wasn't screaming in anger. She didn't understand the point we were trying to make.

'And you were listening to music.'

You could tell that Cathy was struggling to find ways to slither out of the situation, and if I'm right, she didn't have much success.

If I was truly listening to songs, who were the artists, huh?'

'Queen, Beatles — I remember a bit of Abba as well,' Darren chimed provokingly.

Cathy was now turning back to pink as if the situation had just happened. 'Well, Ms Pilate said that those kinds of music genres sharpen your brain!' she huffed.

I facepalmed myself, loving every second. 'That's *Mozart!'*

'Mozart, Queen, same thing,' she murmured.

'They're honestly not.'

'Whatever!' Cathy groaned and strode off in a snooty stride.

Darren looked at me. I could see a laugh already beginning to bubble up. But before he could let out a single note, the bell rang for the first lesson.

'Well, see you at lunch,' he sighed.

Darren and I were *never* in the same class because the teachers knew we wouldn't do our work if we were together, and we had to lend a hand at least twice a week.

'Bye.' We walked in opposite directions to our classrooms. I met up with Toby, my desk partner, on the way.

'Yo, Hayden!' he yelled, putting an arm around my neck. 'You OK, mate?'

I snorted. 'As I've ever been.'

Toby wasn't my *best* friend, but he was better than nothing. He had short, brown wavy hair that always seemed to stay put in one direction.

'What's your secret?' I'd asked him once.

'Gel,' he'd replied as if it were an ingredient in a magical potion. 'Six layers of any gel of your choice.'

The first class was English and guess what? We had a substitute teacher. Just my luck.

'Bonjour, Class 9B!' the teacher announced. Her accent was foreign and it sounded French. Plus, she'd said *"bonjour,"* and I'm pretty sure that meant "hello" or whatever in French. 'I am Madame Bernard; zis is pronounced '*Mad-am Bernard*.' As you might tell, I am Français.'

Toby looked at me and smirked. 'She's a sub teacher.'

I nodded, but I wish I didn't know.

'Why couldn't Darren have her? I'm rubbish with foreigners!' I moaned.

11

Toby nudged me. 'Don't be so rude!'

I sighed. 'I know, I know! I don't mean to come across rude, it's just that I go blank whenever someone talks to me or asks me a question in a foreign language. Remember when we had Mr González and he asked me to say a full sentence in Spanish?'

'Yes, and you freaked out. Why?'

I rolled my eyes. *'Because* I'm rubbish at languages, especially French. I'd much rather stick with English, thank you very much.'

'Just concentrate really hard and you'll wrap your head around it eventually.'

'I'll try, for the sake of you shutting up. Now shush before we get...'

'Boys!' Madame Bernard yelled, looking our way.

'Knew it,' I grumbled.

'Do *you* want to do ze leçon?' Madame Bernard questioned, trying to pull a serious face that ended up looking as if she was constipated. 'Pronounced *'le-song',* by ze way. Since you are talking you must already know zwhat you are doing?'

'No, Madame Bernard,' we both muttered.

'Are you going to stop ze — what shall I call it — ze chatter?' She made a chatting sign with her hands.

Toby and I looked at each other.

12

'Yes, Madame Bernard,' I mumbled.

'Hopefully, Madame Bernard,' Toby quietly muttered.

Madame Bernard's face turned the colour of blood. She was *raging!* 'Excuse me? Zwhat is your name?'

'T — To — Toby.'

'Toby! Shall I move you to a different table by yourself?'

'No, Madame Bernard.'

She sighed. 'I understand that you do not want to do ze French all ze time, but it is important that you learn it because when you go to France, it will be very useful.' The teacher had an accent that made her voice falter when pronouncing some words.

Toby mumbled in agreement once more, which allowed us to move on.

'Zwhat is an *"idiome?"* 'she asked.

Masie raised her hand. 'You mean an *idiom?*'

The teacher shook her head as a sorry. 'I am not very good at ze English language.'

Masie chuckled. 'Well, an *idiom* is a saying that's not *actual.* Like, saying the Maths test was a piece of cake. 'It definitely wasn't,' Mitchell interrupted.

'The test wasn't *actually* a piece of cake, it's just a saying.'

13

Madame Bernard nodded. 'Good. Are there any rewards if you do something très bon?'

'Hmm...' Trevor started, 'Let's just say that our school is super negative, so we don't have any good rewards.'

Madame Bernard nodded slowly. 'Ah, I see. I will give you praise instead, eh? Well done — what is ze name?'

'Maisie. And I wouldn't mind a scholarship or two...'

The teacher ignored the silly comment. 'Well done, Masie.'

For the rest of the lesson, every object that Madame Bernard wanted, I had to fetch, which was a real pain, since she was more annoying than Canada (OK, maybe not *more* annoying. Level, at the most). She asked me to find her *breath mints* one time! I could tell why she wanted them.

* * *

'I lost all of my lunch money,' Kylie Hatchet moaned.

'What's that, then?' Darren asked, poking at her lunch tray.

Kylie rolled her eyes dramatically. 'I was moving onto that if you'd shut it and actually *listen* to me.'

Darren put his hands up for Kylie to continue.
'I have to use my mum's money until I do chores to pay for my own.'

Nobody was paying attention to Kylie, so she stopped waffling and ate her lunch.

'Oh yeah!' Samuel yelled suddenly like he'd just remembered something. Everyone in the lunch hall looked at our table.

'Samuel Godfrey, stop your childish shouting at once!' Mr Stan, our head teacher, shouted. It happened that he was on his way to the staff room at the very moment Samuel had screamed.

'Sorry,' Samuel muttered, 'Anyways. I saw the noticeboard in the corridor and...'

'Me and Hayden already saw,' Darren piped in. 'Yes, we know, the teachers are wondering if anyone would like to be a new cloakroom monitor.'

Samuel munched on a crisp and shook his head. 'That must've been earlier because I saw Mrs Siobhan put up a sign about a new school performance!'

'Tell!' Kylie demanded.
Samuel slowly chewed another crisp until we were all desperate to hear what show we were doing. 'It's Annie,' he finally announced.

Kylie's smile nearly bounced off her face. 'Shotgun being Annie!' she screamed excitedly. Nobody noticed how loud she was, which made Samuel a bit annoyed.

'So *you* get away with it when *you* scream?' Samuel barked.

Kylie ignored him. 'I am *so* Annie. You don't have a chance against me.'

Darren shook his head. 'There are auditions, you fool! And I think Isabella Goodwin will be Annie, anyways. She has her dark skin and the really puffy dark brown hair, doesn't she?'

Samuel and I nodded, but Kylie grunted and left to put her tray away.

That afternoon was exciting because Madame Bernard was gone and my mind had unblocked. But it was also terrible because on Monday afternoons I was placed with Craig Hill in P.H.S.C.E.

'Hayden!' he shouted, running up to my desk.

'Shove off, Craig!' I griped, even though he wasn't touching me.

He dumped a bunch of unnecessary stationery on the desk and sat down over-enthusiastically.

'Guess what?' he asked, grabbing my wrist.

I snapped my hand away. 'Whatever, Craig.'

'We're doing *"Nannie"* for a school play!'

I ignored him until he repeated it again.

16

'OK, OK. And it's *"Annie,"* not *"Nannie,"* duh.'

The guy had no friends, so I felt bad for him, but I promised myself never to be his *only* friend. Yeah, I'm nice like that.

Everyone was chatting when Miss Selene told us all to quiet down.

'Mr McCrery's class is doing a mock test,' she explained. 'We have to keep our voices down. This will help with their GCSEs in the future.'

On that note, everyone settled down. We all knew that Miss Selene wouldn't be too happy if we made a lot of noise. And would you like a bunch of year nines shouting in the middle of a practice test that could change everything?

'We will do a nice, calming and relaxing activity today, partly because of the mock tests next door, but also because you'll be doing your auditions for *"Annie"* after this session,' Miss Selene carried on.

'Annie?' Sarah questioned.

Miss Selene looked confused. 'Have you not been told about this?' She frowned. 'Wasn't there an announcement ?'

Everyone shook their heads, apart from the people who were on my lunch table (excluding Darren as he's in a different class).

'I'd be a perfect Annie!' Isabella shouted.

I looked over at Kylie. She tutted and mouthed *"whatever."*

17

'Ms Harborough *definitely* should've announced this over the tannoy' Miss Selene murmured to herself. Ms Harborough was our No. 1 on-the-top school receptionist. She always alerted the school whenever there was a big event. Seems she was losing her rhythm a bit. 'Anyway, take out your event books and jot it down, please.'

At the start of every year, we got given an event book. Instead of the school wasting ink and paper printing letters that the majority lost, we had to write events down in our book and take it home every other day to let our parents know what was happening.

There was a *lot* of noise as everyone ran to retrieve their event book before the lockers at the back of the classroom got crowded. Unfortunately, I was close to the front, so I sensibly waited to retrieve my book.

'What shall we write, Miss Selene?' Shae asked.

Miss Selene closed her eyes in thought. 'Good one, Shae. Well, I suppose you can put, *"Annie the Show"* — and then fill in the date whenever the word gets spread. I doubt it's going to be soon, though. The real thing should be in a couple of months.

She nodded, tossing her peachy blonde fringe to one side. Her fringe probably took up half of her hair; she'd always cut it short so the tips were only *just* touching her neck.

'Scribble that down while I talk, OK?'

We all bent our heads and wrote the first bit of the notification in a matter of seconds. Sometimes, people would pretend they're very slow writers and actually be doodling instead of writing. That only worked if you were at the back of the class, though. Trust me, I've tried with Mr Farrington. 'Good, good. Now, everyone knows Annie, right?' Miss Selene asked, expecting us to all have heard the name.

Everyone had heard of it apart from Craig. Extra-typical.

'I thought it was *"Nannie."* Still, never heard of it,' Craig commented.

'Well, you will soon,' Miss Selene replied, not bothered to explain the whole thing. 'Sorry, Shae and Hazel, I keep picking on you, but these girls are excellent examples. They like to do calming activities before something stressful, like auditions, right girls? Auditions can be quite stressful.'

Shae and Hazel nodded.

'So I have given you the most laid-back task being undertaken in the entire school at this time. This is something that shouldn't be a lesson in Year 4, let alone secondary school. You can either choose from colouring, drawing, making a poster or making a slideshow. Whatever you choose can be based on *anything*. Slideshows are done on computers. Mr Oliver should be popping in soon and giving us a few.'

As if on cue, Mr Oliver came in with a stack of a dozen laptops. The teachers like to call them *"computers"* because computers came out six years earlier than laptops, and apparently, they've had more experience with computers.

'You had to be quite well-off to have a computer,' Mr Stan had once explained. 'Nowadays, there's quite often one per home!'

There was excited chatter around the classroom. Some people wanted to go on the laptops purely to have a laugh over rude things. I knew Sienna was doing a drawing as she's awesome at it.

'I'm drawing Sonic!' Craig exclaimed.

I nodded. 'Yeah, great...'

He tugged at my arm to make me face him. 'Yourself?'

I turned the other way. 'Dunno. What's it to you, anyway?'

Weirdly, I could feel Craig's smile moulding upside down.

'Wow, Hayden. You don't have to be so rude about everything. I'm only a guy, yet you people

20

treat me as if I'm an alien! Yeah, I'm weird, sure, I like comics and Sonic and uncool stuff like that, but it doesn't mean that you should treat me like dirt. I'm just looking for friends.'

'Sorry, Craig,' I muttered. 'I have other things to tend to. Go and find your own friends.'
Still, I felt guiltier than ever saying that. Who would've thought a guy like Craig Hill could say such a powerful thing?

Miss Selene gave a small cough and we all stopped chatting. 'Just a warning, Ms Winter might be coming in and out to take about three or four of you at a time. You'll be viewing the scripts for Annie so you know what parts there are. You'll all have a chance to do so, but you'll have to wait your turn. Oh, and I'd better say, we're not doing all the little details, OK? For example, we wouldn't do the part when the cards paint the red roses white in Alice in Wonderland, would we? But another thing like her eating and drinking the disguised potions is a vital bit.'

'We're doing Alice in Wonderland?' Kylie buzzed.

Meaghan Lopez gawped. 'Imagine me as Alice! I'm an even better fit than Isabella as Annie!' It was true — well, the first bit anyway. Meaghan had long, puffy, blonde hair and big blue eyes.

21

Sometimes, she'd wear the black headband she got from some hair store in town.

Miss Selene slowly shook her head. 'Kylie, Meaghan, calm down! We're not doing Alice in Wonderland, OK? Why would we be doing *two* performances, anyway?'

The girls both groaned and muttered, annoyed.

'Right, where was I?' Miss Selene sang, getting back in the mood by shaking her head. 'Ah, yes, Ms Winter will be coming in and out with some of you so you can have some time to view the script and select the roles you want, OK?'

My mum had made me watch Annie three times, so I knew all the parts. And there was one character I wanted to be in particular. She told me to watch it because it helped with *"film review homework"* — Pfft, yeah right. I bet she wanted to make me suffer for two hours (apologies to Annie lovers).

Sienna raised her hand.

'Yes, Sienna?' Miss Selene asked.

'Are we doing the old Annie or the new Annie?' she asked.

There was a twinkle in Miss Selene's eyes. 'Oh, good question! You clever thing, I thought you'd never ask! Would you rather me tell you now or find out in the script?'

22

The majority of us wanted to know immediately, not including Craig and the other weedy kids.

'Since the grownups will be more familiar with it, we are doing the old Annie.'

There were some groans, some cheers. I didn't want to do the old one. It was more complicated and had older words.

Miss Selene told us to start on our drawing/colouring/poster-making/slideshow-making (she actually said all that).

I looked over my shoulder to try and see who was doing what. Connor Evans was creating a poster about *maths!* He thinks all the teachers love him — and he's not wrong either. He's too good at everything — literature, maths, science topics, languages. It all gets a bit too much.

I was going to lean over to my desk partner, thinking it was Darren, so we could laugh at Connor, then I realised it wasn't Darren. So, I went back to my work and thought of ideas for a poster or slideshow.

Sienna's desk was in front of mine; I was in the second row, she was in the first, and Connor was in the third. Since she was so creative, I decided to ask her what I should do.

'What do you like, Hayden?' she asked back.

I shrugged. 'Football? Cricket? Triple burgers?'

Sienna carried on talking to me whilst colouring in something on her paper. 'So why don't you create a poster about football then?'

I considered it. 'The girls don't like football. When I have the chance to show my poster in front of the class, all the girls will moan.'

Sienna turned to face me. 'I like football.'

I smiled at Sienna and started on my bubble writing. To be honest, I'm quite good at it, but Sienna is *definitely* better.

After twelve children had read the script with Ms Winter and most people were halfway through their poster, Miss Selene asked how we were coming along.

She looked over at Sierra's work (Sienna's twin) and told her to show the class her work, probably because it was so good.

She held it up, and in big, bubbly writing it read 'gymnastics' with a cartoon gymnast doing a cartwheel next to the lettering. The writing was pink, of course. The only downside was, Sienna was *just a tad* better than her sister.

At that same moment, Ms Winter came in and picked Kylie, Turro, Hannah and Lexi out from names on a chunk of stapled paper in her hand.

'Thank you, Ms Winter!' Miss Selene called.

We got another forty-five minutes to finish off our posters. In that time, everyone, including me, had a chance to view the script. I wasn't *too* disappointed, but doing the new Annie would've been five times better.

My poster was looking *sick*, to be honest. I'd gotten Sienna to help me draw a football border, and the bottom of the A3 page was designed to look like a football field. We were allowed to Google things, so I watched a tutorial on how to draw a cartoon of Cristiano Ronaldo and Harry Kane.

'Nice!' Sienna complimented.

I shrugged. 'We both did some.'

Soon after, everyone had showcased their posters or whatever they did, and Miss Selene personally congratulated me on mine. I thought it was pretty great too.

'Good job, everyone!' Miss Selene commented. 'If you put all your sheet paper in a pile over here, and the slide-showers send me their slideshows by email. I shall be thinking of you in the auditions!'

Everyone stood up and tucked their chairs in. A month ago, all the chairs would have been completely out and *not* tucked in, but when Georgie the caretaker moaned about having to tuck them in himself, we'd all been threatened with detention.

We were met by class 9F in the hall. It happened to be Darren's class.

'Guess what?' he bragged, not waiting for me to reply. 'We got to watch Happy Death Day with popcorn and all. It was the *best* horror movie I've watched in my life. There were so many jump-scares and we all giggled afterwards. Mr Sokolov let us put our feet up on the tables and switch the lights off, as well!'

'Cool,' I murmured.

Darren crossed his arms. 'What did you do?'

I pretended not to hear him.

He pulled a face and repeated the question, but slower, '*What did you do?*' He said it as if I was a three-year-old.

I fiddled with my fingers. 'Well — uh...' Compared to what he'd said, what I was about to say was probably equivalent to saying *"I saw a bug."*

'Class 9B and 9F!' Ms Winter said, clapping her hands multiple times.

Darren frowned and mouthed *"tell me later"* He 100% knew that what he did could never top anything anyone else in the school was doing. So much for doing the most laid-back activity around.

Ms Winter clapped again. 'Slight change, we are now doing the new Annie.'

Everyone, including the people from Class 9F, cheered.

'There shouldn't be *too* many differences — maybe the storyline is tweaked in some parts, and the script is obviously different — but that's all. The new scripts have been printed already. I will split you into 12 groups of 5,' Ms Winter carried on, 'then, I will read out the parts you could perform in our play…'

'What play is it?' Connor shouted out.

Ms Winter glared at him and for about twenty seconds, Connor wasn't the favourite. 'I am sure I have *just* told you, and Miss Selene *certainly* would've told you, Connor Evans. In fact, it was a strict order from Mr Stan for us teachers to tell the forms that we're doing the play.'

Everyone turned to Connor and gave him the *"mhm"* face.

Connor turned red. Serves him right.

'As I was saying… I will read out the available parts, and you'll choose which one you would like to audition for. I know that Class 9B has been shown the scripts, but those were the old ones. If you'd like to come along, then come grab a paper from the pile next to me. These old things are only temporary; on the day you'll have nice coloured folders. Bear in mind I *will* be reading it aloud as well. I suggest that the not-so-confident readers get a script sheet and have a go. You can read a few lines ahead of me that way.'

Everyone started talking about the parts they wanted, and there were a few groans from people who probably found out that their best mate wanted to audition for the same character as them. Ms Winter coughed to regain our attention, then returned to her talk. 'Everyone will be doing the same scene, that way we can judge who incorporates the best ideas and who's the most confident actor. You *can* add in your own bits, as long as no UFOs are swooping down to take Annie off to her real parents, OK?'

We all giggled at the thought of that: *"Annie the Parody"* I'd call it.

'I'll put you in groups of five. If there is anyone who is left with an unwanted role, I can easily group members so they can fit into the role they want.'

Blah, blah, blah. Then you'll perform it, more boring talk, and then...

Finally, it came to the grouping.

'How many have we got?' Ms Winter counted us in threes. 'Good, good.'

Next, she came around and numbered all sixty of us children. When she got to twelve, she restarted at one.

'Number 1s over here,' she said, pointing to a spot on the floor. 'Number 2s...' and so on.

28

I was group number 11, and so was Talia Roberts, Ayo Omiata, Stacy Fence and Connor. Ms Winter read out the parts. I became increasingly pleased that we were doing the recent Annie, not the one staged in the 1900s.

'As you know, we have a change of plan,' Ms Winter explained again. 'We had complaints from many children…' She eyed a few people, luckily passing me, '… so we decided to change it. Most wanted to do the recent movie version. I bet you lot are more familiar with it.'

I fist-pumped the air.

Stacy and Talia instantly fought over who would be Annie, whilst us boys shrugged and picked a part.

'It would make sense for me to be Will Stacks; you know why,' Ayo said.

True fact. His skin was chocolate coloured and so was Will Stacks'.

'Yeah, let Ayo be Will. I'm Annie, though,' Talia announced.

'No, I am!' Stacy pouted.

Connor laughed. '*You?* You're as pale as a sheet of paper!'

Stacy took it badly. Her eyes watered and she started murmuring something. I wasn't surprised. Let's say… she had less-resistant waterworks.

Stacy slowly spoke. 'I — I'm n — not pale at all. In fact, I had a tan not long ago in Spain!'

Connor heaved exasperatedly. He was one of the people who didn't know about Stacy's sensitivity, so he'd always say whatever he pleased. 'Wimp. Annie stood up to the mean boys that hurt the dog. That won't be possible for Blubby over here.'

'Oh, shush,' Ayo muttered.

'What?' Connor teased, although he heard perfectly well.

Ayo would've turned red, but obviously, he couldn't because of his cocoa brown skin.

'I said shush!' he yelled. That, unfortunately, drew Ms Winter's attention.

'Ayo! Whatever is the matter?' she asked, striding over to us, a grim look on her face.

Ayo scowled at Connor, and Connor smirked back.

'Oh, Ms Winter!' Connor whined, putting on a fake tone. 'Ayo is yelling at me for no apparent reason!'

'*Apparent,* huh,' Ayo mumbled.

All that time I'd been a bystander, not saying anything.

So when Ms Winter looked at *me*, I was a bit "*meh*"

'Hayden. You're the spectator here. What happened exactly? Oh, and I do hope I'm not dealing with toddler arguments here because I might as well *twiddle-toddle* away now!'

Connor, Connor, Connor, more Connor, everything Connor, I thought.

I'm sorry, I lied when I said I was a bit *"meh."* It was the opposite — it was more *"yeah"* let's say.

'Connor's been horrific to Stacy, calling her rude and inappropriate names,' I finally snitched. It wasn't too obvious, I don't think. I mean me trying to make it sound one hundred times more harmful and serious than it actually was.

Ms Winter scoffed. *'What* rude words?'

'You wouldn't want to know,' Ayo sighed.

'Tell. Me. Now.' The teacher sounded a bit delusional saying those three words.

I nodded at Ayo to let me take this one. ' *"Wimp"* and *"Blubby."* '

'I did not!' he exclaimed.

Stacy looked shocked. 'He — he did! He's lying!'

Ms Winter shook her head solemnly. I knew she thought that this was toddler drama, just like she'd predicted.

'Listen, I suggest Talia be Annie,' Ms Winter announced. 'And I don't want to hear any more of this nursery talk. You know much better than to argue s'much on something that's barely a problem.'

31

Talia smirked like Connor, and for a second, they looked related.

Stacy nodded. 'I understand.'

And guess what? No tears!'

'Now get on, you've only got an hour, and that's for practice *and* performing.'

In the end, Talia was Annie, Stacy was Grace Farrell, Ayo was Will Stacks, Connor was Lou — ha-ha! — and I was Guy Danily.

We all suited our roles since Talia had the same sort of complexion as Ayo and the dark brown hair. She'd most likely need to get it curled at the most if she got the role as her hair fell just halfway down her back or was usually shaped into a style. There was no hope, anyways; Isabella was Annie for another group. She attended drama club both in and out of school, and she was truly perfect for the part.

We all got given a script, but they weren't highlighted since it would take an awful amount of work to highlight sixty scripts. Anyways, so far, we were doing well, apart from Connor's rubbish Spanish accent.

The scene we were doing was the end scene where everyone was gathered around the bridge. All of 9B and 9F sat down to watch a video on the projected screen. At that point, most people had the talking bits down, leaving only the acting to be done.

'We need to do the dance and all,' Talia whispered to me.

I stayed focus on the screen whilst talking. 'And?'

'We need park benches, don't we?'

'Yeah, but let's use the P.E. benches next to the wall, then,' I murmured back. 'They're still technically benches.'

Talia nodded and winked at me.

'OK, 9F and 9B!' Ms Winter announced. Have you had enough information about the final scene, then?'

We all replied. Some said *"no"* just to hear the closing music.

'I have the best idea!' Stacy said once we were back in our groups. 'I'm awesome at dance, so me and Talia could choreograph the ending dance routine with you!'

Ayo chuckled. 'I'm not holding *Talia's* hands.'

Talia frowned. 'Well, it's show business, Ayo. I don't want to, either, but if you want Will Stacks as a part, I suggest you get on with it.' That put Ayo in his place.

A smile crept up my face. 'I actually quite like that idea, Stacy. I think we should totally do it.'

Even Connor smiled.

33

'Just *one* more protest?' Ayo begged.

Talia scowled. 'Whatever.'

'There's a bit where Stacks *picks Annie up...* I'm not up for that. Talia looks quite heavy.'

That triggered Talia more. 'Excuse me? 50 kg, thank you very much! That's lower than average, duh! But I do agree with you, there are some bits we have to exclude.'

'Yeah, you guys are right,' I said slowly. 'But that won't stop us from doing a

Supercalifragilisticexpialidocious performance, will it?'

Stacy had memorised the dance choreography and started showing it to Connor.

'And left, left, right, right, no, *my* right. Yes, see! Then repeat.' She was trying her best to tutor Connor, and it wasn't working very well. 'Now with counts, OK? Five, six, seven, eight and one, two three, four...'

Connor was quite good at it in the end. Soon, he had the whole routine down, five minutes flat. Stacy should've been teaching Ayo and Talia the routine, but they watched Stacy and Connor do the whole thing through and as a result, knew it off by heart. As for the lifting bits, they ignored it and twirled.

We watched the two dance and clapped once they finished, causing a bit of unneeded attention.

I stood there practising my lines and actions, and the rest went over the dance with props, taking breaks to perform their parts as well. The truth is, Guy wasn't in the last scene of Annie, they just had to add a few bits in for him to say. One of them was, *"Annie, I'm sorry. I didn't mean to do all this. Forgive me. Have a candy."* That one was a bit weird, especially the *candy* part. But, hey-ho, what can you do about an American script?

Ms Winter said she'd save us the trouble of singing and probably let the internet do the work. I was much better off mouthing the words, anyway.

We had our audition ready in twenty minutes, so once we'd nailed it, we practised over and over, as professionals would do.

'Psst,' I heard close to my ear. 'Look, theirs is so good!'

It was Miranda George and Henry Tomlinson. They were staring at Talia and Ayo doing their routine.

I turned to face them. 'Eyes off, pests.'

The pair both went back to their audition, though I doubt they hadn't snuck in a move or two.

Ms Winter clapped twice. 'Okay, Classes 9F and 9B. Please sit on the chairs in front of the stage, we'll have Group 1 first!'

Muhammed Stansky, Maria Hedge, Tracy Evans (Connor's sister), Craig and Katie White stepped on stage. They had a very odd cast: Maria was Annie, Oliver was Guy, Craig was Will Stacks, Katie was Grace and Tracy was… *Lou*?

Katie still had her script on stage, and there were a few laughs.

'So, you lied to me?' Maria started.

Craig stepped forward, and in a deep voice, he said, 'Annie, I'm…'

'They aren't my real parents? I thought I could trust you!' Some other cheesy stuff like that. Will Stacks (Craig) said sorry to Annie (Maria), and more people laughed at how bad an actor Craig was. Then, the music played, and they mouthed the words, not having a routine to the song. *My* group were the only ones who'd thought of it.

Afterwards, it was Group 2, then 3, next 4, and so on. They just did the basic, boring auditions everyone else was doing. But it was Group 5 that drew the most attention.

It was Miranda's group, and they were *OK* until the music started. *Our* routine. Our exact dance choreography, only a bit raw.

'Hey!' I said, nudging Talia.

She stared at me, not noticing the problem. 'What?'

I pointed to the stage and Talia looked. Her eyes grew wider.

'Our…' she muttered, then shouted, 'Our dance!'

Ms Winter abruptly stopped the music and frowned at Talia.

'That was going so well, Group 5. I wonder why Talia spoiled it so much! I am very disappointed!'

'But Ms Winter…'

Ms Winter silenced her. 'Another word and I'll send you back to class.'

Talia shushed and went hot in the face.

'I — hate — Miranda,' she growled. Talia and Miranda had history. *Bad* history. Miranda was always the one to *"accidentally"* spill her lunch on Talia's shirt, or steal her skirt once she was changed for P.E.

Speaking of P.E., how on *earth* would Ms Winter allow us to transport the P.E. bench on to the stage when nobody else got to? We hadn't even used it in rehearsals!

Two

Rodger's

ur audition had gone well. There were a few rumours of us stealing Miranda and her group's dance, but other than that, we did well. Miranda's team's routine wasn't that clean, anyways, since they only got seven minutes to practise it. And best of all: no one cringed!

Sadly, we weren't allowed to use the benches because the others couldn't either, as I thought. But that didn't matter.

Ms Winter said she'd tell us what parts we'd gotten on Friday. And it was Monday.

* * *

Mum came to pick me up.

It was odd, I hadn't seen Canada all day, not even at pick-up time. Normally, I'd see her in school hanging around with Tiffany and Beth. If not, I'd see her waiting in front of the car, ready to go home.

'Where's Canada?' I asked, slinging my backpack over my shoulder.

Mum pointed to a bronze-coloured man, and there were my sister and Tiffany.

'She's going home with her friend, Hayden,' Mum explained. 'For a trip to Alton Towers.'

I laughed so hard I nearly toppled over. 'That's funny!' I blurted, trying hard to breathe, 'I thought you just said *"she's going to Alton Towers!"* '

Mum stopped and put her hands on her hips. *'I did.'*

It was still hard to believe, but by the look on Mum's face, she was dead serious.

'And I get a reward?' I asked.

Mum sighed. 'It's Tiffany's sixteenth birthday. *Sixteenth*. Listen, you boys wouldn't have heard of it, but she's having a Sweet Sixteen…'

'Oh, I've heard about that nonsense,' I interrupted. 'Even though I'm sure it was only in America.'

39

'... and her parents want it to be the best it can be.'

'And what about Beth?'

Mum sighed. 'Her parents are super protective. They won't let her go anywhere more than two hours without them. Beth figured her parents would be like her personal bodyguards and not let her step twenty centimetres out of their reach, so she chose not to go altogether.'

I was alright with that. Maybe Beth could come around to our house instead? She was like a stepsister to me, although she hadn't come in a few months.

Mum opened the door, and as soon as she did, Zoey and Baxter (Bax for short) came barking up to us. Yes, Zoey and Bax are our pet dogs. Zoey is a Shih Tzu, and Bax is a Cockapoo.

'Oh, stop 'em from coming out,' mum ordered, pushing Baxter away with her foot.

'Who's my little Zo-Bo?' I cooed, scratching Zoey under her chin.

Mum went into the kitchen, probably to bake the lasagne pastry. I sat in the doorway, playing with Bax and Zoey.

I don't know if dogs can purr, but the sound Zoey was making sounded like one if they could.

It was quite upsetting for them being cooped up in the house. They were normally at a doggy daycare for a few days a week as they were a bit of a nuisance to train and most of the family were out during the day. Today wasn't one of the days they went though, so they were extra attention-seeking when everyone got back.

I went into the kitchen. 'Hey again, Mum.'

Mum greeted me back, not looking up from the stove.

'Can I take Zoey and Bax to Rodger's house?' I asked.

Mum carried on cooking, then, at last, she turned around and said, 'The harnesses and leads are in the storage cupboard now. They're too fiddly to keep getting off the study shelves without knocking something over.'

I smiled at her and ran for the storage cupboard. The dogs came bounding after me. I wasn't surprised, they were like my baby lemmings.

'See you, Mum. I'll be back in a couple of hours!' I shouted.

'You better,' she shouted back.

I attached the pink harness to Zoey and the blue harness to Bax, then attached the leads.

'Good dogs!' I beamed, stuffing a bag of treats in my pocket. I knew they weren't *only* for them; Zoey and Bax *loved* Rodger's dogs, Bolt and Cooper. Bolt and Cooper loved treats. Also, mine needed a good walk.

It took only ten minutes to reach Rodger's house on Parkfield Road.

I rang Rodger's doorbell and saw him check the door; even though it must've been blurry from the inside, Rodger knew my silhouette.

'Hey, Hayden!' he sang. 'How was school?'

We went to different schools, so at least three times a week we'd go around to each other's houses. When he moved to the area over two years ago, his parents decided that he would attend Parkfield Private Boy's School (PPBS). Like Ridge Meadows, some students could also board, but Rodger was a day student.

You see, Rodger's parents didn't think my school was good enough for him since they were very educated and posh. But even *they* couldn't afford Ridge Meadows.

'School is… school, I guess. Is it OK that I brought Zoey and Baxter?'

Rodger grinned madly. 'More than okay! Come have a seat inside. My dogs will bark like crazy when they see the sight of you all.'

He offered me a chocolate biscuit that looked stale. The chocolate had also melted, so I knew I would find myself with sticky hands if I accepted it.

I shook my head. 'Not hungry.'

Rodger shrugged and gulped down the rejected biscuit.

I observed his appearance. As usual, his shaggy, black hair needed a comb and I could see the tangles, and his green eyes shone even in the day. His clothing looked a size too big for him, although he was a bit on the pudgy side.

'Movie?' he suggested.

I had the best idea. 'Happy Death Day. Class 9F got to watch it, and apparently, it's *epic.'*

Rodger frowned. 'Hate horrors.'

'Oh, c'mon, wimpy, just for...'

Rodger scowled at me. 'Nobody ever calls me *"wimpy."* What's that movie called again?'

Jenn, Rodger's mum, made us sweet and salted popcorn. We had a *humongous* bowl each.

She had straight, black hair and was very skinny. Jenn worked as a Business Development Manager. She helped people promote their businesses. She regularly wore beige cardigans with a white shirt neatly tucked underneath, finished off with a long, black skirt and fishnet tights. Rodger said Jenn was normally dead serious and was *"Mrs Calendor"* to her clients for some reason, but when she was at home with Rodger and me, she was playful old Jenn.

'Dibs on sweet and salted,' Rodger cried.

Jenn rolled her eyes, sighing in exasperation. 'They're both sweet and salted, Rodger.'

'Oh.'

'And Parkfield's is supposed to be doing you good. Huh, so they say!'

Happy Death Day was on Showbox, which happened to be loading *very* slowly.

'Twenty billion years later,' Rodger muttered, in a funny voice.

As soon as he said that the download ended, and the movie began.

Brace yourself, I thought. *You'll be needing a pillow to cuddle for this one.*

Halfway through, my popcorn ran out, and Rodger was a quarter of the way through his second bowl.

'I need a refill,' I told him.

I went into the kitchen to find a bowl of popcorn, and on the wall, a shadow that looked exactly like the baby in the movie appeared. I ran to the extra bowl of popcorn and stuffed a load in, leaving bits everywhere, before quickly leaving the kitchen and returning to the living room.

'What is it?' Rodger questioned.

'Meh, it's nothing,' I lied, casually throwing popcorn into my mouth.

Rodger gave me that look the teachers do, the *"tell-me-the-truth"* look.

'OK...' he slowly mumbled, clearly not believing me.

The whole movie got a lot scarier, now I was thinking of the baby, but I tried my hardest not to show it. Rodger looked like he was enjoying it so much — even though he had said no to putting it on in the first place.

Finally, the movie ended, and I was filled with a mixture of relief and shock. I didn't know it was so scary; Darren acted like it was Mickey Mouse compared to what it actually was.

'Happy Death Day 2?' Rodger inquired.

I shook my head. 'I think me and the dogs ought to go home.' That wasn't *really* the reason. I was too spooked to watch another horror movie for the next month. But Zoey and Baxter were getting tired as well.

'Oh yeah, I forgot about the dogs,' Rodger remarked. 'They've been chasing each other's tails for the last hour and thirty-six minutes! You could stay for a *little* longer, though.'

'Sure, OK. What should we do?' I asked. Anything to get my mind off the baby shadow.

'I dunno, maybe tell me what freaked you out in the kitchen?'

I should've seen it coming. 'I saw a shadow of the baby mask, OK?'

Rodger laughed. And laughed some more. 'Oh, is that it? Listen, my cousin, Rosie, is seven. *Seven*. She has baby dolls galore.'

He led me into the kitchen and turned on the light. There on the counter was a baby Annabelle doll I'd seen in plenty of adverts.

'There, you dunce!' he laughed, hitting me round the head.

I felt like one too. 'OK, thanks,' I mumbled, sounding chilled. I really wasn't. You can't un-see something, so the image remained in my mind.

'Great. Xbox? I've got two controllers,' Rodger offered.

Rodger had *two* Xbox's and *two* screens; they both used to belong to his older brother who now lived across town with his wife.

'Wow!' I exclaimed. 'Lucky.'

Rodger shrugged. 'I only use one.'

We played Rocket League, and Rodger and I were on the same team.

'We're *so* gonna win,' Rodger jinxed.

We lost. I mean, we were against a pro, no, a *god* at the game. So we were bound to lose.

Rodger smiled uneasily. 'Minecraft?'

I shrugged for the fifty-fourth time today. 'Might as well.'

Rodger and I had a restaurant build-off. I thought I'd win since I had more experience, but it turned out Rodger had *even more.*

'Good game,' I congratulated. 'But I bet I'll beat you in 2v2.'

He looked confused. 'What's "2v2?" '

What? That was the funniest thing I'd ever heard. Every human being had to know what 2v2 was.

'Who are you?' I joked, dramatically gasping. 'That's an *insult* to the master creator of the game, the wise old owl of them all, the father elf...'

'It's you, admit it,' Rodger sighed.

I held my breath. 'You are... correct. Yes, I made it. We did algorithm in class and then they introduced it as a club and I just *had* to check it out. Turns out, we got to make super cool games, and if I remember my sign-in, I could download 2v2!'

Rodger looked slightly impressed. 'That's funny, we have that at Parkfield's. Oh, and a debating club. But go on, show me your game if you're so thrilled about it.'

I installed a game downloader Mr Solitine had shown the algorithm club.

' "2Game4You," ' Rodger read aloud. 'Hm, OK. So, remind me what this does?'

I had pleasure in explaining everything to him. 'This software lets you create games as well as open them! You just sign in to your account and you can play the game. Here, I'll download it on your Xbox, then I'll send you a game invite so you can join me.'

I did exactly that, and in a matter of ten minutes, Rodger had loaded my game.

'*Wooooah*,' he admired.

The atmosphere was an orangey glow with tall offices and one-tier stores dotted everywhere. Angry barbers were stalking around the place, and if you got too close, they'd chase you with their shavers.

'So what's the point of the game?' Rodger asked once I'd toured the main map. 'Is there a reason why everything is so... Slaughter Race-y? Or do you wander around, aimlessly looking for something that's not there.'

I shook my head. 'Oh, no, only losers make those sorts of games.'

Rodger coughed. 'And that's why I thought what I thought.'

Blanking him, I carried on. 'The aim is to make a car. First, you have to find a job or dumpster dive in one of the dumpsters. With the money, you can buy car parts, or you can find them in the trash, but that's a rare spawn. Anyways, it's tons of fun.

They keep some of the crucial car parts in the barbers, and as you can tell, he's not a very happy bloke.'

My friend nodded his head in approval. 'Bravo, Hayden. This seems like a whole lot of coding you did.'

I shrugged. 'Meh, it only cost about a gazillion computer lags. Anyways, have a try.'

Rodger had a go and was surprisingly bad at it. When he found a dumpster, he only scratched the surface, then grunted, *"Nope, not here"* and he ended up applying for a job at a food store. He never ranked up.

I stretched. It had been a long day, and I thought the dogs and I had better be going before Mum rang the police.

'The dogs are getting worn out,' I said. 'Bax has even started snoozing! We'd better hit the frog and toad.'

I got my dog's harnesses and leads and called their names. Zoey came bounding back to me and I had to give Baxter a little shake to wake him up. Zoey started yipping to be harnessed.

'OK, be patient or I'll do Bax first.' Interestingly, the dog understood, probably by the stern look on my face, and stopped making a noise.

Rodger looked over his shoulder. 'I wish Cooper and Buster were like that.' Buster was a French

Bulldog and Cooper was a Border Collie. Cooper obeyed quite well. Rodger said that sometimes he'd take his dogs to his grandfather's farm, so Cooper could round up the sheep.

'Don't worry, it took weeks to train these and we had the help of the doggy daycare,' I beamed. I fastened the last snap buckle and stood up, dusting dog hair from my trousers. 'Well, see you in a couple of days! Have a good time at school!'

'I won't,' Rodger called back.

I shut the door behind me, careful not to lock my dogs in the house. Thank goodness it was still light; otherwise, I'd have slept at Rodger's and left in the morning. After watching *that* movie, the dark was the worst thing I could possibly be in.

'Here,' I coaxed, bringing out a bag of Bonio Dog Treats. The dogs knew what the treat bag looked like, and started jumping up at me.

'Steady, there, Bax,' I ordered. My dogs loved treats. I could smell them too, and if *I* was a dog, I'd be going crazy. As a human, maybe not so much.

Zoey had short brown, white and black ears. Her back was brown and her belly was pure white. Her tail went from brown to white ombre, and I'd added a pink bow to the top of her head. Sometimes, I'd use my pocket money to buy her pink dog clothes, and everyone out on the street would coo at her. Zoey *loved* attention, so she'd always go up to people and rub against them.

Baxter was what they call *teddy bear* coloured. Light brown all over, except for a patch of white near his tummy and on his nose. His fur was so curly that even straightening tongs couldn't straighten it. The vets had told us that his fur was perfectly okay; just every two weeks we'd have to give him a wash to flatten down the mad curls. Zoey cleaned herself much more, so she only needed a wash once a month.

'Good boy,' I said to Baxter, giving him a treat. He gobbled it down, leaving crumbs everywhere. Zoey ate hers slowly and perfectly, leaving some. I knew Bax would gulp his down in seconds, and he did. Some day, I'd stop him doing that, as he could end up with diabetes, but he was still only young. I'd let him do what he wanted for a little longer.

'Mum, I'm home,' I called into the letter box.

Mum opened the door and pretended to look at her *"visible"* watch. 'And you're an hour and a half late. What took you so long?'

I shrugged. 'Well, we watched a movie that was an hour and thirty-six minutes long, and it takes me ten minutes to walk home, so...'

'Does that add up to the time you wasted? The movie was an hour and thirty-six minutes including the credits at the end?'

I nodded.

Mum scowled at me. 'I'm guessing you stayed for a *little* bit longer after the movie finished because you *never* stay for the credits in movies. I know my son.'

I smiled uneasily.

'Go and eat your dinner, Hayden. You might want to warm it up, though. You better be thankful you're not grounded.'

I half expected Canada to be picking at her food when I reached the dinner table, then I remembered she'd probably be having pizza or nuggets at Alton Towers.

'Not fair,' I mumbled over and over, which actually helped.

Mum entered the kitchen and heard me muttering. 'You do know that the first sign of mental issues is talking to yourself,' she joked, resting her arms on the tabletop. 'Listen, what's not fair?'

'Everything,' I grumbled.

Mum shook her head. 'Who is it that gets to see Rodger every week?'

'Me,' I mumbled.

'Who is it that gets to go to McDonald's every other Saturday with Darren?'

'Me.'

'Who is it that went to Harry Potter World for four days with two of his best friends?'

'Me.'

'And who is it that's gonna get grounded if they come back more than twenty minutes late from somewhere?'

'Me — wait what?'

Mum chuckled and switched on the kettle. 'Want a cup?'

I nodded. 'Only if it has caffeine. There's a football match tomorrow.'

Mum nodded, even though I saw her add a bag of decaffeinated tea in my cup.

She started humming a soft tune that she'd once sung to me as a toddler. Well, that's what she told me.

'*Let me root, root, root, root for the home team...*' she sang.

I stared at her, and for a split second, her eye caught mine.

'We used to sing that song at every football match we went to, Hayden,' she explained. 'They got the best singers to sing that, and I was one of them. I wish I could slap my past-tense self for messing around with my friends so much; I should've just stood there and sung. See, Hayden, there's no better time than the present.'

Three

The Big Day

The next morning, I woke up early and had a bowl of Cornflakes. I was about to make another bowl for Canada, and then remembered: she was having endless fun at Alton Towers. I know that *I'd* had a lot of fun trips with my friends in the past, but I'm younger than Canada is. Shouldn't she be having a spa day or something? Even worse, Mum reported she wasn't texting at all. She was supposed to be coming back tomorrow, though I started to fear she wouldn't. She was missing school and everything.

'I'll have a chat with Tiffany's dad. Thank God they are back tomorrow afternoon,' Mum worriedly muttered And it wasn't just jealousy that was annoying me. Canada was the most annoying person on earth, don't get me wrong, but she was my *sister*. I wouldn't be able to bear it if something happened to her. You don't know how faulty they make the rollercoasters sound on internet reviews.

I dropped a spoon into my cereal, and splashes of milk flew everywhere. 'Could you — perhaps — call her dad *now*?'

Mum chuckled to herself. 'You truly love your sister.'

I hesitated. 'No — it's just I'm worried about her phone.'

'Ah,' Mum giggled, nodding. I knew that she knew I was genuinely worried about Canada, but she didn't push it.

Mum joined me at the breakfast table. She had toast and coffee.

It was a bit awkward up until she said, 'Listen, I chose your name because it means *"fire."* I chose a fitting name. And your sister's name, Canada, I don't know what it means. Most people would not think of Canada as a name. But I think it's lovely, don't you? Sometimes, you have to wing it and find the meaning yourself.'

I had no idea whatsoever why Mum was blabbering on about names, but I figured I'd soon find out.

'But your name, *"fire"* describes you. I thought I ought to tell you someday.'

55

'OK, cool. Just one?' I asked.

Mum looked confused. 'Just one what?'

'Sip.'

Mum stared down at her coffee as if it were made of an explosive. 'Fine.' She gave in and slid it across the table.

I had one sip, then another, then another, until Mum slapped my hand away from the cup handle.

'You are *very* bad at counting,' Mum chuckled. 'You said *one* sip, and here you are working your way halfway down my coffee!'

'Sorry,' I spluttered.

'Go and gather all your football kit, you've got a match today.'

Like I'd forgotten. I was so worried. We were playing against O.M. Juniors. They had a big reputation of winning every JCF — Junior Cup Final — and this *was* the finals! It was *"go big or go home"* for Grisworth FC.

Mum must've noticed me trembling. 'Oh, Hayden, what is it? You love football — even more than I love the gym!' Mum did have an obsession with going to the gym one to three times a day. She was ready to go now, her hair tied in a ponytail, and wearing Nike gym-wear and Adidas trainers.

'No, no,' I protested. 'I do love football and want to do it for years on end, it's just — Mum, listen, it's O.M. Juniors. They've won the JCF four times in a row before, and that's only in a row. Altogether, I think they have seven or eight JCF trophies. Our team, Grisworth FC, only has two.'

Mum shrugged. 'Please, Hayden, believe you can,' she coaxed, picking up two 10 kg weights. We had a load of those randomly sitting underneath the breakfast table. 'Anyway, I'm off to the gym. They don't have heavy weights, so I've got Dad to buy me these. Oh, by the way, he had to go to work early, bless him. There are about four meetings he's scheduled for.'

I nodded.

'Have a good day at school, honey. Remember your snack and lunch money. The bus...'

'The bus comes at half seven, and it takes ten minutes to walk to the bus stop.'

'Good! You better get moving, quick!'

I gathered my snack, lunch money and a backpack for school and waved to Mum. She pulled something out of her pocket — my phone.

'Forgetting something?' she asked, swaying my phone around in her hand. I took it off her and frowned.

'See you, Mum!'

We were running a bit late, so I only had seven minutes to reach the bus stop. Normally, I got to school with loads of time to spare, since it's better than arriving late.

phoned Rodger, whose lift with Jenn normally went in the direction of the bus stop to get to school.

'Hi, mate, could you possibly pick me up at the nearest bus stop on the way to Parkfield's? I'm running late.'

There was feedback on the phone.

'No? Oh, crumbs, I think this is my last warning,' I grunted back.

Rodger said he was sorry and some other stuff.

'Nah, it's fine, I think Mrs Clauseton might give me a ticket, which isn't that bad.'

Rodger thought a ticket was like a speeding ticket — as if I drove — and he started asking me a bunch of questions like: *"what car do you have?"* and *"isn't it illegal to drive at thirteen?"*

I facepalmed, although he wouldn't be able to see me do it. 'In our school, if you're given a late ticket more than three times in one week, you receive a detention.'

I could hear the guilt in Rodger's voice, but I told him there was a small chance of me being given a *fourth* ticket instead of detention, if I came up with a good excuse, that is. It all depended on which front desk lady I happened upon.

'OK, thanks mate, bye!' I hung up. I was sort of saying *"thanks for nothing"* but it was the polite thing to do anyways.

I got to school at 9:17. Since I missed the first bus, I had to take the second bus fifteen minutes later than the first.

I arrived at the front desk, panting from all the sprinting it took me to finally arrive there. Grisworth is a very big school, so in just getting to the front desk, you could easily waste a minute or two.

It was Mrs Clauseton of all people. She looked down her glasses at me. 'Where's your book?'

I forgot to mention: we have small notebooks where we keep track of our tickets. Every time you're late, you have to give the teacher the book, and they mark your tardiness down. Every time we went to school, we had to check our books with the front desk ladies. And nobody could get away with it, either, since the front desk was a few metres away from the entry point into the school building.

Reluctantly, I pulled out the notebook from my blazer pocket. Mrs Clauseton studied it for a while before tutting annoyingly.

'Hayden, Hayden, Hayden,' she sighed. 'What are we going to do with you? Two tickets last week, three this week — you're on a late *streak!'* She pored over the page like it were an ancient artefact. 'Last ticket, eh?'

I put on my sweetest, kindest face. 'I'm so sorry, Mrs Clauseton. It was all this and that this morning, so it wasn't really possible to come early, if not on time.'

Mrs Clauseton raised her eyebrows. 'What are you implying, here?'

Here it was.

'That you — you let me have a *fourth* ticket?' I pleaded. 'I promise it won't ever, ever, *ever* happen again.'

Mrs Clauseton smiled, and for a second, I thought I was safe. Then she laughed. A lot. 'No child has *ever,* in the time I've been at this school, has *ever* been given a fourth ticket by me. A *fourth* ticket? Who would've heard of it!'

'How long *have* you been here, Mrs Clauseton?' I asked, trying not to smile.

Mrs Clauseton shook her head. 'Thirty-*seven* years, and don't be cheeky.'

I tried so hard not to laugh, but a small giggle managed to escape.

Mrs Clauseton ignored me and wrote a date down in my notebook. 'Here. 8th June, there's your detention date. I expect better from you, Hayden. It should take you fifteen minutes to get to school, not fifty.'

I stared down at the page in disbelief. 'You're *not* giving me detention for being late, are you?'

Mrs Clauseton nodded and handed me a timetable paper. 'I'm sorry. Now get to your classroom before you receive yet *another* punishment.'

Mum would *kill* me when she found out I had yet another detention. I just don't understand how you could get suspended for being late! Stupid school and their stupid rules...

'Maths,' I groused. 'Seriously? We should have something named *"brain warm-up class"* so we don't break our brains from working too hard!'

'Talking to yourself, Slayden?' a shrill voice cooed.

I turned around and saw Petunia, one of the older girls.

'Oh, shut up,' I muttered.

'You're late for class. Better hit the frog and toad, your teacher won't be very happy!'

Petunia used to be my sister's really good friend, and then Tiffany joined the school in Year 10, and Canada decided she was a better friend, obviously. She's only been hanging around Tiffany for a year. Still, I didn't mind Petunia calling me pet names.

'Yeah, I would've been there if someone didn't stop for a chat. Want a cuppa with that?'

Petunia laughed. She had the most high-pitched voice in the whole of Year 11. 'I'm sorry, Scruff. Catch you later! I'd leg it if I were you.'

I ran down the hallway. *I'm doomed*, I thought.

I finally arrived at the ICT class, and Mr Oliver glared at me. It looked like everyone had already settled into the lesson, and they were busy typing away on their laptops.

'Want to take a seat, Hayden?' Mr Oliver asked, 'or are you too good for everyone, so you arrive late? Because we have all the time in the world, you know. It's cool, just pop in anytime. That's how it works, right?'

'No, Mr Oliver.'

I put my notebook in the tray on Mr Oliver's desk. He was the detention supervisor.

'This your detention?'

The question I was dreading to hear. 'Yes, Mr Oliver.'

He did the face all teachers did. I'm pretty sure Darren told me to become a teacher you'd have to learn how to pull that face. 'Go and sit down, Hayden. I'll let you off today — your homework has made up for it. But I'm warning you, next time it'll be detention.'

I smiled with relief and sat down .

From the corner of my eye, I noticed a small card next to Simone, who sat at the desk next to mine.

'You're telling *me* you have detention too?' I gasped. Simone wasn't the type to be given a detention. 'What for?'

She shunned the question, so I asked her again.

'Oh, for leaving the school grounds, that's it.'

I could tell she didn't want to talk about it, so I left her alone and waited for the next question.

At the break, Darren came over to me.

'So, three tickets, eh?' he laughed.

'Hmm,' I replied, pretending to be bewitched by a Twix bar. Darren looked at me and laughed harder.

'Thought you'd be allowed to pass with one last warning?'

How on earth did he know? Have we known each other for so long that he can read my mind?

I nodded, and Darren tutted just like Mrs Clauseton had.

'And Mrs Clauseton was like *"I expect better from you, Hayden"* wasn't she?'

'Leave it, Darren,' I hissed. 'Mr Oliver cleared the detention date anyways. He said he'll tear up my date card and bin it. So stop going on about an event that isn't ever gonna happen.'

'Just trying to help,' he muttered.

After the break, it was time for the football match. I'd taken a banana and an energy bar for a snack. Mum had told me to as they were good sources of energy. Darren was going with me. He too had an energy bar.

We were chatting about the upcoming match and all our tactics when Darren told me the worst news.

'Tom Ventnor's playing for O.M. Juniors.'

I instantly fell silent. Tom Ventnor was an *awesome* player for Grisworth FC, our team. He was the best person to be a striker and was the one who'd won us one JCF trophy, and now he was playing for our rivals? In the *finals?*

'What? Why?' I cried. 'That's not fair at all!'

'O.M. Juniors have a really injured player, and they needed another substitute, so for good sportsmanship, Tom is taking their place.'

'Why can't they make do with one less sub, though?' I whined.

'Because it's the JFC rules that each group has three substitutes, and we had an extra one! So Tom goes *"I'll be a sub for Juniors, Coach!"* and boom, he's on the other team,' Darren explained.

I felt like confronting Tom, right there, right now, but then again, Darren said he was a *substitute*, so hopefully, he wouldn't be swapped onto the pitch.

64

'Well, we still have a chance of beating them, don't you think?' I remarked reassuringly.

'No, not really,' Darren replied.

It was nice he thought Grisworth FC didn't really have a chance of winning, wasn't it? But to be honest, I agreed with him.

The next lesson was P.E., but our football team had to get on the school coach to go to a football court somewhere in Milton Keynes. Tom came on our coach as well, and everyone tried to avoid him.

'Nobody wants to sit next to Traitor over there,' Simon Bosky chuckled. Everyone laughed. Tom paid no attention to them. It was like that for the whole journey. All the boys sat at the back except for Tom and shared fake tactics so Tom could hear and know our *"plan."*

'You know I can hear you?' he spat.

Alfred Smith, the captain of Grisworth FC shouted back, 'We'll be quieter then!' He then made a gesture for everyone to speak louder.

Eventually, Coach Brown told us to keep the noise down.

'We have a player for the other group on this coach, and we don't want him hearing our strategies!' he advised. 'Let's *hush* a little — OK chums?'

We all said *"sorry"* and started talking *even* louder.

Mr Brown shook his head and said it was our fault for sharing tactics.

'So, I'll be midfielder for a change,' Alfred practically shouted.

Sam raised his hand. 'I'll be a striker.'

Alfred nodded. 'Good plan.'

Tom looked back and I could see the confusion on his face. Normally, Alfred was a striker and Sam was a midfielder. They would be, we just wanted O.M. Juniors and Tom to believe our fake plan. Then, they could set up *their* positions, thinking it would defeat ours. Actually, we'd already strategised without Tom a few minutes before we boarded the bus.

My phone beeped; Mum had sent me a text.

"Remember to smash them! Love you!" Darren tried to read the message on my phone screen, but I hid it away from him and texted back: *"Just about to go on the pitch, bye!"*

I knew that would stop her from texting again, as there was no point because I wouldn't reply.

'Your Mum?' Darren asked, imitating what my Mum sounded like. ' *"Oh, I love you! Have a good day at school, remember your phone, lunch money and snack! Take out the dogs when you get back."* '

It was actually spot on. 'You've been around my house too many times.'

66

We arrived at the pitch in twenty minutes, and O.M. Juniors were already doing laps at the side of the field.

Tom was the first person to run out of the coach, and he joined his *"team."* Unwisely, he started sprinting up and down the side of the field, already using up his energy.

I was the last to leave the coach since I was at the *very* back with Darren.

Coach Brown was tapping our heads as we came out, either saying '*on-pitch*' or *"substitute"* I was on-pitch, unsurprisingly, as a defender. Alfred was a striker (of course) and so was Darren, the lucky thing.

'I'll be seeing you on the opposite side of the pitch, Hayden,' Alfred chuckled.

I pulled a quick smile.

Coach Brown got us doing burpees, jumping jacks, sit-ups, press-ups and more painful hyphenated exercises.

'I've — got — a — stitch,' Harry groaned.

Coach Brown gave him a thumbs-up. 'Good boy!'

Harry raised an eyebrow. 'Are you seriously congratulating me for having a stitch?'

Coach Brown nodded. 'It means you are working hard, Mr H. If it's truly *that* bad, put your hands on your hips where it hurts and push.'

Harry turned red, because O.M. Juniors heard a few metres away, and it sounded as if he was constipated.

'Thanks, coach,' Harry replied, turning red. 'Yeah, thanks a bunch.'

Even players from Grisworth FC were laughing. Darren was, so I nudged him in the side. 'He won't play well if he's embarrassed half the time,' I muttered.

Darren nodded, and shouted, 'Yeah, that'll help you lose the stitch!'

He thought that would lose everyone's attention.

Pfft.

* * *

Many of the spectator seats were unoccupied at first, but parents and others who had come to see the match had started to snap them up.

'Oh, look, there's my Dad!' Darren shouted, waving to a blonde-haired guy. He had black shades on and looked like he'd been going to the gym daily since he was ten. His pearly white polo-shirt was buttoned-up and had a cobalt blue line at the very bottom of the collar. He had denim jeans secured by a pure black belt with a gold buckle. He had the sort of perfect, natural tan everyone envied. His cream blonde hair flew in the perfect direction as if there were an invisible fan blowing it.

Darren acted cool about having a dad who looked just like Ken, something I would never be able to do.

'I've rarely seen your dad,' I stated, 'and now I have seen him again, I think I would've mistaken him for a Hollywood actor.'

My friend chortled. 'Oh, yes, he's been a couple of places. He's a model. And the reason why you haven't see him in ages is because he'd often been in Washington in America over the last few years doing magazine covers.'

I gawped. 'And you never told me?'

Darren shrugged. 'Don't like people making it a big thing, that's all.'

If his dad was a model, what was his mum?

'What does your mum do again?'

'Fashion designer,' Darren replied. 'Works well, huh?'

I nodded. 'So your mum designs clothes for your dad to model?'

'Exactly that.'

'Did your mum design that?' I asked, pointing to Darren's dad's outfit.

69

Darren shook his hands, gesturing "in the middle." 'My mum owns the company that sells the clothes, but a worker actually made the outfit. It's a simple design, you can find that sort of stuff in any design company, no biggie.'

I wanted to go on and on about Darren's dad, but I knew the match started in five minutes. 'The last question, I promise. You ready? What's the name of your mum's company and what's your dad's name?'

Darren facepalmed himself. 'That's three!'

'Oh.'

'Whatever,' he continued. 'And how do you not know the name of my dad? You've met him before.'

'Once.'

'My dad's name is Derek Crosby. My mum's company is called — I'd rather not say.'

'Oh, go on,' I persuaded.

'It's Fashquet, OK?'

I tried not to laugh. Fashquet? What was Mrs Crosby thinking? I was intrigued. I had to check it out.

'Is there a shop as well?'

Darren rolled his eyes. 'Fourth question, and yes.'

'Where?'

'It will say on the website if you type in www.fashquet.co.uk. Why are you so interested anyway?'

I took a step back. 'Oh, it's not me who's interested,' I insisted, and I realised it came out rudely. 'I mean, I love the idea and the clothes and everything, but I think my mum would prefer it more. Be ready for about £1,000 coming your way!'

The whistle blew for us to get on the pitch. Tom looked more confused than before; the positions we'd confirmed on the coach didn't match the positions we were in now.

Then, he realised our plan and frowned. I could tell he'd already told O.M. Juniors our placement because some of the team started scowling at Tom.

I smirked at him and he shot a look of daggers back.

Just before the game started, I had a chance to look around the stadium. There were rows upon rows of seats, all of them now occupied. Every so often, there was a door planted in the wall for entry and exit.

The seats were packed with adults and children, curly-haired toddlers, blonde-haired teens, formally dressed adults, and so on. I looked for my mum, but I knew it was for nothing. She'd probably still be working out at the gym.

The majority of the stadium spectators were there for the O.M. Juniors, but the small section of Grisworth FC supporters was cheering as loudly as possible in the circumstances.

The referee put the whistle to his lips and blew once to indicate the game was about to start. When he was certain we were all in our places, he blew it again.

Sam managed to get the ball and pass it to Harry, but Harry soon got tackled by an O.M. Juniors player. They dribbled it down the pitch, already coming closer to the goal. That was my cue.

As the other player got nearer to our goal, I edged closer to the direction in which he was approaching and tried to tackle the ball away. He made it past me, so it was up to Liam — the goalkeeper — to save the shot.

I could hear the tension in the spectators' voices, so I decided to help out a bit more. It was only a minute in, and O.M. was about to score their first goal already.

I switched my planning mode on and brainstormed. Then I thought of something. It was a risky thing to do since the boy was already twenty yards away, but I still did it.

He was running so fast it was hard to track his next move, but I tried anyway and lunged into a slide-tackle. I eased the ball off the other player and it "stuck" to my feet. Grisworth FC fans screamed as I looked for someone to pass the ball to.

The O.M. Juniors player moaned and muttered, 'He thinks he's better than me?'

Liam looked like the world had been lifted off his shoulders. I could understand the pressure of being a goalie, I'd been in that position a few times.

The nearest Grisworth player was too far away, so I passed the ball to Liam, making sure I did it at an angle so the other team's player couldn't swipe the ball off me.

I turned around to get back to my main spot and saw the boy who had nearly broken into a shot before I heroically tackled. Suddenly, I realised it was Tom, his shoulder-length brown hair following him everywhere. This motivated me even more, and I knew my team would also be excited I'd put off "the traitor." A sudden surge filled my insides.

The match was going exceedingly well and Alfred had managed to score a goal for us. He'd tackled another player who was quite close to the goal, and at the speed of light, he'd taken a shot. The shot was so powerful that the opposing team's goalie was mesmerised and forgot what he was actually supposed to do.

'Move it, lazy!' the coach of O.M. Juniors shouted. He was wearing one of their red and white vertical striped hoodies, and on the back was printed the number 1 and "BEST COACH EVER!" Pfft, yeah right. I don't think he's heard of Coach Brown yet.

Alfred did his celebration routine — a backflip — and even the O.M. Juniors fans cheered.

The match went downhill as soon as O.M. Juniors scored with three minutes to spare. Everyone knew it was going to have to go into penalties, but Grisworth FC (without luck) tried to squeeze in a late lucky goal anyways.

Three minutes past and the whistle blew.

O.M. Juniors fans cheered so loudly it drowned out the Grisworth FC fans. Everyone knew that we had no chance at penalties — O.M. Juniors had the best strikers and always won the shootouts.

We were given two minutes to sort out who was doing what. Coach Brown decided who was taking the shots, and I was one of them. I used to be a striker and I was great at it.

Four other boys, Alfred, Brody, Simon and James were each taking a shot as well.

'Line up!' the ref hollered. I and the other four boys stood in a line in front of the goal. Alfred was going last because if the score was a tie, he'd be certain to get it in.

'Up first, we have James Wilfred from Grisworth FC!' the commentator announced. The Grisworth FC players cheered, and the O.M. Juniors players laughed.

James took a few steps back and ran for the ball. He kicked it with such force a divot of grass came out of the ground. It was a shame since the O.M. Juniors goalie thought and responded quickly; the shot was at the perfect angle for the ball to line up and be caught by his cup-shaped hands in an unusually accurate piece of coordination! It was almost as if the ball came to him! James looked crushed. I sympathised even if I was miffed. It must be the worst feeling to start by losing a penalty for your team.

'And a perfect shot for the O.M. Juniors goalie, William Spanksby! Next up, we have Lewis Donaldson, fighting for a goal for the Juniors!'

Lewis looked redder than ever. He was jogging on the spot, warming up for the big moment. He soon ran up to the ball and fooled our goalie by making a decoy move to the left when he was actually shooting right. I would've expected Liam to know that trick, but it went in anyway.

The O.M. Juniors fans cheered like mad. They were winning 0-1.

'What a goal!' the commentator cried. 'Now, ladies and gentlemen, we have Simon Gregory from Grisworth FC!'

The commentator had their own tiny room at the very top of the stadium. They weren't professional commentators, and they didn't talk about the match after it was over like the TV pundits, but it was cool pretending I was a proper footballer when there was a commentator. Embarrassing as it was, I helped Simon out by shouting and chanting his name as loudly as possible.

'Simon, Simon, Simon!' I shouted. All of my team joined in, and some of the O.M. Juniors players were cheering as well.

Tom started shouting his name, too, but he soon got shushed by a boy that was probably their captain.

Simon revved up, got in his starting position and went in for the shot.

'And — it's in!' the match commentator shouted. 'Now, for O.M. Juniors' second shoot, we have the captain, Adam Fursheca. I, Scott Pickley, am excited for this lad.'

Adam did the same starting move, and then went in for a shot, but stumbled with his footing. The ball wobbled a metre or two in front of Adam, ending up nowhere near the goal.

'Oh, and it's a sore miss! Not much power in that one!' Scott chuckled.

Adam turned red. 'I demand a retake!' he screamed. 'My — my laces were undone!' Everyone in the stadium was silent, and all eyes focused on Adam's laces.

Then, the commentator breathed into his mic, 'All eyes on Adam. Looks like they're triple knotted! Someone's been chewing on the Fib Fudge!'

Adam shouted in protest. 'No, I'm not! It simply felt like they were untied!'

The commentator carried on, 'We'll let him keep his spot, but that goal certainly doesn't count and he definitely will not get a retake!'

The coach of O.M. Juniors beckoned for Adam to go to the side-lines. He patted his shoulder and whispered something to him, and Adam grinned from ear to ear.

'OK — next up we have Brody Junes from Grisworth FC!'

Brody kicked the ball higher than most shoots, a clever choice since the O.M. Juniors goalie was not as tall as our goalie. It went in, and so did a cheer.

'Darn it,' I saw the O.M. Juniors coach mutter.

Scott cheered. 'Gone for a tall one, there! Grisworth FC is winning, but all could change, depending on this shot from Ralf Cludo!'

Of course, Ralf had to score. It was a Ronaldo-worthy shot as well.

So that left Alfred and me.

'You'll smash it,' Alfred told me.

I smiled, even though I hadn't taken a penalty in months.

The commentator looked down at me. 'Here we have...' Scott looked down at a sheet or something, '... a speedy and smart defender!'

All the pressure descended on me. If I got this in now, there was a chance of us winning.

It was all a blur when I took the shot. I couldn't remember what had happened. But then, I heard the loud cheers and a voice booming, 'It's a goal!'

I saw all of my teammates and the Grisworth FC supporters cheering.

Alfred came over and shouted, 'You did it!'

I wasn't that amazed, partly because I didn't know what was going on, but I celebrated even so.

'If O.M. Juniors get this one in, there's a chance of them taking the win. Here comes Max Crest!'

Max was tall and thin, with a mop of curly, dark brown hair. I could tell already he'd score. And my instincts were correct.

'It all depends on Alfred Stone to get this one in. Go big or go home, people!' Scott cried.

Alfred looked as confident as ever. He stepped up to the penalty line, looked at the ball and smirked as if they were distant enemies.

He put all his life and soul into the shot, charging at the ball. He took note of all the tactics Coach Brown had taught us, making sure to use the right part of your foot, looking at where you want the shot to go; you could tell he was trying. It was a perfect effort as well.

But the goalie was too quick.

The Grisworth FC fans were devastated, and so was Alfred.

When he returned to the team, his eyes were watering. 'It's Tom,' he whined. 'We've lost. Pack up, boys, let's go, we're done here.'

Coach Brown patted his back like the O.M. Juniors coach. 'You did awesome, boy. And you never know, Tom could be off today and completely miss!'

What I also heard Coach Brown mutter wasn't very helpful, though.

'Not very likely,' he mumbled, mixing it into a cough.

The commentator coughed into the mic to stop the noise. 'Uh-hum. Sorry. The last shot of the day, Tom Ventnor!'

Tom acted as if the ball was his enemy, and kicked it so hard and quickly, the whole thing blinded me. Once again, it was a blur. Not my sort of confusion blur, an actual "I-can't-see-it" blur.

The volume of shouting and screaming was immense.

'Our Junior Cup Finals winners: O.M. Juniors Football Academy!'

Grisworth FC was forced to congratulate the other team and shake hands with them. As I shook their hands, I pressed down as hard as possible on their fingers.

'Sore loser,' the tall boy named Max Crest muttered.

'Bad winner,' I replied.

After five minutes of walking around in circles, trying to figure out who we'd shaken hands with and who we hadn't, Scott Pickley announced the man of the match.

'Now, for the moment you've been waiting for, our man of the match award goes to...'

There was weirdly ominous suspense as everyone fell silent.

'... Tom Ventnor, for scoring the winning goal and playing like a star!'

The O.M. Juniors' side cheered and shouted Tom's name. One lady, with the same looks as Tom, was shrieking her head off.

Tom collected what must've been his 27th or whatever trophy. Grisworth FC was only there to see a bit of the collection, and all of our supporters had already filtered out of the stadium. Some had even left when Alfred missed and it was Tom up next. So much for a substitute.

* * *

As soon as we got back from the match, everyone thought we'd won because of Tom's trophy. Tom had pleasure in telling everyone that wasn't the case.

'No, they lost,' he boasted. 'This trophy is because I won man of the match. The coach of O.M. Juniors was so mystified by my warm-ups that he swapped me onto the pitch before the match had started.'

Everyone congratulated him more than they had in the stadium, and Tom carried around his trophy to show everyone who asked how the match went.

I tried to ignore Tom for the rest of the school day because I knew as soon as I saw him, he'd bring out his trophy, and maybe even "accidentally" shove it in my face. But if I told him to stop gloating, it would show I was affected by it.

'Good job, mate!' I congratulated when he was passing me.

Tom smiled. 'On what?'

I knew he just wanted to hear me say it, but again, I didn't care.

'Winning the game and getting the man of the match. Pretty sick, man.'

I saw the smug look on Tom's face. 'Yeah, it is. What a shame you lost. I bet you would've won if I were on your team.'

'Mm,' I muttered through gritted teeth.

Four

A Hole New World

I t was twelve o'clock. I know, I know, why did I stay up so late? Well, let's just put it into one word: homework. Well at least, I'd gotten it out of the way before the weekend.

My Saturday morning routine wasn't hard to repeat, and soon I'd have left home with my favourite — a PB&J sandwich.

I'd secretly wrapped it in tinfoil to take to Rodger's house. We were going to go to the park together. I looked back at the street sign — Libra Harp Lane. That had been a tradition since forever — looking back at the street sign whenever I was leaving without permission, just in case it was the last time I'd ever see it (not that I'd leave without permission when I was young or anything). Mum and Dad were still in the house, but they probably wouldn't notice me gone and think I was upstairs on my Xbox.

Surprisingly, I was correct.

I arrived at Rodger's, but he wasn't there. His parents were, on the other hand.

Jenn wasn't looking as cheery as usual, and her long, black locks were tightly kept up in a ballerina's bun. Rodger's dad, Caesar, was smartly dressed in a black boss-suit and his hair was waxed into place.

'Hello, Mr and Mrs Calendor, where is Rodger?' I asked, standing tall with a grin on my face. Trust me, you don't want to look slouchy when you're facing the Calendors. They'd probably pull you in for a private yoga lesson to fix your posture.

'Oh, Rodger's at his tutoring session,' Mrs Calendor replied. 'Has he not told you about that? He does it every other two days. Quite a friend you are!'

'No, no, I've heard all about his tutor,' I retorted. Sighing, I added, 'Well, thanks for the notice. Tell Rodge...'

'Rodge?' Mr Calendor questioned, pulling a face.

'... I mean, tell Rodger I was here.' And with that, I walked away.

As I was making my way to the park, a loud noise rumbled in the distance. I can't explain how sick I was of all the storms lately. But it was blue skies ahead, not a single cloud in sight.

Then I suddenly realised it wasn't a storm.

I carried on walking towards the park, deciding I'd be one of those loners who went by themselves. Still, the sound followed me.

I tried walking quickly, further away from the noise, but no matter how far I went, the roar followed me. I picked up pace and started to walk quickly. Far too quickly.

A stitch formed in my side, so I entered the small cafe at the mouth of the park. Once sat inside, the rumble went away for a while.

I unwrapped my PB&J sandwich (it's a peanut butter and jelly sandwich – mostly a thing for the Americans) and ordered a flat white coffee with the five pounds in my pocket.

Having finished my refreshments and dropped my styrofoam cup in a bin, I exited the cafe, careful not to awaken whatever the sound was.

But then I heard it again. Louder, this time. I walked further and further away from the park with no idea where I was heading.

More walking — quicker and quicker still. I was speed-walking. The stitch in my side grew, now feeling as if it was slowly tearing my ribcage apart. Where was the sudden surge within me coming from? I was moving quicker by the second.

Again, the sound rumbled like a vicious tornado. And that's when I decided to sprint.

It was a small wonder I wasn't split in two. My stitch was practically killing me. And yet, I ran.

Ahead of me, I saw a ditch. Or a black hole. Or both.

No, it's just an illusion, I thought, Keep on running.

I tripped on what must have been fresh air. Then I fell.

Everything was black. Everything was still. All was silent. My fingers were numb and I couldn't feel a thing. It was like my senses had been snatched away. The last thing I remembered was the black hole. The only thing I was sure about was that I'd been knocked unconscious and was just waking. I'd forgotten my name. My brain was buzzing with questions I couldn't answer, like "Where am I?" and "Why can't I see?"

Just then, I heard something. It sounded like thudding on a hard wooden deck. Then the sound multiplied until it was louder than a conch horn. I heard mumbling around me, but not in English. No, this was more a conlang suited for a Martian.

I felt a sharp poke in my left arm, and I tried to cry in agony, but no sound came out. Just then, my vision cleared, and before I got a proper look at the blurred figures, a dozen hands seized my arms and legs and marched me off.

* * *

The next time I woke up, I could see, hear and feel, which was a great relief. What I did see now were two hairy green creatures, each about the size of a toddler. They were grinning like mad scientists and speaking their unknown language.

'AGH!' I screamed.

'Hekoa unam!' one chimed, waving its four-fingered hand. 'Disepta colest?' The hairy figure held out a plate of what looked like cactus, only red.

'No, I — I'm fine,' I stuttered. I figured it probably meant something like "Eat this, you vermin!" or something like that.

After offering me the red cactus, they escorted me to some sort of dorm.

I didn't get the chance to see much of my surroundings, but on the way, I noticed lots of buildings made of wood. Duplicates of the same figures were cleaning or crafting or something else I didn't recognise as belonging to my experiences on planet Earth.

When we reached the dorm, one of the creatures belted out something like "Romin arona!" and spread his arms as a welcome.

The room had half a dozen bunk desks, which are basically bunk beds but with the bottom bunk as a desk.

A girl sat on a carpet, despite all the bunks. She was alone, playing what appeared to be some sort of card game, even though most card games are played with at least two people.

'Crocid Mae,' another green hairy figure beamed. He was sitting down on the carpet playing a card game with the girl whose name seemed to be Mae. Now I think of it, he wasn't there before — had I really been gone so long I'd turned crazy?

The girl stood up and dusted herself off as if she was covered in cobwebs.

'Yep, I'm Mae. And these guys are the Nurogons,' she cheered, pulling the Nurogon she'd played cards with to her side.

I looked Mae up and down. It looked like she'd been dragged through a bush and had been raised in the jungle half her life — her ginger hair was unkempt and hanging loose, her ragged jeans were ripped, but not in a trendy way, and her arms were scarred for life, it seemed.

'Ho — how do you understand these beasts — Nurogons?' I questioned. I probably should've kept quiet, because the girl's look became dangerous.

'Once you're here for a while, the effects start taking place. This is the land of the Nurogons; you can be everything you've ever wanted.'

As she said that, I started to remember my name, letter by letter.

H-A-Y...

'Hayden,' I marvelled, as it finally came to me. 'My name is Hayden.'

The Nurogons that had escorted me into the room (there were about seven of them) cheered and chatted, and suddenly I could understand them.

'Welcome to Nurogonia, the Land of the Nurogons,' one rejoiced.

* * *

The last few days had been challenging. I had to decide whether or not to try the food in this new world, and I would've starved if it wasn't for the tip one of the Nurogons gave me — the food instantaneously knows what you'd like to eat.

That was quite a bonus. At each meal, I mostly ended up eating half of my seventh helping.

By the third evening in my new home, Nurogonia, someone had called it, I wasn't hesitant about eating one bit. But sometimes, the food wasn't tasting so good, so I'd end up having soggy lasagne or chicken pie with neon-yellow sauce.

The Nurogons told me to greet "everyone" I saw, and I did. By doing this, I gained a few pals. One, by the name of Grisella, started tutoring me. She taught me their language and how to pronounce numbers. I think she had said they spoke Nurogonian. Every time she saw me, she'd say in her shrill voice, "Hayden, let's revise numbers 100-200 in Nurogonian!" And I'd make a stupid excuse and run away before she could call me back.

Mae was becoming more of a friend than an acquaintance to me. She helped tidy the dorm, set the table, even clean the toilets. We'd also traded stories of when we were back in our homeland on Earth. She relayed that her mother would teach her how to knit and bake cakes. Apparently, her mother worked as a Business Analyst, which I thought was a pretty decent job.

'What about your dad?' I'd asked, which I almost immediately regretted asking.

Mae had put her head down. 'Died when I was two... Enough about me, what's it like at yours?'

Dr Rubeka taught me Zumorse and Nurogo code at one of our private dorm lessons. She added a desk in the corner of the dorm and called it "The Doodah Desk."

Every Potlku and Ishkop (those weird words are Nurogonian days of the week) she'd bring out a stack of papers and timed me to finish them all, causing our lessons to be up to three hours long.

Mae sat in the corner, either reading or secretly watching me and smirking. She remarked she'd already had her lessons and they couldn't possibly teach her anything more (cough, cough).

'Did you do your homework last lesson, Hayden?' Dr Rubeka asked me.

I struggled for words. 'It's not exactly done, but I did make a start.'

Dr Rubeka raised a bushy eyebrow. She looked like the other Nurogons, only taller, slimmer and smarter. Oh, and she wore glasses and a scientist's coat.

The Nurogons were four-fingered, two-toed, freckled, muddy-green creatures about the size of a tall toddler. They had long dark green nails, droopy eyes, sloppy noses, big white teeth, hunched backs and large folding chins. Clusters of hair sat on their sideburns, the top of their heads, the tips of their large pointed ears and the tip of their tails. They were often seen wearing a white toga with a red sash.

'Show me,' she demanded rather crossly.

I looked at the small duffel bag next to my feet and brought out Ishkop's homework from the side pocket.

'Here, all done, pages 10-50.'

I pushed the papers to face her, and after a few seconds, a spurt escaped her tight-closed lips. Then she started laughing. She laughed and laughed. Finally, once she'd caught her breath, she spoke.

'Y — you think I,' she pointed at herself, occasionally still getting the giggles, 'I — Dr Rubeka, smartest Nurogon in Nurogonia — believe that you,' she pointed at me, 'did not hand me another day's homework?'

Busted, Canada would've said.

'Hayden, that's unacceptable.' I looked back to find Mae Greens, standing in the other corner of the room with her arms crossed. She looked so serious, which was one in a million for Mae.

'What are you doing here, Curls. Go and find the plunger or whatever.'

'Actually,' Mae smirked, 'I finished toilet duty a few hours ago, Pith Smith. Since someone doesn't have a very long attention span, someone else had to check off the job.'

'Go. You shouldn't be here, Mop,' I grunted through gritted teeth. I didn't dare look at her, she'd just see how mad I was.

Mae scoffed and left the room.

Once she was sure she was gone, Dr Rubeka started chuckling to herself again. 'She's a bit moody!'

I laughed along with her. I knew Mae was still five metres within the room, probably hiding behind a wall or something, but I didn't care.

Then, Dr Rubeka abruptly stopped chortling and faced me, looking dead serious.

Oh boy, I thought, I'm in for it now.

'You can do half of your homework here with me and throw away the rest,' Dr Rubeka sighed. 'I understand you can't finish it all, and maybe I've been giving you a bit too much. We'll scrap the revision; I think you've done enough of that. But the parts you struggle on is a definite keep. You can sort out what papers you'd like to do now and throw away the rest. And I've got a brand new charger for your coding device.'

I sighed with relief. 'You're a life-saver.'

When I missed my family, which was all the time, the Nurogons let me look at their present actions in a book called the Okaloma. I'd only be able to see them for a few seconds, but it always made me more upset than ever.

Every single time I took a look in the book, I'd see Mum crying or Canada with her head in her hands or Dad desolately drinking a cup of gin.

I was missing them so much; I couldn't believe how Mae did it. She told me she'd been in Nurogonia for a few months now, helping with the resources, doing tasks, waiting for her quest. Every night, at least one tear with the lettering "FAMILY" on it would find its way striding down my cheek.

I just wondered if they were missing me as much.

Five

Welcome to My World

Hey, I'm Canada, Hayden's sister as you know. This will probably be the first and last time you'll see me here; writing isn't my hobby.

The last few days have been challenging for me, so Mum suggested I keep a "diary." But who can be bothered to waste a fiver on something you're not gonna use? So I chose to write my thoughts on a laptop.

Well, I guess there's nothing more to say other than I don't accept sympathy. I don't like all that sappy stuff. But I will take chocola — empathy, I mean. You've been warned.

* * *

Mum had a chat with the police for the fourth time, sobbing her eyes out. Since Hayden had gone missing, there wasn't a time I'd not seen her crying over the last few days. She'd cry herself to sleep, not that she got more than half an hour of it. Every time she had fainted, she regretted it so much, because she thought she would miss out on a huge event, like Hayden coming back or the po-po finding clues. Mum also thought if she fainted and fell too hard when Hayden returned (if he ever would) she wouldn't remember him.

I had to walk myself to school instead of Mum or Dad driving me. It took ages to walk there and back, so sometimes Tiffany's dad would pick me up, or sometimes he'd shout at me and say he's sick and tired of having an extra body in the car.

Of course, I was the one who had to explain to the teachers where Hayden was, and they all said they're very sorry and shall pray for him. I knew they were just saying that — most weren't religious.

'Have a — have a g — good day at school, C — Canada,' Mum sobbed. She had a doctor's appointment that morning about her digestion. She was only having water and a banana a day, so the doctor's stated they would either have to tube-feed her (which I couldn't imagine happening) or she had to start eating.

I reached the bus stop just as the bus doors were going to close, and screamed, 'WAIT!'

Mr Macken, the bus driver, raised an eyebrow at me. 'Late, Canada?'

I hesitated. 'I — I'm sorry, a lot is going on in my life right now. And I was only late by a few seconds, anyway.'

Mr Macken tutted and gestured for me to get on. 'Boarding was a minute ago, and Mr Stan did say you're supposed to arrive at the bus stop five minutes before boarding, so that's six minutes late, young lassie.'

I took a seat next to Beth and she greeted me.

'Oh, hey,' I muttered, exhaustedly.

'You had a good sleep?' Beth asked.

I nodded. What if I drifted off in class? Then I would get a detention, surely.

Beth looked at me. 'Listen, you don't have to keep all your feelings to yourself. You have friends like me and Tiff, don't you? If anything is troubling you, tell us. You do know that?'

I nodded, even though I knew it was a bad idea to tell Beth anything; once it's with Beth, it's with the whole school.

I stepped off the bus, so tired I used the railings to lean on. Mr Macken helped me upright, letting out a small chuckle.

'Is your spine screwed on properly?' he asked and pretended to repair something on my back.

I laughed with him, though it still hurt. It hurt to do everything — walk, run, laugh.

I wondered if it would be possible to make it through school, especially P.E. Maybe I should've called in sick or made a fake note saying I can't do P.E., then forge Mum's signature at the bottom.

Beth walked into school with me, patting my back, which was the last thing I wanted.

'Ah!' I cried.

Beth pulled her hands away. 'Oh, I'm sorry! What did I do?'

I strained to straighten myself back up. 'Nah, it's fine. I'm a little bit — you know — crooked.'

Beth raised an eyebrow.

At that moment, her hair was tied up in a loose, quick bun, her go-to hairstyle. Beth's white shirt and black tie were stainless and pure white. Her black skirt was level with her knees, but she said she liked it that way.

'A little bit crooked?' she exclaimed. 'I think you need to see the nurse.' Beth attempted to drag me towards the nurse's office to the right of us.

I pulled away and shook my head, saying I'd be fine, but seeing the nurse wouldn't have been an altogether bad idea.

We collected our schedules from the front desk and headed off to our lockers. That's where everyone usually hung out and chatted about stuff.

'Oh, really, my locker was number two hundred! I got an XXL one,' I heard Blanche say to Isabella. 'Purely to keep all of my designer gear in, you know?'

Beth looked at me and rolled her eyes. ' "I got a million bucks for my birthday," ' she imitated in a silly voice, ' "but it wasn't that much." '

I giggled for a few seconds. I was either becoming less tired or getting used to being tired.

Isabella smiled. 'Lucky, I got my locker for half the price!'

'Oh my gosh, I can't believe it! You've been living a very frugal life, Izzy.'

Beth went up to Isabella to comfort her and tried to put her arm on Isabella's shoulder, but she pushed her away.

'I'll do it myself, Beth,' Isabella muttered.

Beth backed away but also mouthed the words "stop it" to Blanche. Blanche raised an eyebrow.

'So, this...' Blanche burst out laughing, shocking everyone. 'So this kid thinks she can — ha! — she thinks she can tell me t — to stop!'

Everyone laughed along, even though it wasn't funny. Well, everyone except me.

She stared straight at me. 'Are you alright, State?'

Blanche used "State" as a nickname for me since she believed Canada was a state in the U.S.A. Blanche was a bit dim, you see. She'd have pleasure in saying "in a state, State?" whenever I was struggling or in a bad situation.

I hesitated to reply but found my words eventually. 'I'm not laughing because it's not funny, Bleach.'

All of the boys made an "oooh..." sound, and soon lots were gathered around Blanche and me.

'I — uh — you daren't try that one on me! Did the teachers choose you as a homecoming queen?'

I shook my head firmly. 'But they did choose me to represent the whole school in Multi-Debate.'

I could feel Beth smiling, and I knew the smile was partly because I had taken over the situation for her and let her slide away.

'You!' Blanche called, pointing her bony finger at Beth.

Not so smug anymore, huh? I thought.

Blanche beckoned for Beth to come, and she scooted over from the shadows.

'I cannot believe you forgot all about Breakfast in Bed!' she randomly exclaimed, forgetting I was there.

Beth focused, then her grim face expanded into a grin. 'B&B! Oh, way back in Year 4, right? That was the life!'

Blanche giggled. 'We should totally do it again, eh, what do you think?'

I winked at Beth, and she winked back. I trusted her enough not to fall for Blanche's silly games.

'I think... yes, of course!'

I stared blankly at Beth, and Blanche nudged her and breathed something in her ear.

'Yeah, I'm done with Canada,' she shouted, striding through the locker room, arm-in-arm with Beth.

'I...' I didn't understand what I'd done wrong. How could Beth do such a thing? I remembered being more of a friend to Tiffany, but Tiffany and I were in different forms and classes. Beth was all I had left.

'So, I'll tell my dad to book two-person massages and manicures at the spa, then you can come to mine for a movie? We have a 150-inch flat-screen TV, so we can watch a movie or something,' Blanche babbled.

'150-inch?' Beth asked, shocked.

Blanche nodded. 'I'm so mad at Daddy for not buying a 200-inch one. They're not expensive, like, I think they're ten grand?'

'I am so being your BFF,' Beth squealed.

She looked back at me and blinked hard. This time, I knew what it meant. We'd called it "The Double-Wink." It was such an old invention I wasn't sure Beth would remember it. But things come in handy, eh?

One Double-Wink told me she'd find a way to pretend to be friends with Blanche, embarrass her and expose her and still get away with it.

I looked back at them strolling down the hallway and smiled.

At lunch, Blanche and Beth sat next to each other on a six-seater table, even though there were two-seaters in the corners.

I caught Blanche looking Beth up and down, and then saying, 'After school, half three, you're coming to mine. I cannot have you looking like that with me. I don't deserve it.'

Beth nodded and beamed, 'I'd love that!' I could hear the waver in her voice. Although it was a scheme, she actually sounded affected by it. I could tell it was harder than it looked to put up with Blanche and not merely punch her in her perfect face. 'But — I'm going somewhere with Canada.'

I was shocked. I thought she'd be with Blanche 24/7, she obviously wanted to share her ideas with me. Or make Blanche jealous?

Blanche pulled a face. 'That person?' she exclaimed. 'Oh, you'd rather hang out with me, trust me.'

Beth smiled. 'Yeah, but my mum forced me to go to her house. She says I need to "befriend" her since she's — you know — lonely. Also, if I wanna get a car in a couple weeks, I need to do something "compassionate." '

I scoffed, forgetting it wasn't actually true. For a second, I thought she was using me to obtain a stupid car, plus Beth's mum, Tess, told me herself she'd allow Beth to have a car for Christmas when she was seventeen. How could she not know that?

Blanche frowned. 'I was willing to pay for you...'

'You pay for friends?' Beth questioned, clearly shocked. There was a horrific rasp in Beth's voice and she clutched her throat in agony.

'... but I don't see the point of paying for someone who will not be here. Daddy gives me fifty pounds a week to buy my friends, but I could obviously keep the money if you want?'

Beth's eyes grew larger, but she managed to keep her cool. 'Oh, I'm not saying I don't want it, it's just...'

Blanche smiled. Now she was manipulating Beth. 'I'll give you five pounds a day, only on school days. Starting tomorrow. So that gives you...' Blanche counted on her fingers. 'Sixteen pounds? Wait, no, no, twenty pounds.'

'Twenty-five, actually. Twenty-five a week, if we're excluding weekends.'

I watched the two girls shake on it, and I have to admit, I sort of wanted to be in Beth's position. Twenty-five pounds a week? I thought. That would help me and my family out incredibly.

'Oh, I'm so upset you have to attend P.E. with Canada!' Blanche whined.

I was slyly loitering around them near the bin where they were. Beth's elbow was leaning on the bin, and every now and again Blanche would give her a look of disgust.

I was in a position where I could see and hear them, but they couldn't do the same for me, due to the stage curtains.

'I know right! She'll probably stink up the gym room!' Beth complained, laughing at the last sentence.

I observed them laughing together and tried not to believe Beth was enjoying her time with Blanche.

Blanche stretched out her arms, waiting for a hug. 'See you after school, Beth Bug!'

Beth stared at Blanche's open arms in shock. I did the same.

Beth Bug was my name for Beth. I had a "No Use of Nickname Beth Bug Unless You Are Canada Smith" policy. And Blanche being Blanche had to step in and break the law.

'Excuse me?' Beth stuttered.

Blanche rolled her eyes childishly. 'I said "See you after school, Beth Bug!" '

Beth nervously chuckled and stepped back. 'Yeah, I'll see you too, Blanche.'

For a second, her eyes caught mine behind the curtains, and before Blanche could check behind her, I pulled the curtains over my visible body parts.

Blanche looked behind her. 'Huh?'

Beth smiled. 'Uh, nothing, just a — just a cockroach! Well, gotta go!' With that, Beth ran out of the lunch hall and turned left.

I took the second exit well away from Blanche's ability to see. I knew Beth was waiting for me, since the P.E. block was to our right, not left.

I exited the lunch hall and searched the perimeter of the massive building, eventually finding Beth hiding behind a rubbish skip.

'Did she see you?' she whispered as if we were secret spies.

'Uh, no, not on my watch.'

Beth let out a sigh of relief. 'She's getting on my nerves.'

I patted her shoulder sympathetically. 'I know, and I'm sorry. What's your plan anyway?'

This time, Beth smiled. 'You know that diary she keeps?'

I was shocked. 'Blanche of all people keeps a diary?'

Bethany facepalmed herself. 'She keeps a diary on her real and fake friends and how much she'll pay for them. Apparently, she told me at lunch she only tells her friends this and nobody else knows she pays for pals. So I've come up with a plan to find her diary, rip out all the pages with writing on them and stick them up on the walls all over the school.'

I didn't know what to think of the plan. It was big-time revenge on Blanche, but I sort of felt sorry for the girl. You never know, she could be acting like this for a reason.

'So, what'd you think of it?' Bethany asked devilishly.

There were a few seconds of silence, then I decided to come all out.

I raised my hands. 'I'm not into any of this. Sorry, but I can't. I'm already having a hard time at home; if I get just detention it'll mess everything up. See you in P.E. Let's hope for the best — we're on the same netball team.'

Beth slowly nodded. 'I — I understand. I guess I'll see you too.'

I turned back and waved, and for a second I thought I saw someone hiding behind a bush beside the skip. The thing had long, blonde hair and — Blanche!

What a surprise! Typical high school: you set someone up and it turns out they did the exact same to you. Double-crossing is a major crime at Grisworth.

Blanche knew if she became best friends with Beth all over again, it would trigger my jealously, but she knew Beth was too good a friend to leave me just like that, all on my own. She knew it was all a setup, and in return, she set us up.

I had to warn Beth, but it was a silly idea to tell her in front of your enemy.

High school had gotten a lot harder.

Six

Golden

T he hole moved locations often. One time it was in Essex, next in Brighton, then it somehow ended up in New Jersey. The only person who had control over where the hole ended up was Lord Nurogi, Master of the Nurogons.

Colusko, a fellow citizen, had told me all about Tempoku Nurogi, Lord Nurogi's temple, and how he would answer in clear detail if you had any requests. I'd decided to ask him about my family visiting, or even me going home.

As I stepped up to Tempoku Nurogi, a shock of nerves washed over me. My friends the Nurogons reported that Nurogi was only in a good mood when he'd slept for a good sixteen hours. They'd also told me, the way to get into the temple is to

bow at the entrance and repeat his name seven times.   I   don't
know why. I guess seven is a lucky number for the Nurogons.

Tempoku Nurogi was marvellous. It was exactly what I'd imagined heaven to be like, with smooth golden walls you could see your reflection in perfectly, surrounded by twenty-metre-tall pillars. There was yet another gold theme on the temple, this time the turrets on top. The turrets had a small window, and I could almost see a tiny figure peeping out. I walked up the polished, quartz steps to find myself looking at a — would you believe it — golden door. The handles were like Darren's door handles — big brass loops you could slip your hand into.

'Lord Nurogi, Master of the Nurogons,' I stuttered as respectfully as possible, with a stiff bow. It felt silly repeating the phrase seven whole times to a door. But as my voice started to crack and my back ached from all the bowing, the door let out a deep rumble, and for a split second, I thought I was about to get eaten alive by a grizzly bear.

In front of me was the master himself.

'Guj mig sreda,' Nurogi boomed. His voice was at least three times as loud as I would've expected since he only appeared about an inch taller than the other Nurogons. 'You may speak,' he boomed, so I took the opportunity.

'Lord Nurogi,' I remarked, adding another stiff bow for effect. 'I would like to ask if it would be possible to change the location of the hole to Libra Harps Street.'

Mae had told me all about how the black hole changed locations, and how Lord Nurogi would occasionally cause it to follow specific people. If he could get the hole to follow my family...

Surprisingly, Lord Nurogi answered back with a half-smile on his face. Also, in English. 'I already understand you want your parents and family to join you in Nurogonia. I have several requests from other fellow Nurogons to spawn the hole in highly exotic places. And I also have several other fellow Nurogons asking to ban humans from this place. I cannot fix all your problems, but I will give your family a decent amount of time to come — three days — and if they do not enter the hole, I will have to move on to the next request. You are dismissed.'

'But, Lord...'

'YOU ARE DISMISSED!' he boomed.

I decided to leave. Even half a mile away I could still hear the faint echo of his voice in my mind.

I knew my family would never make it on time. We were late for most things. That's why we got "The Bell."

After a short time, a mob of Nurogons surrounded me and started asking questions. I wasn't in the mood for any of them.

'What happened?' one asked.

'Did you get punished?' another questioned.

'Why so glum?' a Nurogon enquired.

'Oi!' a voice cried. Mae pushed her way to the middle of the circle and made a gap so we could exit.

'I suggest we get some rest,' she ordered. 'Then, you tell me everything, OK?'

I was too tired to argue, so I let her lead me to the bunks.

A tray of two green smoothies and a plate of egg sandwiches were set on the bedside cabinet. I didn't feel like eating at all, but Mae somehow managed to persuade me.

'I told the food and drink to taste like hot chocolate and milky cookies,' she said, 'as a treat.'

She handed me the tray, and I hesitated. 'I'm — I'm not hungry.'

Mae folded her arms, picked up the tray and placed it on her own lap. 'You've got to cheer up! Should I go tell the head dream councillor to make you have sweet dreams?'

I shook my head solemnly.

'Then what's the matter?'

I took a breath. 'I — I — I can't.'

Mae frowned. 'So, you won't tell me?'

I shook my head again. 'Goodnight, Mae.'

She cursed under her breath, but at least she left me to myself for a little while.

That night, I dreamt about walking back up to Tempoku Nurogi and entering without bowing or repeating anything.

'I demand to see my family!' I boomed.

Lord Nurogi looked down blankly at me. 'Castaway! You weren't supposed to be in this land anyway!'

I stared straight back at him. 'Send. Me. Home,' I growled.

Lord Nurogi looked at me and smiled. 'Goodbye, exile.' And with a click of his fingers, the floor disappeared and I found myself in a free fall, tumbling through black skies and nearing the ground. Twenty metres from the ground — fifteen metres from the ground — ten...

* * *

I woke up, breathing hard. Looking at my alarm, I realised it was only two in the morning. I flopped back down onto my bed and tried dreaming about something else, hoping the head dream counsellor wouldn't inform Lord Nurogi of my vision.

'Morning, Hayden!' Mae called over to me. Then she remembered she was in a mood with me, and added, 'Not that I care or anything.'

I gave her a dirty look. Sometimes, I have to be the bigger person, I thought.

'I'm sorry. Yesterday just wasn't my day. But now I have something to tell you.'

Mae looked up, her eyes twinkling.

I hesitated to tell her but eventually told her everything.

'Does it mean something?'

Mae shrugged. 'Talk to the Counsel of Dreams about it then, they'll have all the details. They see your dreams.'

* * *

'So, what was it again you needed mending?' I asked Mae, who had made me tag along to one of the huts just to mend a possession of hers. 'And why is it so important?'

Mae rolled her eyes. 'I've told you a thousand times, it's my practice staff! If I want to ever become a Dream Counsellor than I have to practice, and Chiko told me there's no other way than to get one of these!' She waved a split-ended red stick in the air with an air of impatience.

'You're actually going to apply for a job here? But what about home? What about your family, what about...'

Mae tensed.

Oh, shouldn't have mentioned family, I thought. 'Mae, I'm sorry. I...'

'It's not that, stupid!' she hissed, her voice eerily quiet.

I stared at her. 'Mae, are you...'

But when I followed her gaze, I noticed why she was so tense. I noticed why she had been staring.

'Do you hear that distant, splashing noise?' she whispered, horror etched in every syllable she spoke.

I nodded slowly. 'But the waters are never this viol...'

I couldn't finish my sentence, for not far away, a shrill scream could be heard.

'AAAAGH!'

It was the voice of a child's — a female voice at that.

Then a second voice followed.

'Botilda! Botilda! Someone help me!'

It was a female who spoke this time. Her cries of help persisted, each more panic-stricken than the other.

Mae gasped. 'Look! Hayden, LOOK!'

There was no need telling me once, let alone twice. I could see the image clear enough myself, an image I did not want to see.

A young Nurogon, probably around six, was bobbing around helplessly in the thrashing water beneath us, struggling for breath. The few times I saw her face she appeared to be on the brink of death.

'God knows what lies beyond the waves...' Mae muttered. 'HAYDEN, NO!'

But I was already making my way steadily towards the Nurogon. Well, as steadily as you can be when you're attempting to swim in conditions like this.

I drew sharp intakes of breath as sharp rocks grazed my knees and legs, clearly drawing masses of blood with each cut. The salty water struck my wounds, causing agony I had never experienced before.

115

I heard Mae's faint screams calling me back, but I didn't listen, I didn't care; my only focus was the Nurogon now only seconds away from falling off the edge of where the water ended... As Mae said, who knows what lies beyond it? But it couldn't be anything good.

The Nurogon's head disappeared underwater and did not reappear. She couldn't have fallen off already, she had just passed out. Botilda, her mother called.

Taking another breath, I plunged underwater.

It wasn't clear water at all. It was muddy-green and full of algae. No fish could be seen, but neither could the bottom. It seemed that the farther I travelled, the more pain I had to endure. My skin was burning — what was this substance?

I swam to the surface and took another long gulp of air, before diving again.

There she was. The Nurogon named Botilda, sinking away into the murky depths of the water. Her arm — if I could just grab her arm...

I felt my hand clasp around her wrist. It was limp and lifeless, but I didn't care. My lungs were searing with pain, screaming for air, but they could survive another few seconds if I could make it to the surface in time.

I swam up as fast as I could, my hand still firmly clasped around Botilda's wrist, my other one outstretched in hope that I would be able to grab hold of a bridge leg.

Just as my eyes were beginning to close and my head was starting to roll, I felt something — one of the bridge legs.

My hand was above the water, but I was not. I heaved with all my might and forced Botilda up onto the bridge, she had been left with no air for longer than I had.

I was about to force myself up as well, but I was out of time. I got one last view of my surroundings. Just one metre away from the edge of the water. Surely I would lose my grip and get carried away by the water, to certain doom?

And this was my last thought, because a split second later, I felt my head roll, my eyes shut and I was plummeting into darkness.

* * *

'Hayden? Hayden?' Mae's frantic voice was right above me. My eyes flickered and I caught a brief image of her flaming red hair.

'Mae, calm down. He will be fine,' a male voice assured.

I didn't know what was going on. Sitting bolt upright, I shouted, 'I — *what?*'

'You're alive!' Mae screeched as she pulled me in for a hug.

None of this made any sense.

'Wait, can someone explain...' I looked around wildly.

The male voice chuckled, and I turned to see a Nurogon wearing glasses and a doctor's coat.

'I am Dr Ujoko, Hayden. And I'll tell you what's happened.' He pointed to a paper in his hand.

Tenderly, I took it off him and read the front line.

"Yrnja hmrjn dovg mojn," it read.

'Young human saves day...' I processed the words over and over. 'Young human saves day... young human — me?'

Mae looked sternly at me. 'Yes, you, Hayden! You jumped into the water under the bridge when you saw that little Nurogon drowning! You heroically lifted her out when you were just a metre or two from the edge. Everyone was sure both of you weren't going to make it. But when you got her out of water... and then I was sure you'd fall off the edge — when you passed out and all, and...'

'You do realise I still have no clue what you're talking about, right?'

Mae frowned. 'Oh, I'm being such a prat, of course you would have no clue, you've literally drowned... you've been in here for three days, by the way, asleep.'

Now it was my turn to frown. 'Three days?'

Dr Ujoko coughed. 'Mhm?'

Mae and I both looked over at him.

'I am ever so sorry to interrupt, but I do have a way for Hayden to remember this event as clear as day. Three words, in fact. Staff. Screaming. Water.'

Mae stared at him weirdly. 'Uh, thanks, dude, but I don't think it actually helped?' She said the last five words sarcastically.

'No, Mae. I remember,' I whispered.

She looked struck.

'Yes. You wanted me to go with you and mend your stupid practice staff, and then you went all tense and weird and I asked you what was wrong. And then we heard screaming — a female voice screaming for someone named Botilda or something — and we saw her. The Nurogon, drowning. You said you didn't know what lay beyond the water. I didn't want an innocent baby Nurogon to die, so I jumped in and tried to catch up with her.

'I saw that her head didn't return to the surface, so I dived to try and locate her. When I saw Botilda, I grabbed her and pulled her along with me, now attempting to find a leg of the bridge. I found one after a while, heaved her onto it and was gonna do the same for myself when I passed out.' Everything came rushing back to me. My head started to ache with all the information I was consuming.

'Agh!' I moaned.

Mae gasped once again, as she had done so many times. 'Help, please, help him!'

Dr Ujoko merely shook his head. 'No, Mae, it is natural for the brain to ache after a procedure like this. It will soon pass; he's just in a bit of shock. It's not nice to remember you nearly drowned.'

And he was right. I hadn't realised what had happened until he spoke those three words. I didn't want to believe it, but my brain was forced to.

'Where is she?' I asked.

Mae raised an eyebrow. 'Hayden, what do you mean?'

'Botilda. Is she alright?'

Dr Ujoko and Mae shared a worried look.

'She — she didn't make it?

Mae shook her head frantically. 'No, no, of course not. She's just...'

'She's healing in another hut, Hayden,' Dr Ujoko continued. 'But another doctor, Dr Hemila, her name is, doesn't think it'll be much longer before she's gone. I checked her and think the same.'

I sat up again, although this time nobody stopped me.

'So — but how?' I cried.

'The Nurogons, Hayden,' Mae whispered, 'have a weaker immune system, especially the younger ones. When she went underwater... if it were water on Earth, she would've lived, but the water in Nurogonia is different. The farther you get to the edge, the more breath you need. Botilda passed out and wasn't able to return for breath for a very long time, Hayden.'

'There is a chance she'll survive, right?'

Dr Ujoko looked at the floor. 'She's only got a few hours.'

This time, I jumped up, ignoring the weakness of my legs.

'I need to see her,' I said. 'Where is she?'

'Hayden, no don...' Mae reached out to grab my arm, but Dr Ujoko held hers back.

'No, Mae. He deserves the right to visit her in her last hours. Let him go with you, you will take him there and that's an order.'

Mae shot one last look at the Nurogon and led me out of the room.

'Please, Hayden, you wouldn't want to see a dying Nurogon!' she pleaded once we were out of earshot of Dr Ujoko.

I took a deep breath. 'Don't try to stop me. Just take me there.'

Seven

My Time is Over

❦

otilda passed after the visit. She was with her parents and her younger brother in her last moments. They wanted me to be there too, but Mae refused on my behalf.

Her parents offered me many things in return for my attempt to save her life, but I declined every one of them.

'I can't bear it anymore,' I murmured one day.

I was sitting on my bunk, staring blankly at the ceiling above me.

'What?' Mae muttered.

None of us was in a good mood, it had been a few days since Botilda died. Every day I was thinking of how I had failed to save her. I remembered her lifeless body when I visited her, and the shimmer of gratitude in her eye when she saw me. She had managed to utter a "thank you," but even that caused her immense pain.

'I need to go,' I said loudly. 'I need to, Mae. I can't stay here.'

Mae glared at me. 'What do you mean? Hayden, you can't go now! You have to stay, you haven't finished your quest, you...'

'You don't understand!' I shouted. 'I'm sorry this had to happen. But I've made my decision, I don't need someone looking out for me all the time!'

And with that, I stomped out of the room.

My feelings of despair at not being able to save Botilda were made worse by the fact that my family had missed the deadline. It was excruciating, waiting, knowing there was no way to prompt them. All I could do was hope and pray that instinct would somehow lead them to the hole. To be honest, I'm not sure why I waited. Lord Nurogi hadn't given me a chance to say what end of the street to park the hole in. With so many side streets leading off Libra Harps, unless the hole was parked literally outside our house, I wasn't sure there was going to be much of a chance of my family happening upon it.

Nurogonia is the place of dreams, I was told, and I dreamed of leaving the place. I couldn't bear

124

it anymore. One night, I dreamed so vividly about leaving, Kioksi, the chief of Dream Controlling called me the next morning.

'Hayden, I have recently seen you dreaming of leaving Nurogonia. Is anything troubling you?'

I felt guilty but did my best to be honest. 'I don't know what to do here. Nothing seems right. I don't belong here. And with everything that's happened, everything that's going on...'

Kioksi sighed. 'See, this is the problem with allowing you humans here in Nurogonia. You never stay for very long. I do understand, yes, but if you want to leave, that's up to Lord Nurogi to decide.'

I headed to Tempoku Nurogi, disregarding the curious looks from Nurogons passing by. It looked more glamorous at midday when the sun was at its highest point.

I prepared a speech in my head for when the door opened: "Lord Nurogi, I have served my time in Nurogonia, and I am prepared to return to the human world. I don't want to cause any more commotion."

And I said exactly that. Lord Nurogi stroked his chin. 'Very well, you may return to your dimension. Who knows, I dare say you will return someday. But for now, Nurogonia will miss you, Hayden.'

I never thought in a million years he'd be that calm about it. I thought I was a very important part of Nurogonia, but it turns out their toilets don't need cleaning all the time!

'To get out, you must climb these stairs,' Lord Nurogi started, pointing to a staircase, 'and speak your destination. You must also close your eyes in the process, or you will be stuck in Nurogonia for eternity. It has happened before. Sultan, a fellow Nurogon, was once human but opened his eyes on the way to the human world. He is stuck as a Nurogon forever. I will despair to see you go, Hayden, but I know what you mortals are like, and I understand Nurogonia isn't the best place for you to settle in. Leave, and remember us Nurogons. I will spread the news that you are gone.'

I climbed the staircase, a wave of joy and anxiety washing over me. I would miss Mae but there was no time for proper good-byes. Strangely enough, I realised, I would miss Nurogonia, but as Lord Nurogi had stated, Nurogonia wasn't the best place for me to settle in. And I'd barely stayed there — thinking back now. It felt as quick as a blink.

'You will return to Nurogonia again, whether you want to or not! This is not the last time we will see you!' Lord Nurogi shouted behind me. I guessed that was some sort of warning, although I secretly thought that was never going to be true. For a second, he sort of sounded evil.

When I reached the top of the stairs, I called out "Libra Harp Street" closed my eyes and took a step forward.

'Farewell, The One!' Lord Nurogi hollered.

* * *

My eyes couldn't adjust to the sight of my home. I was used to seeing it every day, but now that I'd been gone a while, it seemed so strange — like Nurogonia was somehow the best place for me. Well, I had thought the same thing when I'd returned from holiday, so hopefully, it was a phase.

It took me a good thirty seconds to ring the bell. Imagine ringing a could-be criminal's bell. That's how I felt, for some random reason.

After some time, I heard footsteps click-clacking towards the door. A shadowed figure opened it and gaped.

'C — Canada, come, n — now,' Mum stuttered. She liked to dress fancy; however, this time, her red sleeveless dress, which showed her knees, hung loosely on her now bony frame. Her normally silky, blonde hair wasn't curled at the ends as usual. Instead, it hung limp on her shoulders and she was not wearing a drop of make-up. She looked gaunt — haggard almost.

I let Mum take a breath because it looked as if her heart was stopping. 'H — Hayden?'

'M — Mum?' I mocked.

She stepped outside to where I was standing and gave me what seemed like an endless embrace.

'Oh, Hayden, Hayden, Hayden.' She carried on sniffling with tears streaming down her face. 'Where on earth have you been my dear boy? You were nearly the death of me. You would not believe the number of asthma attacks and the number of times I fainted while you were gone. I had to visit a therapist! We got the police and everything...'

I stared at Mum and grabbed her arms. 'Calm down, Mum. Police? They would think you are delusional.'

Mum shook her head. 'Oh, the police know. I'm not delusional at all.'

I frowned. 'Mum?' I murmured.

'Yes, dearest Hayden?' she whispered back, a crazy but loving look on her face.

'How are we supposed to get out of this?' I inquired.

Mum smiled. 'Oh, Hayden. What was I supposed to do? I said I'll call them as soon as we heard anything.'

I relaxed but then tensed again. 'And you think they won't question me? What am I supposed to say?'

Mum went blank. She realised what had happened. 'It was the right thing to do. We had no clue where you were and still don't,' she mumbled.

'Mm-hm,' coughed a voice. I looked behind Mum and saw a teenage girl with a short T-shirt, ripped jeans and blonde hair tied back in a tight pony.

'Canada!' I shouted. She walked towards the door. For the first time in forever, my sister opened her arms and let me in for an embrace.

'You're still a moron, though,' she snapped, pushing me back, 'On a serious note, don't ever go off like that again, OK? Ever, and I mean it. What were you thinking? You idiot, you got us all so worried!'

I hesitated. 'Careful now. You better treat me right from now on. You see... Lord Nurogi, who let me come back, told me I'm destined to return to Nurogonia... So, yeah, I might be going back. As for the rest of what happened, I don't want to explain that right now.'

'What are you on about?' she cackled. 'And you call Mum the delusional one! Who is Lord Bogey or whatever? And no "How are you, Canada? How was Alton Towers, Canada?" or anything?'

'How was Alton Towers, Clownada?' I grumbled hardly believing she was managing to make this about her.

'Horrible. Tiffany was being, you know, off, and there was an incident on a nearby ride. Yeah — let's just say the rollercoaster went — uh — off track.'

'Why would you want me to ask if it was that bad?' I pointed out. 'And where's Dad?'

Canada frowned, 'He... since you've been gone, he's been out a little more, there.'

I curled my lip, 'He's at the pub, right?'

'The Ol' Frog 'n' Toad, to be exact. Straight from work and off there. I'll call him now,' Mum added.

Typical Dad. Always taking stress out on beer.

'Please may I — uh — you know, come in?' I suggested, realising I'd been outside the whole time.

Mum practically suffocated me as she pulled me in. 'We were in such a deep conversation we forgot to!'

'We?' Canada snorted.

Mum glared at her. 'Yes, we. It's plural.'

'Pfft, well, I'm off!' Canada scoffed.

Mum shook her head. 'Teenagers, huh?' She started talking about how she'd been so grumpy without me. I doubt it was true, though. Then, she started talking all about when I was gone again. 'I still feel like you're not my son. Are you my son?' She started feeling me, making sure I wasn't a "fake."

'You are! I will be talking about this for days, weeks, months, years!' She gave me seven more hugs throughout her chat. Then, the worst news came. 'Oh, and how could I forget! Your cousin Zoya is here!'

I blinked twice. 'Cousin Zoya? The heck of a good ballerina? Oh, no. No, no, no, no, no...'

'Oh, yes. Yes, yes, yes, yes, yes, she's upstairs,' Mum copied.

I decided it was polite to go and see Zoya. She was a junior professional ballerina with tons of medals. Guess where I found her? Pirouetting over and over in my room!

'Hey, Zo!' I cheered.

She stopped in her tracks and turned to me.

'Ooh, look, it's Hudson!' she squealed.

'Hayden.'

'That is zwhat I said!' she replied in her Russian accent. 'Where have you been, my dear cousin? I heard the news, and I was nearly put to tears!'

I rolled my eyes just like Canada did. 'It's... a long story. Let's say, magical creatures, cleaning toilets and learning codes. Oh, plus the black hole.'

131

Zoya gave me a look of disbelief and shrugged it off. 'If you say so. I will not deny my greatest cousin, Hudson.'

Ignoring her insult I asked her a simple and relevant question.

'So, Zoya, how is ballet? Any shows, or um, whatever you do in your baby classes?'

'I do not do baby classes!' Zoya retorted. 'In fact, I do the highest level of junior ballet in the county! It is hard and tiring and makes ze muscles very weary!'

I snorted. 'And because you do ballet a lot, it makes you really dumb!'

'Excuse me?' she shouted, clearly offended.

'Because you spin so much, the fluid that makes normal people dizzy isn't there for you, since you trained so much you got rid of it! That makes your brain smaller since you're missing the fluid.'

'And who says so?'

'Google and BBC Radio 2,' I smirked. 'You can't beat that.'

'I have heard of zis, and it is not true. The fluid is in ze ear, not ze brain! Hmph!'

'If you say so, Little Miss Perfect,' I chortled.

'I am not zis Litt…'

'OK, OK, I get it, chill, sister!'

'I am not ze sister!'

I rolled my eyes for the second time. Maybe it's best I don't ask, I thought and left the room failing to find the opportunity to ask how come she was at ours.

Dad came crashing in as I came down the stairs. He hugged me fiercely, sobbing into my hair. I felt heartbroken. He looked heartbroken, drained and a shadow of himself. He wouldn't or couldn't talk about where I'd been. I reckoned it must have been the denial he had been trying to drown out.

'Haydee Baby?' Mum called from the kitchen a little while later. 'Come here for something to eat.'

'I told you not to call me that,' I grumbled sauntering into the kitchen.

Mum completely ignored my statement. 'I was thinking, would you like me to throw a Search-Over Party, to let everyone know you're here?'

I scowled. 'Two things, one, no, and two, why even bother when you knew what I'd say?'

'Well, Aunt Al already said she's jolly well worried and when she heard of the idea of a Search-Over Party...' 'You've already told people.'

'... she nearly cried. Oh wait, she did cry.'

I sighed. 'Well, that's just great. Tell me, what day is the Search-Over-whatever-it-is?'

'Tomorrow.'

'What?' Now I sort of wished I stayed in Nurogonia. 'However much you try to bribe me, I will not — and I mean no, no, no — will not be there.'

Mum smiled. I knew that smile. It meant, "just wait and see." I didn't have to wait at all, because Mum tried me straight away. 'OK, how about the new iPhone you said you wanted?' I sold out.

Eight

The 'Big' Event

Mum had really planned a whopper. There were spotlights, stacks of pizza, hamburgers and all sorts of foods, including soup for vegans and vegetarians. And I was certain that the vegan and vegetarian foods were there for Mum and Dad to squeeze in one last attempt for us to change our minds about the whole "vegan" concept.

Mum told me before if anyone asked where I was, I should say I had been kept in school for a very long detention I couldn't get out of. Like, seriously! Made me worry a bit how unable the last week or so had made her. Or was it that there wasn't enough time before her hurriedly put together party to cook up a decent story? Mum did seem to believe me about my actual whereabouts though. Apparently, she'd caught a glimpse of a very odd hole somewhere down the road, but it seemed like an illusion. She'd only seen it for half a second, then — poof — it was gone.

'So, my Haydee Baby,' another aunt cooed, 'where were you all along?'

I hesitated, and in the end, decided to make up another excuse.

'There was this stay-over-no-phone school trip I had for a week, and I forgot to tell Mum and had no way to contact her,' I mumbled, in a rush.

My aunt gave a side look and tutted, 'You know Aunty Peggy doesn't like that. You should always tell Mummy and Daddy or even me about things like that.'

'Sorry, Aunty.'

'Mm, now, it's OK, my little Haydie-Waydie. We all make mistakes. Your cousin, Gordon, comes home with a detention card every day! That's his mistake!' Aunt Peggy chuckled.

'Hahaha,' I faked-laughed along.

'Guess what, Hayden?' Mum asked once she'd finished serving the food out to guests.

'The last time you told me something using that tone you planned a massive party I didn't even want. So, should I trust you, or not?'

'I ordered a cake. The iced message is "Found You!" Isn't it sweet?' she sang.

'Uh, thanks, I guess.'

I walked around trying to find Zoya. I needed to try and make amends. I didn't get a chance to do so before she left the day before. Canada had mentioned she was back here. Apparently, her mum had found temporary work in England, somewhere not too far off. Zoya had come to ours as she was on school holidays back in Russia. I didn't get why they didn't come to stay at our house, but Canada explained she was in an Airbnb near her workplace.

It was so crowded I could barely find Zoya. When I did she was pirouetting in front of tons of adults, showing off to all of them.

'Wow, Zo!' Nan Pam cheered.

'Whoah, she's quick!' Uncle George exclaimed.

'She zis my sister, but she's a show-off, too' a boy grunted. I looked over at him. He had the same confident air as his sister. An exact copy of her, wearing a casual T-shirt and jeans with shoulder-length fair blonde hair and blue eyes, but a boy. Sometimes I'd get my twin cousins mixed up.

'She needs to come with me now anyways!' He had a more English accent than Zoya.

'Alexei, zis is not ze time!' Zoya moaned, still twisting and turning.

Alexei scoffed. 'Mother called and told me we need to get ready zis instant! She is picking us up very soon.'

'Oh, Alexei! You have spoiled ze fun!' Zoya grunted. 'And why are we leaving already?'

Alexi frowned and tugged at her arm, making her abruptly stop spinning.

Zoya didn't budge. Even though she looked extremely light and skinny, it was a great effort for Alexei to pull her along.

'Am I zat heavy, twin brother?' she snapped.

Alexei pulled a look clearly stating: "Don't embarrass me here, OK?"

Once the party was over — it went on for another four hours — I had a big nap. More like an early sleep, to be honest. I didn't get a chance to say goodnight to Dad, he was still at the pub. Mum had tried calling him, but it went straight to voicemail. He'd left before soon after the last of the guests departed. She explained he was still a bit overwhelmed and I could tell the party had been much too soon for him. He needed to take my return in.

'Nighty, Hayden,' Mum called to me upstairs. 'I love you!'

'Love you, too,' I shouted back, half-asleep.

The next morning, Dad was at the breakfast table before anyone else. He was reading a paper, and he only noticed me as I sat down.

'Oh, morning, Hayden, get yourself a piece of toas...'

I smiled up at him.

Dad closed his newspaper and squinted at me carefully. It looked like memories were coming back. I could almost see them flashing in his eyes.

Then he froze.

I thought it was normal for a few seconds, but he remained frozen.

'Uh... Mum,' I called.

Mum came downstairs. 'What is it?' She turned to look at Dad. 'Oh, your father did that all the time when you were gone. He'll be back soon.'

We waited a further fifteen seconds before Dad was able to speak again.

'Hayden? Hayden! Oh, my son!' he exclaimed getting up from his chair.

His eyes were bloodshot and he had eye bags that looked like they weighed a million tonnes. He looked like he'd pulled an all-nighter. To be honest, I think he had.

'Are you... OK?' I asked.

Dad rubbed his eyes. 'Best moment of my life. Still can't believe you are home safe.'

Dad and Mum had an argument about who dropped me off to school, so I suggested they both do it.

'Hm, but I'm driving!' Dad called.

Mum had a face like thunder. 'Chop, chop, then.'

We arrived at school early as we'd driven there. Arriving early was a bad thing because if you weren't in before-school club, the teachers would give you a job to do. Last month, I was twenty minutes early, and I had to tidy Class 7D before they came in. Another time I was early, I had to colour-coordinate the textbooks in my class.

This time, I had the — Worst. Job. Ever. It was worse than any others you could ever think of, out of this world mad, and something no student would ever expect.

I received a hug from every teacher I came across. Yep, the worst of the worst. It was so awkward; I had to stand there and gradually lose the nerve to embrace the teacher back.

Miss Selene was fine, she understood how embarrassed I was, so she gave me a small present — a highlighted script.

'I gave you Guy,' she whispered, her voice tingling my senses. 'I thought you'd be great at it.'

140

I was so excited I'd got the part I auditioned for I was the one to hug Miss Selene. 'Thank you!' I blessed and ran down the corridor to store my prized possession in my locker.

It felt good to be back at school, but when I thought about Lord Nurogi's statement on my way out I knew for a fact I'd have to return to Nurogonia.

It's fine, I thought, Lord Nurogi will give you time to catch your breath. But I still had a hunch that I'd be returning before too long.

And I knew I couldn't use the school trip excuse on my school friends, so I came up with a surprise holiday with my aunt and uncle. It was a hard sell but better than trying to float the truth.

The first school lesson was maths, then P.E. I don't see why the school should put P.E. on the morning schedule, because then the sweat stays with us all day.

Being twenty minutes early to school, I was also early to class, followed by Molly Digger, Ben Robin and Evie Taylor.

Evie took a seat next to me. She was my desk partner for maths. She had very little equipment: a notebook, a pen and a pencil.

'Not much stationery, huh?' I asked.

Evie shook her head. 'Mm.'

Small talk with Evie was sometimes tedious, but somehow I felt it my duty to try. She never really talked much, which was a shame, since she was a nice smart person who could help me with homework.

She had short, golden-blonde hair tied in a small ponytail. Recently, she'd gotten new, pink glasses she wore for reading. For uniform, she had the usual black blazer, white shirt, black tie and black skirt. I wore the exact same, just with black trousers instead.

Looking down at her shoes I found an opportunity for a chat. We both had regular lace-up shoes, but I she was a definitely a few sizes smaller than me.

'Gosh, looking at your feet compared to mine, I see a big difference. I'm a size 9,' I revealed. 'What size are you?'

She wrote down the number "2½" and I gasped.

'Only that?' I asked.

Evie nodded. 'It's weird — right?'

'What size were you in primary school?'

Evie tried to think. 'In Year 5... In Year 5 I was a size — what was it again? — I was a size 12? 13? I think 12½. I stayed that size till the end of school. Then I got size 1 in Year 7, now I'm size 2½ in Year 9!'

'You're telling me you weren't even a size one when you left primary school?'

Evie innocently nodded.

'I was a 5½! Wait... no, a 6.'

We had a decent chat about shoe sizes whilst Mr McCurry was sorting out his desk and marking books.

I was happy I'd finally found a topic to talk about with Evie, so now, maybe, she could help me with homework?

'OK, Class 9B,' Mr McCurry shouted, 'Ears this way!'

Nobody paid any attention to the teacher, so he did his famous whistle to let us know he was actually there. The whistle reminded me of "The Bell" and how it got more annoying every time I heard it. Even so, I stopped talking to Evie about shoe sizes.

'Molly and Henry will hand out your Maths textbooks, and I will show you simple algebra on the board.'

Everyone groaned. When Mr McCurry said "simple" he might've as well said "impossible." Plus, everyone in the class hated algebra.

When Molly came over to give me my textbook, she glared at me and muttered, 'Don't think about getting Evie to do your homework.'

I was stunned, so I mumbled, 'I — I won't.'

Molly gave me a "really?" sort of look and walked over to another desk.

'I can help you with homework,' Evie said.

I didn't hear her, so I carried on scribbling down every sum Mr McCurry wrote on the board, in case I forgot what something was.

Evie looked at me blankly. 'OK, your loss.'

'What? Sorry, I wasn't listening.'

Evie knitted her brows. 'I can help you with homework, I said. If you'd pay attention and stop doodling in your textbook.'

'Really?'

Evie laughed. 'No, of course not.'

I frowned, not getting the joke.

'Ugh, something called "sarcasm." Yes, I'll help you with homework, as long as I'm free.'

'Thanks, I guess.'

'Has everyone done equation 8? The $2x - 10 = 10 - 3x$ one.'

'Yes!' everyone simultaneously replied.

Mr McCurry looked at Rosetta Divan. 'Rosetta, you're reasonable. What is the answer to equation 8?'

Rosetta flicked through her textbook, the wind from the pages blowing her burgundy-dyed hair.

'Erm… ah, the answer is 57 — no, that's a different equation…'

Some of the boys at the back started laughing, so Rosetta shot them an evil look and they hushed.

'Any time today, Rosetta,' Mr McCurry pleaded after a minute of her searching for the equation.

Rosetta looked up at him. 'I'll take me time if I want to, Mr McHurry. Give me a second's breath, for goodness sake!'

The whole class hushed in tense suspense. Some couldn't help sniggering. All eyes travelled Mr McCurry's way. He looked shocked. 'Alright, then, Rosetta, if you'd like to behave like that, go and help clean the lunch hall with Ms Haughton.'

Rosetta didn't budge, so Mr McCurry repeated the sentence.

'I mean it, young lady, go and help clean up the lunch hall. I cannot be having a horrible attitude in such a lovely class.'

Rosetta grunted and got out of her chair. She did a rude sign at Henry, who dared to laugh. Mr McCurry handed her a detention card on her way out which she plucked out of his hand.

'Date and time on here,' Mr McCurry told her. 'Not highly impressed.' Mr McCurry shook himself back into the lesson. 'So, yes, x = 4. Did everyone get that?' I felt sorry for him. Thankfully, it was the weekend. He looked like he could use the break.

The bell for the end of the lesson rang, and everybody stood up. One of the best things about Mr McCurry: he doesn't ever say that stupid "I dismiss you, not the bell" thing most teachers do. He just lets us stand up and run straight to our lockers for intermission.

Logan O'Dowd's locker was next to mine, and we usually chatted about... stuff.

'So, how has your "Drama Diary" been?' I asked.

He brought out a 300-page A5 notebook and opened it to where his bookmark was placed. 'I figured since Brody and Ayo both get mad easily, we could do this.' He pointed to a bullet point and I read it aloud.

'Steal Brody's fountain pens and put them in...'

'Sh!' Logan hushed. 'In your head!'

I nervously chuckled. 'Whoops, my bad.' Steal Brody's fountain pens and put them in Ayo's locker, it read.

'Hmm, yes. Brody loves his fountains pens. But I think we need to add more of a twist to it.'

'Like what?'

I shrugged. 'Dunno, get some other people involved? We can say we saw Cathy Richards holding them!' I suggested. 'She will get so mad!'

Logan didn't look too sure. 'She'll snitch.'

'Well, just say it was probably another set of pens, not Brody's. Simple pimple, and we get a good laugh without getting in trouble as well.'

Logan still looked unconvinced, but he went with it anyways. 'Fine. But I have a vision, I think that we'll end up being the ones to get told off or someone will find this notebook — wait no — both! Oh, boy, we're in trouble.'

'Stop being a worry pots and get on with life.'

'Operation "Steal Brody's Pens and Put them in Ayo's Locker" is going to take place in three days. Of course I'm worried!'

We'd already wasted three out of five minutes of intermission.

Logan pressed a box of Tic Tacs into my palm, and I smiled and gulped half of it down in one go. Logan, on the other hand, had a maximum of three Tic Tacs and sucked on them for what seemed like forever (it was actually about thirty seconds).

'This is our Mission Ago device,' Logan murmured. 'Tic Tacs.'

As I was planning to ask for another box of the mints from Logan, Cathy came striding over, hands on her hips.

'So I see you have breath mints,' she spat, staring directly at me. I was holding the empty mint box in my hand, and Logan had already returned his very full box into his locker.

147

I looked at Logan and furrowed my brow. 'They're his, not mine,' I surrendered.

Cathy looked him in the eye.

'I don't have bad breath or anything,' Logan stuttered.

'Mmm, yeah,' Cathy hissed sarcastically.

'Look, I don't see your problem here. What's wrong with having Tic Tacs?' I questioned.

Cathy laughed and looked to her left as if there was someone to laugh with, but there wasn't.

'Breath mints are for bad breath,' she explained. 'You need to brush.'

Before Logan or I could argue back, she walked off.

Logan sighed. 'That's Cathy for you.'

All I could think of is the "Operation Steal Pens" mission.

Turns out not all dreams can come true.

Nine

My Atrocious Visit to Darren's

~~~⟨ℭ𝔤ℭ⟩~~~

*O*n Monday after school I was going to Darren's house, so we both got the chance to go on the same bus. We found double seats and sat in them.

On the way to a bus stop nearest to Darren's house, we talked about the match and how Alfred had missed his shot. It was nice to chat about normal stuff again with Darren. Nurogonia felt like it happened many moons ago. Darren had been understanding too; he got that I didn't want to talk much about it. I gave him the same sob story I gave everyone at school. He knew me well enough to know something else was amiss but was kind enough not to pry. 'He was our only chance,'

Darren was saying. 'It was tense, because I knew as soon as Alfred missed and Tom was up, we'd lost.'

'Same,' I mumbled. 'I'm still shocked he did miss.'

We were talking about Alfred when Darren's backpack slipped off his shoulder. He was about to turn around and pick it up when a familiar face helped him out.

'Here,' the boy offered.

Darren was still talking to me whilst the boy was helping him out with the bag, and at last, he turned around.

'Oh, thanks, Alf...' He gulped. 'Thanks, Alfred...'

He turned back to me and his eyes grew larger. I couldn't help but laugh. That's me; when I'm in a bad situation — like someone you were talking rubbishy about is actually sitting behind you — I just have the will to laugh.

Eventually, Darren joined in too, and we were so busy laughing we didn't notice the people staring at us.

I got embarrassed for about, I don't know, three or four seconds? Then I started quietly laughing again.

Finally, we arrived at the bus stop five minutes away from Darren's home. Darren and I thanked the conductor and bus driver and hopped off the bus.

'Oops,' I whispered, a laugh already bubbling up.

'Oops indeed,' Darren replied.

Darren's home was huge. The front garden was about the size of my entire garden. Wait, no, fifteen times bigger. The house itself was modern, with white concrete exterior walls and a black, flat roof that partly expanded off the house. It had freshly trimmed grass and garden lights, illuminating the entire grounds. Even in the day, it looked awesome. I just wished I was coming here when it was dark — I'm sure the light would shine over the whole city.

Darren led me along the stone path to the front door. It looked like it was the front door of a castle, with big rings for handles and a vertical wood pattern on the door itself. He let me bang the large door handles against the door, so I slotted my hand inside a ring and whacked as hard as possible, making certain not to hit my knuckles against the door.

I heard high heels clip-clopping against a stone or marble floor and heard a lady at the door.

'Hello!' came the greeting and the door opened.

'Hi, Mum,' Darren greeted.

The lady had cream blonde hair, just like Darren's, in a low, posh bun. Her hair was secured by a toggle with fake pink petals. She wore tons of make-up, the only ones I recognised being lipstick and blush, but with all that stuff on, she still looked like Darren's mother. She had a sleeveless, light pink dress to match the toggle. The straps on the dress were crossed over, probably some sort of stylish trends boys had no clue about. The shoes she wore were the same colour as the dress, and the heels must've been at least five centimetres high.

'Hello, Darren! Oh, I mustn't forget you, Hayden! How's life treating you?'

I shrugged. 'Good, I guess.'

'Like my Jimmy Choo Violas?'

Darren nodded. 'How much?'

Darren's Mum snorted. 'They are so cheap, I'm ashamed of it! Would you believe it, £1,295! Honestly!'

I raised an eyebrow. 'Cheap? Sorry, Mrs...'

'Call me Lyn.'

'Sorry, Lyn, but expensive in my house is fifty quid.'

Lyn looked sympathetic. 'Oh, I'm so sorry to hear that!'

Darren nudged his Mum and stared at her.

'What?' Lyn questioned, and Darren looked daggers at her, 'Oh, yes, quite expensive as it is, fifty pounds. Hm, yes...'

I could tell Darren didn't want me to consider them rich and snobby, but his mum gave it all away.

He mouthed the words, "sorry" and shrugged. I'd only been to Darren's house a couple of times before. He normally came to mine, but I was used to this sort of thing happening whenever I came round.

Before we moved on, Lyn handed us both expensive-looking embroidered white linen handkerchiefs and grinned like a Cheshire cat.

Darren shook his head. 'We're fine, Mum.'

Lyn didn't look convinced. 'A civilised house should always take a handkerchief around,' she explained. 'The scheduled cleaners often miss spots of dust.'

Darren turned red.

'Take a joke Darren! I mean, it's time for tea!' Lyn laughed.

Once she was ahead, I asked Darren the questions I'd been longing to.

'You have a scheduled cleaner?' I asked, 'When did you get so rich?'

Darren shrugged. 'We're not rich, just — well-off! Listen, let's forget about all of that stuff and have dinner as my mum said.'

We walked down a long hallway adorned with ancestral portraits on the walls.

'See, the Crosby Household has a very rich bloodline. Some say we were related to royals!'

'Uh — royal manure cleaners, Mum means.'

Lyn looked puzzled and then went along with him. 'Yes, we have a very famous bloodline of manure cleaners. Some were good friends with the queen!'

Darren gestured for her to not say that, and Lyn replied, 'No? No, not friends with the — yes, just manure cleaners.'

We arrived in the dining room at last, and it was incredible.

A ten-seater elegant dining table reached down to the end of the room, surrounded by matching cushioned chairs. A fruit bowl was filled to the brim with grapes and mangos and peaches and other exotic fruits. The table was brown, wooden and smooth. Above the table hung a chandelier, throwing off a light yellow effect.

'Only a simple, basic dining room,' Lyn sighed.

I raised an eyebrow. 'Basic? You should see mine.'

Lyn chuckled. 'Don't compare this attic to your mansion.'

It was bizarre for her to say this. She'd never seen my house before, let alone the dining room itself. Even Darren looked confused. His mum was going a bit over-the-top with the "we're-not-rich" theme especially as her outfit gave it all away. I mean it could've easily cost up to — oh, I don't know — £2,000?

'Let's have dinner,' Lyn suggested, nervously tittering.

She clapped, and an old man with neat, grey hair and a moustache entered the room. He was holding a round plate in one hand covered with a cloche.

'Dinner is served, Ma'am and Masters!' the man announced.

Lyn smiled up at the man. 'Hayden, this is Fraloue; Fraloue, this is Hayden.'

Fraloue held out his hand. 'Pleased to make your acquaintance, Master.'

I stared him up and down. He had a side cut with a bald patch going through the middle. His moustache was wispy and — waxed?

After a few seconds, I realised what I was doing and shook his hand. 'You too, sir.'

'Simply call me Fraloue.' The man had a twinkle in his eye. 'That's an order.'

'Fraloue is the family butler!' Lyn interrupted. 'He has been with us for many decades. He has his own room and sleeps here; this is his home. Fraloue is a retired soldier! He used to be in the army, on England's side, of course, but he has retired as a soldier and needed some extra money to keep him going! We don't pay him much; he simply won't allow two hundred pounds a day.'

'Excuse me?' I cried. Fraloue nodded at me.

'We agreed on one hundred and fifty pounds a day,' Lyn explained.

'I'd easily take the other one — fifty, I mean, I'm all in,' I chuckled.

Lyn laughed along with me, but it didn't sound very natural. In fact, it sounded as if she were constipated in the mouth.

'Well, I expect you'd like to know what's under the cloche!' the butler inquired.

Lyn nodded. 'We'd be delighted.'

Before opening the cloche, the butler made what sounded like a prepared speech. 'I present to you a delicate dish created by one of our best cooks, Blessed Jordon.'

He opened the cover to reveal a disgusting-looking pasta covered in bits of lettuce and other stuff.

'This is Cauliflower and Fontina Cannelloni. It incorporates Blessed's special ingredient, which I am forbidden to tell,' Fraloue continued.

He placed the giant plate next to us and also gave us a server. Pushing open the door to exit the room, I caught a glimpse of an all-white kitchen with three stoves and two of every kitchen appliance you could possibly imagine. There were two microwaves at the end of the long expanse of counters, and two sinks. In the corner, just in sight, I caught a glimpse of three massive dish cabinets stacked to the brim with plates and glasses.

'Here you go!' Lin beamed, collecting a huge lump of the pasta using the server and dumping it on my plate.

I stared down at my plate in horror. 'Uh — looks great!'

Lyn smiled at me. 'Glad you like it. I'm expecting clean plates from you, boys! We serve top-notch cuisine here!'

Darren looked at his mother. 'We're not babies, Mum. We'll eat how much we want.' Darren looked at his food the same way I did. 'And it doesn't look like I'll eat any at all.'

Lyn stared at Darren. 'I want to see you eat at least half of the food.' She split Darren's food in half and pushed one portion to the side of his plate.

Banging her fork on one of the halves, she commanded. 'Eat this bit up. Same goes for you, Hayden.'

I felt like a five-year-old. My mum lets me eat freely, giving my dad the bits I don't eat. That's why she only ever cooks a small amount. You end up oversizing the quantities if you make one portion for everyone.

The pasta looked soggy and not delicate at all. Mum normally made me ravioli pasta, and she made every piece light and fluffy. The pasta Blessed had made looked as if a dog had chewed on it before spitting it out. It was lumpy in some places, and there were lots of lettuce sprinkles in one place and none in another. Chunks of broccoli leaves were splatted around the place too, making it look more like a hardened plate of yellow sick than a prestigious dish. The cauliflower Fraloue had boasted about was nowhere to be seen.

It wasn't fair at all, because Lyn gave herself the smallest portion of food. It would take me about two spoonful's to eat, but she slowly ate her food so it took her five spoonful's to finish.

'Hey, Mum!' Darren protested. 'How is that fair?'

'How is what fair?' Lyn slyly replied.

Darren pointed a finger at his mother's plate. 'You're having to eat a tiny amount!'

Lyn tittered. 'Oh, teens these days. Have I never told you I was on a low carb diet? So this, in fact, is out of bounds for me.'

Darren focused. 'Uh, lemme think — no.'

'Oh. Never mind. But as we all know, pasta is full of carbohydrates. And they really make me put on weight.'

I would've thought Lyn was at the level where you were so slim you couldn't put on any more weight, but apparently not.

My friend looked at me and muttered, 'We have a set of scales in every room. Only Mum uses them.'

With that, I craned my head in different places around the room and indeed saw a set of scales. It wasn't too far away, and I could just make out the last weight recorded on the display: 42.5 kg. I stared at the scale in shock, then realised I was supposed to finish half of my food and had to get to it.

When I dared to take the first bite of the "delicate" pasta, it proved to be one of the worst ideas in my fourteen years of life.

'I gotta go!' I shouted, covering my mouth so I wouldn't leave traces of extra soggy pasta all over the walls.

'Come ba—' Lyn got cut off by me as I ran through the elegant double doors leading out of the dining room.

I opened every entrance I came across, not having time to close any of them until I finally found a bedroom with an en-suite bathroom.

Rushing through the bedroom, I tripped over something on the floor. I automatically threw my arms out, leaving my mouth uncovered. I sprayed bits of pasta all over the room. Before I had time to fully recover, I heard the sound of approaching footsteps.

I ran into the bathroom and grabbed a wad of toilet roll. Trying to wipe the stains off only spread the mess, so instead I focused on picking up the single lumps of food before whoever was approaching passed the room.

Slowly, I saw a figure draw level to the bedroom door, and I watched as the door inched open.

I looked up, horrified. A lady with an extremely tight ponytail, stern face and strong frame stared down at me. I was kneeling on the floor, picking up bits of the food.

The lady was wearing a black, tall hat that was puffy at the top, and she also had a long, button-down gown with black trousers and shoes. A red ribbon was tied loosely around her neck, and I instantly knew who she was.

The lady stretched out her hand for me to shake it. 'My name is Blessed, the chef who cooked your meal. I see you didn't like it?'

Her name did not suit her at all. She didn't look blessed. Not one bit.

I worriedly shook her hand. 'Uh — no, it's not that I didn't like it, it's just I forgot that — that I, erm, I'm semi-allergic to lettuce. Yeah, I get really bad hives.'

Blessed's eyebrow crept up. 'Really?' She brought out a notepad. 'And what is your name?'

I stared at her and asked, 'What are you doing?'

She ignored my question. 'What is your name?'

'Hayden,' I glumly replied.

'Hay-den,' she repeated, breaking it up into syllables as she wrote it down. 'And have you ever been here before, Hayden?'

I shook my head — an obvious lie.

Blessed looked at me. 'So what connection do you have with the Crosbys?'

'Darren is my best mate. We go to the same school.'

'How long have you been attending the same school?'

I didn't feel 100% comfortable. Would you if you were forced to share all your details with a stranger?

'We were at the same primary school, so... nine years? Ten years? Yes, ten years.'

Blessed laughed at me. 'And never, ever in all those ten years have you been to his house? Is this the case? I think I need to ask Lady Crosby herself!'

Lady Crosby, I thought. How fancy.

'You see,' I explained, pretending to get all sad, 'Darren hasn't had a great life. His father works as a model, you know. He works nearly all day. And you know Lyn — Lady Crosby, sorry, being a clothes designer doesn't help. As Darren normally comes home to an empty house for a few hours, I'm never really allowed to stay without his parents being here.'

Blessed looked at me and I could tell she was suspicious. 'There used to be a girl who came here called Gracie-Jayne. She looked after Darren until the start of Year 8. Did you know about her?'

'No,' I honestly replied.

Blessed shook her head. 'In the event you ever visit again, I have your allergies all written down. Lastly, can I have your phone number and that of your parents?'

I was tempted to shout something like "What are you, a stalker?" but gave her the phone numbers anyways.

'Have a good day, sir, and try to stay clear of lettuce next time around.' Blessed gave me a wave and exited the room.

I blew a sigh of relief.

The chef walked off in a recreation of the one and only "Gordon Ramsay stomp," and I could tell she was gutted someone didn't like her meal.

Mum, if you're reading this, note that if you're ever randomly telephoned and asked about your son's allergies, say he's semi-allergic to lettuce!

Ten

'X' for Xaferios

'How was school, then, Hayden?' Mum asked as we walked to the car after school. I shrugged. 'School was school.'

'And what's school then?'

'School.'

It was an endless cycle.

'Canada didn't have a good day, either. Apparently, a girl named Blanche was horrible.'

I wasn't listening to mum. 'Oh, sorry, what was that?' She sighed. 'Stop daydreaming and get hearing! And... I have to ask you a favour.' I didn't get to say anything before mum continued. 'Can you be nice to your sister? I snorted. 'Pfft. Lemme think — no.' Mum frowned, stopped in her tracks and looked me in the eyes; a sign it maybe wasn't time to joke around with her. 'Your sister is facing many difficulties and challenges at school. Tests, friendships, GCSEs coming up — it's an endless list...'

'An endless list that just ended, huh?' I cheekily asked.

'... so I really want her to feel wanted — like someone actually appreciates what she does.'

'I thought that was your job.'

Mum shook her head. 'Well, yes, but you could help out a little. You could be my smart little happiness colleague.'

I carried on walking and was silent until we reached the car park and found the car. Just as I was going to open the car door, I grunted, 'Fine.'

Mum literally jumped with joy. She wrapped her arms around me, held my cheeks with her hands and looked me in the eye. 'Promise?'

I threw my pinkie at her. 'Promise.'

* * *

Canada was already home; the bus had left early for her class. I found her reading a book called "Anxiety Relief for Kids."

'You don't need that,' I called, grabbing a — what Mum called — Marathon bar from the cupboard. They'd renamed it to Snickers bar a couple of decades ago, but mum said that back in the day she'd have a good old Marathon bar to give her a good kicking.

'Go do your football training or something,' she grumbled, 'because you're not wanted around here.'

I took the book she was reading away from her and read a page. 'Sit in a quiet and comfortable place. Place one of your hands on your chest and the other on your stomach. Take a slow and regular breath in through your no...'

'Give it back, you monster!' she screamed slapping me across the face in an attempt to get the book.

'Ow!' I cried, clutching my face in agony.

'That's what you get!'

I sulked off to my room but got stopped by mum.

'What did I say?' she asked, reddening by the second.

I pulled a face as if I was remembering something. 'Uh, that I should be nice to Canada?'

'Yes, exactly that. Now be nicer.'

166

I shrugged. 'Well, what am I doing now?'

Mum crossed her arms and looked as if she were about to cry. 'Don't give me that. Can't you do any better, Hayden?'

'That's probably the nicest I've ever been to Canada, so... no.'

Mum sighed and walked away.

'Going to Rodger's house,' I told her.

'Be back at latest half seven, please,' she called out.

I wasn't going to Rodger's house. No, I was going to summon the black hole to get to Nurogonia. I wanted to get this "quest" out of the way. I wondered if, for all the fuss, it would be something mundane like clean the dorm for a week or plunge all the toilet bowls in the area. I'd been thinking about it all day, resulting in me getting a headshot in dodgeball (they call it the "Daydream Shot") in PE and getting splatted in cake mix in Home Economics. Plus a gazillion grammar mistakes in Literacy. I had felt the pull. Somehow I knew it was time. It was difficult to explain how or why, but the tugging was relentless.

Suddenly, I heard a voice behind me.

'Hayden,' the voice whispered.

I turned back and saw the worst possible person — Canada. She'd followed me onto the pavement in front of our house.

'Go away! You're not wanted, either. It's only been a minute since you slapped me across the face.'

Canada turned pink as if she'd been slapped, and said the last thing I expected. 'I — I'm sorry.'

Facing her properly now, I gawped. 'How come...'

Canada ignored my question. 'I want to come with you.'

I ignored her for a moment, then ran up to her and hugged her tight. 'You can't.' How did she know? Were they pulling her too?

Canada pushed me back and placed her hands on my shoulders, an arm-length away. 'Listen, I'm serious. I'm coming with you. I have to, you can't do this on your own. I heard your stories. I believe you, Hayden.'

'No!'

'Listen, Hayden, I have this gut feeling that you'll absolutely need me. Please!'

I'd never seen Canada plead so much. It was hard to watch, so I gave in. 'Fine! But you — not me — are explaining to everyone why you're there.'

Canada smiled. 'So... what's next?'

'I summon the hole.'

'On the pavement?'

I looked left and right; there we no cars in view.

'No, on the road.'

168

Canada automatically stood back, giving me space to hopefully summon the black hole. I'd never tried it before, but I was thinking if I prayed hard enough, the hole would successfully appear.

'Lord Nurogi,' I breathed. 'Send me and my sister Canada to your realm. Bestow upon us the quest. Provide us with the best oracle and prophecy of what lies ahead for us. Akrm.'

Once she was sure I was done, Canada took a few steps forward. 'What was that last word? "Akrm," wasn't it?'

I was shocked. 'I — I don't know. I did it without thinking, but it must mean something.'

'I'm sure we'll find out soon. Where's the hole an...'

The ground rumbled, exactly like it had when I first fell into the hole. The road below us suddenly split in two, and a swirling black gap emerged.

'Hayden!' Canada cried from the other side of the hole. 'Jump!'

I took a few deep breaths and counted to ten aloud. 'One, two three, f...'

'Now!' Canada shouted, jumping in! I couldn't leave my sister and I had a feeling the hole would close up in a matter of seconds. I jumped.

'AAAAAH!' I yelled, tumbling through the black abyss.

* * *

'H — Hayden?' I heard her soft, subtle voice and sighed in relief. I was glad to hear my sister but wasn't too happy about the fact we were surrounded by pitch blackness.

'Don't worry, I'm here. Try to find me. We've landed, but I didn't feel a hard thump or anything.'

We both fumbled for each other, and I eventually found her arm and grasped it tightly.

'It's — It's fine,' she stuttered, even though I could work out she was crying. 'We'll be fine.'

We rummaged around to find an exit with no luck.

'I don't want to be stuck in the middle of nowhere forever,' she cried. 'Is this Nurogonia?'

I found her shoulders and worked my way to hug her from there. 'Nurogonia is a lovely place. We'll be found soon, trust me.'

She held me tighter, and I felt her tears rolling down the back of my T-shirt. 'I — I'm so sorry, Hayden.'

Before I could reply, a beam of light cut through the darkness. Familiar shadows multiplied around the room. At least there are walls, I thought.

'Bou wre taufte,' a voice called.

The door opened, and Canada and I were led out. I looked back at the place from where we had exited and saw nothing. It had completely disappeared.

Nurogonia had managed to change in only a few days. They did say time passes much faster in Nurogonia.

It had the same four wooden bridges, all of them constructed in a cross shape. The one pointing north led to Tempoku Nurogi, the one east led to the dorms, and the one south to the workshops; but the difference was the bridge running west. There used to be huts, as the Nurogons lived in them instead of the dorms, but now things had changed and the huts had been moved next to the workshops.

I saw a sign that read "Xafes."

Morkul, a Nurogon, noticed me looking at the building. He had rectangular, small glasses for his tiny eyes and an oval head. He was very witty when he wanted to be and knew all of the secrets of Nurogonia. He knew things before they happened.

'We call it Xaferios. Yes, the sign does say Xafes, but we call the actual building Xaferios. It means "The Place of Quests." '

'So what does Xafes mean?' Canada questioned.

'It's hard to understand, but Xafes means "quests." So just those four letters — rios — represent the words "The Place of." It's complicated.'

'Sure is,' Canada stated.

'The oracle is in there,' Morkul continued, 'and a little bird told me you have a quest...'

He looked at me, his eyes gleaming.

'Me?' I asked, mock shocked. 'Since when did I sign up for this?'

Morkul ignored my question and turned to Canada.

'Hm, a new Earthling. Who is this?' He studied my sister as if she were a precious artefact. 'You two are unusually close, hands 4.3 cm apart — ah, how sweet are relatives!'

See what I said about Morkul knowing everything?

Canada gulped. 'Uh, how did you know t — that?' She sounded seriously spooked.

'Morkul is a Qiento, pronounced kwen-toe. There's no proper English translation since its origins come from Nurogonia. His rank is a Corake Qiento, the highest rank. Think of it like being a senior scientist.'

'Corake Qientos work for Lord Nurogi. They're like his second brain and can tell your relationship with someone. If Tiffany was here, by your position and posture, he'd be able to tell you've been friends for a while.'

'Hm, thank you, Hayden. The boy is correct. I can tell you never knew Nurogonia was such a place and thought it was fictional, though you believed your brother in the end.'

Canada blushed. 'Uh — I didn't expect it to be this good.'

'Foolish Earthling,' Morkul cursed. 'Haveth you no brain? Nurogonia is a place of dreams! Not stupidity!'

I butted in their conversation. Morkul wasn't choosing to be a very jolly figure. Intelligent, but gloomy.

'Thanks a lot, Morkul!' It did sound a bit sarcastic, but he deserved a bit of telling-off anyways. Imagine telling someone off who's a million times your age! 'We better see the oracle, then! No time needs to be wasted.'

I pulled Canada along, and she muttered, 'So I'm the foolish one?' I ignored her and power-walked to the Xaferios to collect our prophecy.

Many Nurogons tried to greet me on the way, but I had no option but to smile at them and quickly pass on before they had a chance to ask what the rush was.

After a good ten-minute walk, we reached the entrance to the Xaferios. Back there next to

Morkul, the building had looked tiny in the distance, but next to it, it was absolutely massive.

I hesitated, knowing that not everything in Nurogonia was one-hundred-per cent safe, but since this was Canada's first time, she went straight for it.

'What you waiting for?' she called back. Once again, like the black hole, I had no choice but to follow after my eager sister.

There was a large patch of land where many buildings stood. Although they didn't look it, all of the structures must've been quest-related.

I looked around frantically for a place to go, and luckily found a building with a headboard saying "Oracilo." Even Canada could suss that out herself.

'The — the oracle,' she groaned. I had to push her upright so she didn't doze off.

I wasn't feeling too drowsy myself, but I sensed it was only a few minutes till I collapsed. They obviously wanted the only entrees to be the best and strongest heroes.

'We're only twenty-five yards away from the Oracilo,' I pleaded. 'You can do it.'

I pulled her along and we carried on like that for about thirty seconds, and finally, we reached the Oracilo and Canada shook herself back.

'W — was I sleeping?' she asked, staring warily at her surroundings.

'Nearly,' I replied. Canada realised she was holding onto my arm and let go as if it were diseased.

The building itself was T-shaped, like the letter, and was made of a coal-like material. It gave me the chills, as it reminded me of the Horror House at the funfair. I was half expecting fake zombies and vampires to jump out at me.

The chill I felt had a tingly feel to it, something I'd felt before — the aura of many Nurogons together. Many as in a couple of hundred. I had felt it when I first came to Nurogonia. Although I couldn't see them all, I had the same feeling I got while I was lying on the floor when I first arrived; that just as many Nurogons were surrounding me.

But this sense had a different "smell" to it. It was many Nurogons, but also one. It was either just me and my head playing a game of hot potato or there was one Nurogon so powerful they had the aura of hundreds.

'We're close,' Canada warned.

'Yeah, I didn't know that before,' I grunted.

We'd already gone through the first doorway and were now presented with another. As soon as we went through it, long, wooden torches lit up the room and at the far end sat a single chair and desk.

It was what was on the chair that surprised me. A slim, tall half-Nurogon sat on the chair. He wore a plain white toga over his chest with a gold lining and a silver crown on his head. His face was plain and he appeared bored, whilst his eyes were glowing purple.

'Nurogese or English?' the character grumbled.

'En — English, please,' I stuttered.

'Names.'

'Canada and Hayden Smith,' Canada confirmed.

He looked through an ancient list of what was probably names. 'I only have Hayden Smith and Mae Greens on this list. It says Mae Greens must have something to do with this on my Xafe sheet. What would you like to do, Hayden?' He showed us a flash of a smaller but just-as rusty-looking paper.

I scowled. 'What are my options?'

The Nurogon looked back at the smaller paper as if it were a file and he was the secretary. 'Uh, let's see. It says in small print at the bottom, "If there are any extras, they either leave and never return to Nurogonia, or stay and proceed on the quest, dropping out someone else." So you can dismiss Mae Greens from Nurogonia and proceed with the quest like this,' the oracle spread his hands to resemble Canada and me, 'or switch around your choices.'

I bit my fingernails, something that was a usual pastime. And something that also meant I was coming up with a ploy.

'OK,' I announced, smiling.

Canada shook her head, and mouthed "Not me."

'Get rid of Canada and do the quest with Mae Greens, please.'

She gawped at me and turned her head, obviously shamed.

The Nurogon pulled out another piece of paper, this time a fresh one. He also brought out a feather and a pot of ink. How old was this guy?

'If you'll please sign right — here. That would be lovely.'

'Thanks, uh, Nurogon?' I stated, unsure of his name.

The Nurogon grimaced and said, 'It's Harkui. Why does nobody know me? Am I that anonymous?'

I ignored him and speed-read the sign-in form. Very slowly, I picked up the inky feather and pretended to write my signature.

'Done yet?' Harkui asked.

'And — yeah, I'm done.' I slid the paper back over to him and let Harkui have a few seconds of inspection.

'All good, now — hey, wait a minute, you didn't actually sign the slip!'

177

I shook my head innocently and looked over the sheet again. 'I did, look, here.'

'Sorry, but if the quest form isn't signed then the quest will be cancelled and Nurogonia will be in severe danger. There is also a very high chance of your world being affected. What do you think about that?'

Canada gulped. I was searching my brain for an answer.

'Uh, well, when a human signs with Nurogese ink, it doesn't show up to the Nurogons. Canada, you can see that, right?' I blurted.

Canada nodded. 'Uh, yes, I see it. Very clearly, in fact.'

Harkui shrugged. 'OK, what was your choice?'

'To have Mae Greens over her,' I snapped, pointing disgustedly at my sister.

Harkui wrote something down on another piece of paper. 'This change cannot be undone. I'm gonna put it in "The Finalizer," as you humans would say. As I said before, this change cannot be undone whatsoever.'

I slammed my fist on the desk. 'Go for it.'

The oracle lit a torch in the corner of the room, and we were able to see more clearly.

The floor was dust brown, and the wall was the same coal-like stone. It had no windows or electric switches for light, merely the Viking-styled torches. At the far end was a chipped cupboard bolted with a corroded lock. Behind Harkui was a wooden door that looked like it could give you splinters from a distance, and of course behind us the door we had come through.

When Harkui went to open the door, Canada and I paid close attention, squinting to get a better view.

He brought out a small, steel box. It looked like one of the square coffee makers, but "The Finalizer" had many red and blue buttons.

So there was some technology in this room. I was happy now I was sure I hadn't teleported to the Dark Ages.

'This is the tool,' Harkui announced, doing the following as he spoke. 'The paper goes in the slot hole, then we press a few buttons — and there! That'll never come out again! There's a secret storage compartment somewhere here...' Harkui tapped the bottom of the machine. 'Alrighty, how would you like to get rid of Canada? Demolish, stay or evict...'

'Actually, Mae, me and Canada are going on the quest. I lied. I didn't write anything on the form. I said that the ink could not be seen by Nurogons to let both Mae and Canada come along. C'mon, you should've seen that coming. Some oracle you are!'

179

Harkui facepalmed himself. 'How could I be so torue!' He stomped over to the cupboard, waved his hand over the lock and a purple mist appeared.

Canada and I gasped, and Harkui let out a grunt in reply.

The lock crashed to the ground, leaving a mini dust storm. Harkui pulled out a load of papers and let them fall to the dusty floor.

'There has to be a policy about this!' He carried on searching, papers flying everywhere. 'Ah, here! "No Nurogons with the hair over 75 cm..." Eurgh! Fine, you get your way, Earthlings. Your prophecy will be given to you once Mae Greens is here.'

I was about to run out of the door to find Mae when Canada called back at me to stop.

'It's fine, I got it,' she stammered, breathing heavily.

What she did next left me gawping to this day.

Canada closed her eyes, took a few exhales, and opened her mouth.

'Puyew Mae johac!' she shouted.

Mae landed behind me. She looked normal: ginger, curly hair in a low ponytail, a golden grin on her face, her usual green hoodie, blue denim jeans and red sneakers. She wore the same clothes, but she looked older, more mature. Considering she'd just been summoned without notice, she looked happier than clothes fresh out of the dryer.

'Guess what Hayd...' She glanced over at Canada and frowned. 'Who's this?'

'Mae! So glad to — uh — see you. This is my sister Canada. She's coming on the quest with us. Isn't it exciting?'

Mae scowled. 'No. Has she got any clue about Nurogonia? Have you been here before, Blondie?'

Canada got all up in Mae's face, and I could already tell it was going to be difficult to get the two to get along.

'One: don't ever call me that, two...'

I stepped in between the girls. 'Guys! You're on a quest with each other, OK? Calm down! Mae, this is my sister's first time in Nurogonia.'

'Pfft,' Mae grunted.

'Trust me, she's the one who summoned you here. She's capable. Already she's mastered Qiento Level 3,' I argued.

Mae acted as if she didn't care at all. 'Whatever. How old are you, anyway?'

'I'm fifteen. What about you?'

'No younger than you.'

Canada rolled her eyes. 'That doesn't actually answer my question, June.'

'OK, fine, I'm fourteen in two months.'

Canada cackled right in front of her. 'Haha! Youngling and Earthling. Could you get any worse than that?'

All the time Mae and my older sister were bickering, Harkui was trying to reach down and grab the sheet of paper that was stuck on its way up The Finalizer.

He coughed for our signal. 'I've got a prophecy button on here, but it seems to be broken — Ah, here, upload most recent prophecy.' Harkui jabbed at the button several times, and finally, a sheet emerged from the slot.

We all turned to the Nurogon and stayed silent.

'Great-o! Let's see...

Flying on the wings of a legend, a myth,

You will find yourself a dangerous ally to conjoin with.

This associate, as one might say,

Is the exile, evicted, castaway.

You will stumble across the deputy lord,

And find all the possessions she may hoard.'

We were all silent for several seconds.

'The exiled, evicted castaway?' Mae repeated, clearly confused, 'We're gonna be joined by someone who is a threat to Nurogonia...'

Harkui raised an eyebrow. 'Think, girl. You will know him — I mean, the person, but these two,' he pointed at Canada and me once again, 'will not know her — I mean, whatever!'

'Another girl?' I grumbled. 'That's the last thing I need right now.'

Harkui chuckled. 'Hm, I will not give away any more. Even by merely saying the gender may trigger your senses. I do not want you knowing every little detail about your quest.'

'Do tell us!' Canada pleaded.

'You sound like a four-year-old,' Mae laughed.

Canada glared at her.

Harkui clapped his hands to get our attention. 'I am Harkui, your well-working oracle. Most oracles only speak from a script, but I have a working brain and say what I please. I also say your quest begins tomorrow and you will need to have packed by tonight. See Torkie for transport details and Nomki for resource details. Good day!'

He sounded like a kid put on a TV advert — like he was reading off a script.

'Where are we bunking?' Canada asked.

Mae pointed East. 'This way and we're packing, not bunking. I wouldn't believe you're a Year 9.'

'Pardon, I'm a Year 10. Mind you, you're only a Year 9, aren't you?'

Mae ignored her and went for the door. She probably knew where to find Torkie and Nomki. I didn't.

* * *

183

Canada and I followed her to the dorms, where she got her backpack and gave us two spares from the storage cupboard.

'Here,' she said, passing me the Galaxy Hype rucksack and giving Canada the ugly, muddy brown travel backpack.

'I'm sure there are better ones,' Canada protested, leaning in for a peek.

Mae practically shut the door on her nose. 'Nope, that's the only good one.'

Canada pulled a face but left it there.

We continued to follow Mae, and she led us to a small, wooden hut at the very end of the hut area. Small stone steps led up to the entrance, and Mae went up them like they were the steps to Disneyland.

She knocked hard on the door with her knuckles, and after two seconds she knocked again as if we'd been waiting five minutes.

A plump, hairy Nurogon with a red toga opened the door. He had a wispy moustache and very little hair.

'The name's Nomki, what is your...' He looked at Mae and smiled, then he did the same to me. 'Hayden! Mae! And — who's this?'

Canada stepped forward. 'Canada — pleased to meet you.'

184

Nomki smiled at Canada as well. 'You've obviously been selected for a quest! Nobody ever comes to me for anything! I have all the packaging supplies in Nurogonia, though, so I can be extremely helpful. Why don't you all come in?'

'Our pleasure,' Canada replied meekly.

Nomki's hut looked like he'd been a magpie half his life. The sofas were tattered and boxes upon boxes were stacked in every possible corner of the room. The carpet in the middle of the room was dirty and I could've sworn I saw an earwig or two slither over it.

I peeped through a doorway leading to the kitchen. The sink was covered in cobwebs, same as the rusty, old cabinets. The cabinets seemed to be full of plates and glasses were stacked on the counters, not leaving a single space to cook, despite the oxidised stove.

I looked through another doorway and saw the worst room. It was the bathroom. I walked in a little bit more to see that the sink was leaking brown water, the bath was rusty like the cabinets, and the toilet hadn't been flushed. For a while. What was in the pan, I'll leave to your imagination!

And on top of all of that, the whole place stank of something rotten.

'Not the neatest place, but I can certainly call it home!' Nomki chuckled.

'Yeah...' Canada said, wrinkling her nose.

Nomki threw some boxes aside. 'Let's see, I thought I saw my quest boxes here sometime last year.' The dippy Nurogon kept searching through all the boxes, until finally, he came to a regular cardboard box.

'In here is food and money. You have some pre-cooked food and fruit or something. There's more than enough to last you a week'.

Food. From this dump? I shot up a prayer for our bowels.

'And here's the best part, apart from the arsenal.'

Nomki pulled out a wad of cash. It must've been around $2,000.

'Why dollars?' Mae asked. 'Don't know about you, but we're British. What happened to pounds?'

Nomki raised an eyebrow. 'I thought you'd know this, Bravy, I mean, Mae. Whatever you buy, let me tell you now, they will accept any form of cash. Plus, I was human for a while and owned my own company in the USA. I'm rich.'

'In dollars,' I added.

The only time I'd spent a dollar was when I'd found one on the road in Disneyland when I was seven. I picked it up and begged to go to a store where I bought a pack of Candy Corn. Now, double the age, I got to spend a couple grand of it. I imagined getting Xboxes and PS4s, along with loads of games for them...

'Hayden? Hayden!' Mae was waving her hand in front of my face.

'Oh, thanks for the cash, Nomki,' I mumbled.

Mae rolled her eyes.

Canada gave her a look. 'Excuse me, that's my job. My eyes are practically made for rolling.'

Mae ignored her and turned to me. 'Nomki was just saying he's going to show us the best bit when you zoned out.'

Nomki nodded. 'Through this way, I'll lead you to the arsenal.'

He led us through to the stinky, old kitchen, and in the corner was a handle. On the floor. At first, I thought it was something out of place, but as I got closer, I realised there was a square on the floor around the handle. A trapdoor. Impressive, I thought.

Nomki went over to the trapdoor and pulled out a key from a nearby drawer.

The click of the key was satisfying, but it soon ended. 'Follow me, kids.'

As we climbed down a faulty ladder, a wave of nerves washed over me. It didn't look good yet. My view of the room so far was obscured by darkness, and I had a feeling that torches wouldn't suddenly illuminate the room like at the Oracilo.

When I reached the bottom, the room wasn't as bad as I thought. In fact, it was awesome.

The walls were a deep, luscious lavender and on the floor was a navy-blue carpet. It had seemed dark at first sight, but the room was really quite pretty. Boxes were stacked three-high, those at the top had their lids flapping open a little.

Nomki pulled down one of the single-stacked cardboard boxes and opened it. 'Let's see... Vinni, Xetrox, Kipa, Luwsen and some others. Perfect! Come get yourself a dream master, kiddos!'

I was the first to reach into the box. I closed my eyes and pulled out a short, steel staff. I read the small print on the side.

It read "Apocalypse."

'What do I do with this?' I asked, nearly throwing the thing back in the box.

Nomki smiled. 'I see you have a special one. Apocalypse has chosen you, the leader. Its touch is fatal, destroying any enemy. Go on, say her name.'

'Apocalypse,' I stammered, unsure of what would happen.

I wasn't quite ready for what did happen. Red particles and mist flew around the staff, so I couldn't see what was through it. It lasted for about four seconds, then it cleared.

I stared at what I was holding for a while. For starters, it had elongated so now it was three times as long, and the red mist had actually dyed the staff red.

The weirdest thing about the staff was an odd shape had appeared on top. It looked like the target sights on a gun. The outline was a thick black and you could stick your hand through the middle of the shape.

'How is this ever gonna hurt people?' I asked, confused.

Nomki smiled mysteriously. 'Ah, that is for you to find out, not I to tell you!'

I whined. 'I so hate it when people do that. I don't see why you couldn't just tell me! It will make the quest shorter! C'mon, man, say it.'

Nomki simply shook his head.

Mae and Canada were looking through the box, trying to find the best weapon in there.

'I see what you girls are doing,' the Nurogon chuckled, 'and it won't work. Hayden's already taken the best weapon in the box, Apocalypse. The staff chose him, the leader of you all.'

'Technically, I should be the leader, I am the oldest,' Canada exclaimed feistily.

'Oh, sweet!' Mae squealed.

I looked over at her and saw her "weapon." It wasn't much compared to mine — sort of lame, to be honest.

Her staff was baby pink and quite normal.

'It's called... the Dreamatiser!' Mae exclaimed.

Wow, they really had a thing with "isers" in Nurogonia.

With that, the staff formed pink dust and (surprise, surprise) Mae's staff elongated just like mine into a longer baby pink staff. At the top of her staff was a cartoon sort of cloud.

'I see you've picked the cheerful staff, Dreamatiser!' Nomki announced.

'Sure, I'm pretty sure it's "Dramatiser," ' Canada corrected. 'Now that's the one that suits her best.'

'Sure means unsure, Canada,' Mae mocked.

I stared at the useless staff. 'I thought you didn't like pink?'

Mae nearly choked. 'Who said I didn't like pink? I love pink! I know, I seem like a wild girl, but trust me, pink is the best ever!'

I widened my eyes. Mae didn't seem like a girly-girl. I guess because you like pink doesn't mean you like make-up and unicorns and bracelets and rings as well.

Nomki studied Canada and smiled. 'Futorious! Of course! Come here, my dear Canada.'

My sister walked over. 'What?'

Nomki closed his eyes and hummed an eerie tune. Canada looked seriously creeped out.

'Uh... hoarder dude? Are you okay?' Canada asked, poking him. 'I don't wanna be in some kind of ritual with you, alright?'

Then, slowly but surely, something began to rise from the box. There was a huge clatter of metal being clanked together, but eventually, a white staff appeared.

'This is Katropolis, Nomki announced. As you see, nothing happens when I say your staff's name. I am in charge of the staffs, and you will never be able to see it, but I instantly decide whose staff is whose. Once it is yours, nobody else can transform it into its lethal form. The only weapon I didn't have the control over was Hayden's. As soon as he got it out of the box, it was his.'

I smiled. Nomki was a nice guy, he made me feel special. A little bit bonkers and a bit of a collector as well, but still a nice guy. His home was starting to feel cosy.

'Go ahead and say the staff's name. They are not like a pet where they have to get trained to know their name. They know it as soon as they hear it. Go on, say Katropolis — what are you waiting for?'

'For you to finish your silly saga.' Canada grumbled. 'Fine, I'll do it. Katropolis. Wait, wha...'

The force of Canada's staff was so strong it knocked her back into the boxes. When she got her balance again, she blew her fringe out of her face and smirked. 'So you say Hayden's got the best staff?'

'Or is it that yours isn't trained?' Nomki quipped.

'Well, how do you think she's supposed to train an object that can't talk? And you did say they don't need to be trained,' Mae pointed out.

'You see, the Dreamatiser will find a way to communicate with you...'

Canada scoffed. 'You did this a few minutes ago! You make it sound as if we're gonna have to find it out ourselves.'

Nomki chortled. 'Oh, Canada, you make me laugh!'

Canada stared at him. 'I'm not joking.'

Nomki looked at her. 'Dear, oh, dear Canada. Of course you have to find it out yourselves. Us helpers might as well do the quest if you're asking every "difficult" question. And you might not need to use your staffs at all this time...'

Mae changed the subject. 'You do realise we're being joined by "anonymous" — won't they need a staff as well?'

Nomki shook his head. "Anonymous" will bring their own weapon. Now, I don't want to see you lot here for a while. Shoo, I have an appointment with another Nurogon. There's a war-run tomorrow, so loads of them are coming to me for weapons. All of the knives and swords are in some other boxes; they'll use those. Staffs are specially reserved for quests.'

'What's a war-run?' I questioned.

'It's practice in case Nurogonia comes under any sudden attack,' Nomki explained. 'Like the time the nightmares got out. Oh, that was horrible.'

'What time?' I queried. I was very curious.

Nomki shook his head. 'I'll tell you later. And by later I mean when you finish your quest. Goodbye! I'm guessing you're off to see Torkie.'

'We are! Thanks, Nomki! Bye!' Mae called back.

'I wish you luck and shall be thinking of you. Hopefully, you won't die.'

That wasn't very reassuring, but there was no turning back now.

* * *

Once again, Canada and I followed Mae to Torkie's hut, and even she seemed lost.

'I — uh, I've actually never seen or been to Torkie's hut before,' she admitted. 'Legend has it

193

that it's the very last hut, near the outskirts of Nurogonia. Beyond Nurogonia is where the free dreams roam, and — oh, never mind.'

'It would be nice if you actually did mind for a change,' Canada snapped.

'Whatever, Washington, I'll tell you when you're in a case where the information is needed.'

We kept on walking south in the hope of finding the mysterious Nurogon's hut. After what was probably fifteen minutes of wandering around hopelessly, I spotted a murky, moss-covered shack. It was made out of logs, and as a result, the whole building was quite damp.

There was a small stream next to the house, and you could barely tell there was water. I realised I wasn't treading on grass — there was so much algae any fool could've stepped on and through it.

We went to the front of the hut. It had one of those ancient doors I'd seen too much of lately, comprised of vertical wooden panels with circular knockers. Darren also had the same type of doors to his grand house.

But the doors to the shack before us gave off a strangely different aura. I felt as if I should turn around and run. Something seemed wrong about the place — as if something dangerous was lurking inside.

'Well, what are you waiting for?' Mae asked, looking at Canada.

Canada laughed. 'You to open the door!'

'You're the oldest,' Mae protested.

'You've been here the longest. Stop being a chicken.'

'If you stop being a wimp.'

Once again, I had to cut into their "friendly" conversation. 'Why don't you both agree you're being as bad as each other and let me open the door?' I shouted. 'I'm not the oldest, but I'm definitely the most mature. What do you say to me opening the door, then?'

Canada and Mae both shrugged and said simultaneously, 'OK!'

I tried to act as if I was fine with it, but my hands trembled as I reached for the handle.

'Hurry up, we have until tomorrow morning to get to the first QL. It's always like that with quests.'

Canada looked at me. 'Are you some sort of child genius, or is a "QL" something nobody's heard of?'

Mae facepalmed herself. 'A "QL" is short for "Quest Location." What I really meant was QSL, Quest Starting Location. Hopefully, if we ever open this door, Torkie will give us some sort of map.'

'Have you been on a quest before? You know a lot of stuff,' I admitted.

Mae looked down at her toes and sighed, and I knew I'd hit a soft spot.

'I'd — I'd rather not talk about it now... but I'll tell you in the future. Maybe.'

I felt a bit hurt because from experience I knew when someone said they'll tell you later or whatever, they end up never telling you.

Despite all that, I ignored her and knocked on the door.

Unusually quickly, the door opened, frightening the life out of me. I stepped back since my nose was practically touching the door.

'Apologies,' uttered someone with a deep voice.

'It's OK...' I looked up and gasped.

The figure smiled. 'Here for some information? Step right in...'

We sat down on a sofa inside the hut.

'I'm Torkie,' Torkie greeted.

Mae smiled. 'I'm Mae, nice to meet you. This is Hayden and Canada.'

'Hey, there!' He waved at Canada and me.

'H — hi,' I stuttered.

Torkie pulled out a digestive biscuit from his pocket and munched on it. 'My appearance is weird, right? Yeah, most people think that too.'

'Not — not weird, just unexpected,' Canada replied.

If I was the reader, at this point, I'd be rather eager to know what Torkie looked like. That seems fair, so I'll tell you!

Eleven

The Unexpected 'Surprise'

W e headed down to the medicine area. I peeped through the doorway, just to make sure nothing was lurking inside the room. The coast was clear, so I beckoned the other two to follow me inside.

The pharmacy was like a library, but instead of books, potions upon potions lined the tall shelves. Step ladders were in every corner of the room, and I went over to one and pulled it across to a shelf. On the shelf, there were loads of labels, one labelling each glass bottle filled with a potion '#164 - Nose-Hair Growing Potion. Uh, okay? Canada gasped. 'Look, here's a good one! '#56 - Shushing

Potion!' Canada glanced at Mae and Mae rolled her eyes (again).

'I've actually got a reasonable one. #484 - Boost Regain Potion. I'll take that!' I heard a clink as Mae dropped the potion in the mountain-climbing backpack.

'Perfect! Read the long label on the side,' I told her.

Mae brought the potion from her backpack back out and focused on the bottle. 'Oh, here. "Only use ONCE. Instant healing. Effects last for ten minutes. If the user is still not healed, the user will not get affected by it again. Will be sensed with power over a 1-mile radius. WARNING: Victim of potion will be easier to find and may get tracked down. Use in desperate cases." Meh. Still gonna take it.'

'Mae, before you do, see if there are any longer lasting ones,' Canada advised. 'I saw an antiseptic potion that lasted for five minutes, and then I saw one right after lasting for an hour!'

'I'll keep looking, then, Miss State.'

Canada shot me an accusing look. I shrugged, full of fake apology. She knew I'd probably told Mae a few tales. How else would Mae know about the "Miss State" nickname?

Thankfully, she sensibly let it pass. We certainly had bigger fish to fry.

I kept searching, putting aside the "worst" potions and looking for the best of the best as I wanted the top collection.

'Hayden, that was a fire-resistant one!' Canada shouted.

'Yeah, that lasts for thirty seconds! Like I'm gonna take that! You'll be dead by the time you've got it out your bag!' I snorted.

I carried on searching, eyeing the others just in case they had any good stuff.

After a few minutes, Canada came up with a suggestion. 'Why don't we all choose two bottles, then we can meet up once we've got our choices and eliminate the worst one, so we're left with five?'

Torkie had told us we were only allowed to take five bottles maximum because if we took loads, his shelf would be as bare as a baboon's bottom.

'Sounds good,' Mae agreed.

I'd already chosen a bottle, so it was one left to go.

'Is everyone done?' Mae asked once we'd double-checked every shelf.

Canada coughed. 'Yes, hopefully. I saw an empty room with just a big carpet in the middle of the floor, we can discuss everything there.

Mae shivered. 'Why on earth would you have an empty room with nothing but a carpet? I'm done with creepy rituals.'

We entered the room, and Canada was right. It was a big room, about the size of my parent's bedroom, with a single, patterned carpet in the centre. Well, the carpet wasn't the only thing in the room. Wall-mounted heads of bulls, reindeer and lions stared down at us. The gross thing was, the "statues" had real fur and the lion had its fangs bared and they were bloody.

'Those are real?' I stammered.

Mae heaved. 'I wish they weren't.'

I ignored the animals and sat down on the carpet, beckoning for the others to do the same. They followed my example and we sat facing each other.

'Empty your backpacks,' I ordered. The bottles clinked together as they were emptied in a small heap of glass. 'I will pick out a random bottle, read the label and you have to tell me who chose it. Okay, first.'

I picked up an anonymous bottle and read the label. '#1432 - Super-Speed Potion, 30 seconds. Who chose this?'

Mae raised her hand. 'If you're in a deadly situation, like getting chased by a monster, you'll need to run away. If you think about it, with super-speed, thirty seconds is a long time to lose someone. You'll be safe in no time.'

I shrugged. 'I guess. It depends on what the other choices are, and whether they're worth it or not.'

'Ooh, can I choose the next one?' Canada pleaded.

'Uh, sure, go ahead.'

Canada closed her eyes dramatically and selected a glass bottle as if she were at a pageant. 'Oh la, la! #3287 - Dis-Threat Potion - 1 Hour. Look, it says here "This potion will make the drinker a friend to all and will not get harmed in any way. Enemies will become friends, nemeses will become acquaintances, so on. This can be drunk 1 - 3 times." Gosh, this is a keeper! Booyah, suckers!'

I stared at Canada and she stopped and smiled awkwardly. 'OK... that will be a keeper. Bring on the next one!'

The other four were:

#087 - Ultimate Strength Potion - Five Minutes.

#122 - Telepathy Potion - 3 Hours.

#832 - Mind-To-Mind Communication Potion - 24 Hours.

#012 - Regeneration/Healing Potion - 1 Minute (ONE TIME USE ONLY).

'Well, which one should we get rid of?' Mae asked.

Canada shrugged. 'The Telepathy Potion is like the Mind-To-Mind Potion, so maybe we should get rid of that?'

'Okay. Is that fine with you Mae?'

'Sure.'

I stood up to return the bottle, but Mae stopped me.

'I'll return it. I mean, I'm the one who got it, I know where to return it,' she insisted persuasively. She sounded like she was begging to put it away. I had no idea why it would be so important.

I handed the bottle to her and pushed her in the direction of the Potion Library.

'Well, she's eager,' Canada muttered once Mae had left the room.

I tittered. 'I think she's the only one of us three who actually wants to do the quest. Personally, I thought it would be something simple, like cleaning the loos or washing the dishes for a week. But no, we always get the hard job.'

'You never know, "Anonymous" might want to do the quest,' Canada pointed out.

'I doubt it,' I muttered.

It had been a minute since Mae was gone, so I started questioning.

'If she really knew where to put the potion back, she would've returned by now,' I moaned. 'Torkie will be wondering where we're at. It's been half an hour already.'

'She'll be back soon, just give her one more minute at the maximum.'

I hoped Canada was correct. The only downside was, she wasn't.

'Thirty more seconds then I'm going for her, okay?'

Canada nodded. 'Thirty. No, forty-five, no, do a minute.'

I raised my eyebrows. 'Since when were you so concerned about Mae? I thought you didn't like her, now you're giving her an advantage and more time!'

Canada shook her head vigorously. 'Of course not! I just want her to keep away from us for longer. She keeps on interfering when I'm trying to talk to you. I do hate you and all, but you're my brother.'

With that, Mae walked through the doorway. 'Took a while, didn't it? I nearly forgot where the shelf was!'

'I think you did forget,' Canada murmured.

'Right, now we've got everything, we'll go and get our transportation and we'll set off an hour after that. Clear?'

'Yes, sir,' Mae stated in agreement.

We found Torkie munching his way through his Golden Ticket Biscuits he said he'd made. He was so content he didn't notice us waiting in the doorway.

'Uh, hello,' Mae chirped.

Torkie jumped up in shock and immediately hid the biscuits.

'Erm, kiddos, that was quick!' he chuckled nervously. Then, he breathed, 'You didn't see anything, did you?'

I shook my head. 'Apart from you eating those biscuits.'

Torkie exhaled heavily. 'I'm so sorry, I can make you another batch if you give me an hour. See, I'll go and...'

'We're fine, Torkie,' Canada sighed indignantly. 'Look, we've got all the bottles, what next?'

Torkie grinned at our backpacks. 'Let's see your picks!'

'NO!' Mae yelled quickly. 'I mean, we, erm, we wanted to keep it a — a surprise, yes, a surprise.'

I pulled a face. 'Did we?'

Mae stared at me urgently. 'Yes, we did. Show us how to get to the QL and we'll go.'

Torkie frowned. 'Hold it there! We have loads of things to get through!'

Mae grunted so hard we all looked at her. She flapped her arms and walked out of the room.

'Teenage hormones? She'll be fine. Come sit on the canapé and we will start our chat.'

'You mean a sofa, right?' Canada corrected. 'Since when were you French?'

'Sofa, canapé, whatever, just sit down!'

Torkie brought out a bunch of papers.

'You really have a list?' I asked.

Torkie ignored me. 'One of you get Mae. We can't really start the talk without her.'

Just as I was about to say the same, Canada shouted, 'Dibs not doing it!'

So I was left to find Mae somewhere in this unusual shack.

'Mae?' I called. 'C'mon, it would be better to get the talk over...' I looked in the room we'd shared potions in, '... with.'

She was sitting in the middle of the carpet. Her hair was messy, her eyes were wild, her clothes were ragged and overall she looked like a hobo. Her hand was raised and her fingers were curled in a meditation pose. She was the one who'd said she didn't like rituals.

She glared at me. 'What?'

I turned pale. 'T — Torkie says that — that we need to g — go for the talk.'

Mae calmly stood up and sighed. She shook herself and returned to her normal self.

Her hair wasn't a mess anymore. In fact, her hair was newly styled in a plait. Her eyes were calm and understanding. Her clothes were neat and washed and smelt of washing powder.

'Ah, Hayden, what a wonderful pleasure to see you,' she whispered, calm and collected. She acted as if she were Mary Poppins, perfect in every way.

I knew if I asked her what the heck had just happened, she'd say "nothing" and change the subject.

'Well, uh, Torkie wants to have — wants to have a chat,' I told her.

She readjusted her hair and neatened herself. 'I suggest we go, then!'

Mae was acting strange and different, like a real lady. I even noticed a laced hankie neatly folded up in her jeans pocket.

When we approached the room, Torkie smiled at Mae.

'Hello, miss!' Torkie chuckled. 'Come, take a seat.' He patted a space next to him, but Mae sat on a pouffe instead.

'Right, first. I look a bit, human, don't I?' Torkie started.

I was waiting for the right moment to tell you. Yep, Torkie's a human. He looked a bit like Tom

Jones, only younger and more relaxed (not saying Tom Jones looks old and stressed). He had white, short hair and a matching pretty boy goatee. He wore an old tee and filthy joggers, finished off with unlaced trainers.

'Here's the backstory,' Torkie continued. 'My mother was a traveller and adored finding different ways to travel the world. I lost my father when I was three. He was never into travelling. Anyway, my mother's name was Hermia, named after Hermes, the Greek god of transitions, travel, trade, and boundaries.

'Hermia's father always wanted her to travel. Transportation ran in the family. Then it was my turn. I was just nine, a normal Nurogon with no reason to go against the flow. My mother died and I was left to provide transportation for the whole of Nurogonia. Back then, we had nothing. No cars, no trains, no bicycles, none of that. The thing we did have were Arosanios. They pushed out our only source, just like delivering a baby. Our only source, the...'

'Forgotten souls,' Mae muttered. 'They gave birth to the forgotten souls. That's how Nurogonia got invaded!'

Torkie nodded. 'Too many forgotten souls were born, and as humans do as well, many of them got diseases or conditions. One with anger problems bred lots of other forgotten souls. You can imagine how it ended. That's...'

'I don't exactly get what forgotten souls are. The way you talk about them makes them sound real; it's weird,' Canada interrupted.

'Because they are real,' Torkie continued. 'Forgotten souls are quite self-explanatory: "Forgotten Souls." Souls that have been forgotten. And they can live as an animal or human. They used to be more commonly found as animals. They can be very dangerous, but despite my mother's efforts to find better ways to get around, there simply was nothing.

'But back then, about forty years ago, we were desperate for a way to get in and out of Nurogonia, and forgotten souls were the only way. Nowadays, the Arosanios aren't all here, but in a very old book about Nurogonia, it says one still stalks the earth, and that's Iola.

'All I know about her is there's a quest to find her and bring her back to Nurogonia. But many Nurogons protest. The Arosanios are dangerous creatures — evil figures — that breed worse things. There is a slight chance Nurogonia will be left cursed if just one of the Arosanios returns. Lord Nurogi still needs to plan a court meeting with the whole of Nurogonia, so we can vote on the quest. Anyway, I wasn't supposed to be telling you all this, I was actually going to tell you how I became human.'

'I was waiting for that,' I answered. 'Tell us!'

Torkie smiled and started talking, putting actions into his words and making it dramatic as if he were telling us the day he killed a dragon. 'It all started on a windy day. Our oracle was the same as yours. In fact, he's been alive for five thousand years now.'

We all gasped.

'He's a scatty oracle, but a good one. He gave me a quest, telling me I'd be the shifter, the transporter. My quest was to find a smooth way to get around until I died or had children of my own old enough (they had to be over eight) to do the job.

'I was sent to the human world as a human. My quest was to bring back one — just one — item that would give Nurogonia a transport advantage. This way, mechanics could copy the one object and make many more of them. I had twelve days to undertake the quest, and it took me fifteen.

'I didn't exactly get clear instructions for the quest, so they can't really blame me. That is most likely what delayed me so much. You won't have clear instructions, either. So here I am now. Bear in mind, I was twelve years old, one day added to the quest for one year of my life. I really regret not doing the quest now, since I'm...'

'It's fine, we don't want to know,' Canada interjected once again.

'Okay, I simply won't say. Of course, I was much less handsome back then than I am now,' Torkie arrogantly bragged, 'but I was still the most good-looking around Nurogonia.'

Mae clapped. She had been silent since she spoke about the forgotten souls. 'Very humble, my king.'

The old man didn't get her sarcasm and patted Mae on the head, making the effort to reach over to the pouffe. 'Thank you, dear Mae! Now, where was I?' Torkie took a list out of his pocket. 'Telling them I'm good-looking, then...'

'You actually bothered to put that on your list?' I tittered. 'Too modest, Lord Torkie.'

Torkie was starting to realise it was sarcasm. 'Erm, just as a joke, I know what you kids are like.'

'Could you explain the Arosanios and the forgotten souls a bit more clearly?' Canada pleaded. 'They sound like good information.'

Torkie sighed. 'The Arosanios were once called Murogons, but now they are far too dangerous to have their name linked to us Nurogons.'

'But you're not a Nurogon anymore...' I mentioned.

The man thumped his chest. 'I am in my heart.'

Tears started to well up in the corner of his eyes. Torkie sniffed and gave out another large exhale.

'The old days,' he mumbled.

Canada, Mae and I all glanced at each other and the girls rolled their eyes.

'Uh, Torkes?' Mae whispered. 'Torkes, you there?'

Torkie shook himself silly and returned to planet Earth. 'Ah, they were dark creatures, the same height as us...'

'You mean the Nurogons?' I butted in.

The man grunted. 'No, I mean us!'

'But you're not them, you're us!' Canada protested, pointing at herself.

'No, I'm them!' Torkie pointed to the wall.

'What, you're wood?' Mae joked, really getting on the guy's bad side.

Blanking her, Torkie continued 'Anyway, they were the same height as us and had wings. Sometimes they'd swoop about, making great delivery people. Not if they were animal, though, no. Yeah, so like on Earth, there were the animals and humans, if you can call them that.

'The only thing in common with the "humans" and animals is they both bred dangerous things, regardless of the species. These things were called forgotten souls. Yes, it's weird how they were already forgotten from birth, but it was like that. You can imagine how fast Arosanios ran out. Once they were all dead, there was no belief in them ever returning.

'But as we are, us Nurogons got our only transport from them. Any forgotten souls that were rideable were used daily. It was a big risk because they were so dangerous, but we did it anyway. Solves your problem?'

'Nope, still as confusing as ever, but carry on.'

'No need to. I'll confuse your simple mind even more. Next step. I will summon your ride. Your ride will have a side pouch, and in that pouch, you will find a map. "X" marks the destinations, and there will be lines from your QSL — Quest Starting Location — to the place you need to search. Follow me, if you want to start your quest and get it over with.'

Torkie led us into a small garden and told us to stand back. He stood in the middle of the garden and looked at his hands. 'This should do it.'

Mae, Canada and I looked at Torkie, trying to establish what he was doing. He stretched out his arms and shook them as if he was warming up.

'Close your eyes,' he instructed.

None of us did so.

'I'm warning you — if you don't, you could get seriously hurt. I had a client who didn't close his

213

eyes whilst I did this.' Torkie sighed. 'Didn't make it out alive.'

We still didn't believe him and stared contently.

'Oh, look, Santa!' he yelled, pointing to the sky.

We all turned our heads and looked up like three-year-olds.

In a flash, I felt the ripple of a blast, pushing me back into a wooden fence that surrounded the garden. The same probably happened to Mae and Canada, because I heard not one thud, but three as we all crashed against the fencing.

'Quick, get up, you'll want to see my beautiful baby!' Torkie stated hurriedly.

'What are you...' Mae squealed, standing up. 'Oh my gosh, oh my gosh! I love it!'

I opened my eyes and rolled them immediately. 'You've got to be kidding me.'

Canada looked and yawned. 'Of all possible choices, you chose this?'

The creature neighed and glared at Canada. My sister backed up and the animal produced the closest thing to a smirk it could.

'Kids, this is Despoena. Despoena, this is Mae, Canada and Hayden. Despoena can take you anywhere on your quest and show you some hidden delights which may surprise you, even earthly ones.'

Despoena whinnied at me and rubbed her head against my chest. I ran my fingers in her soft mane and it neighed in delight.

'Guess who gets the best first impression,' Canada murmured.

Torkie tutted. 'Lucky she didn't catch your eyes falling, Hayden. She'll grow to like you, Canada. She's only two, so she's got lots of learning to do.'

I scoffed. 'She? The last thing I need is another girl on this quest! Let's hope Anonymous is a boy.'

Torkie laughed at what I said. 'Oh, Hayden. Anyway, Despoena is a Pegasus. I didn't create her, I simply summoned her. What's that, Peggy?'

Despoena neighed and Torkie translated.

'She says it's a delight to be here, away from everything else. See, when she was a young foal, there was a terrible storm, and her mother was killed in it.'

Despoena started charging about and butting into things as if to say she didn't want Torkie to talk about it.

Torkie held out his hand and stroked Despoena's long snout. 'I know,' he cooed, 'but it's my duty to tell them. Where was I? Yes, her mother was killed in the storm, and her father had passed away a few months before her mother was due to have her. Despoena was taken in by another herd of Pegasus'.'

215

'When she was old enough to travel on her own, she came to Nurogonia. Everyone else was afraid of her, bless the thing. At last, after she'd scouted all of Nurogonia, she came to my mossy, dark hut at the south end of Nurogonia. I was the only one who'd take her in. We became best friends as soon as I started feeding her Werther's toffees.'

Despoena started whinnying and grunting, so with a heavy sigh, Torkie went into his kitchen to fetch a packet of the toffees.

He returned with the sweet-smelling sweets and opened the brand-new packet.

'Here you go, Peggy!' Torkie remarked, popping a Werther's into her mouth. Despoena neighed in delight and opened her mouth for another. This time, Torkie poured the whole bag (excluding the packet) into her wide mouth.

'Are you sure that's healthy for her?' Canada enquired.

Torkie shrugged. 'She'll be fine.'

I frowned. 'Hm, a shame. I wanted one.'

Despoena looked at me and almost laughed. Creepy, huh?

I looked Despoena up and down, and then I realised she had a black pouch on the side of her body. I unzipped the pouch and brought out a crusty, dog-eared map.

216

I straightened it out and blew the top of it, just to make it as dramatic as they did in Narnia.

Torkie noticed me and laughed. 'It's not that old. I say things start making dust of their own when they're like, perhaps ten millennia? This has only been here for four millennia, I think.'

I couldn't believe I was holding something from that long ago. Four thousand years? I felt as if I was holding an Egyptian or Greek artefact.

'Four millennia? Madness!' I took a proper look at the map. All I saw were lines leading to blank spaces.

Every time I took a good stare at the map, Mae and Canada tried to take a look at what I was so surprised and shocked about, and I pulled the map away every time they did so.

'No peeking!' I shouted, pushing Mae's head back to where it was before.

She protested. 'Just show us! What's your problem!'

I looked at her. 'I'm the natural leader so I get first look.'

Canada and Mae shared a look and both simultaneously muttered, 'Cocky.'

I'm not going to lie, I did feel very offended, but as the natural leader, I had to try not to retaliate.

Torkie broke the silence. 'I think you're all ready to go! Bye, bye, Dessy the Peggy! If these guys are naughty, just send me a neigh. Have a good quest, Hayden, Canada and Mae!'

'Wait!' Canada shouted. 'I don't feel ready enough for the whole...'

Torkie had already pushed us all onto Despoena's back and she was flapping her wings, ready to launch into the sky.

'Farewell, my friends!' Torkie yelled from twenty metres below.

It was like riding into our worst nightmares.

Twelve

Our Literal Breath-Taking Hike

'Among the hills and far away, lived a girl with the name of Mae. She picked the pansies and buttercups, but little...'

'Could you shush for once?' Canada hissed. 'Nobody wants to hear your dainty ditties!' Mae snorted. 'Your wish is my command. Tra la la, sheep go baa, a cow goes moo and so do you, ponies neigh, eat some ha...'Wait, did you just call me a cow?' Canada scoffed.

'Yep.'

I had had enough. 'Both of you be quiet!'

They both hushed and we were all silent for a while.

'Are there any chips in there?' Mae suddenly questioned.

Being careful not to fall of Despoena, I cautiously took my backpack off and searched for potato chips. 'Uh, not that I know of. But there are Nuro Noms. They look like some sort of mini biscuits.'

'Check the ingredients, I don't want gluten.'

I turned the packet over and scanned the ingredients. 'Erm, oh, here. They say "glouttan fere." I tried to translate the words that should've been easy to translate.

'Gluten-free, Hayden,' Canada laughed with ease.

I glared at her. 'I was about to say that!'

My sister raised an eyebrow.

In the end, Mae took the Nuro Noms and finished the whole lot before I could ask for one.

'Is there not another packet in there?' she asked apologetically.

I rolled my eyes. 'Doesn't excuse the fact you ate the whole packet in thirty seconds! If there is another packet, I'll have to eat the contents well out of your reach!'

Mae laughed. 'My Mum keeps putting me on diets. I'm not that fat, am I?'

Canada snorted and I glared back at her.

'No, you're not fat,' I replied.

'Just not skinny,' Canada gleefully added.

I held up my fist to Canada's face and she leaned out of my reach.

'Both of you, stop! You're both wrong — sort of. It's my mother, okay? She's a bit of a posh lady and wants me to be exactly like her. So she puts me on all these sissy diets to "flatten me down." The truth is, I look nothing like her. She's got straight, long, golden-blonde hair and this really curvy but skinny model figure. All I've got are dingle-wings and flaps on my sides! My father told me she once had a tirade because of my figure and hair.'

'What's your father like then?' Canada asked, suddenly interested in Mae's tale.

Mae looked uncomfortable for a second and was fidgeting and hesitating. 'He's gone to — to a better place.'

'Where's that?' Canada asked.

Mae ignored her, so she repeated the question.

'I don't wanna talk about it, okay? All I'll say is he's somewhere far away. Far, far away.'

Mae bowed her head and brought something out of her pocket. I saw the back of what it was and guessed it was a photo. On the back of it was the date 17-05-2009. It also said in scruffy writing,

You'll always be my Mae. Not April, not June, my Mae.

Enjoy your life without me.

I decided not to say anything about it, but Mae must've been quite young when that message was written.

All the way to our QSL, that one sentence echoed in my head. Enjoy your life without me. Perhaps that was the reason Mae didn't want to talk much about her father.

We had been flying for several few hours when I spotted a mountain range and made a decision.

'Pass it here for a second,' I ordered Canada. She'd been studying the map for the last half hour (which was a massive time waster since it was blank) and looked completely baffled by the whole quest.

Ten seconds later, Canada replied. 'Uh, yeah, sure.'

I saw her face as she lifted it from gazing at the map. It was pale and her eyes weren't very straight.

'Are you OK?' I asked her, taking the map as I did.

Canada was slow to reply once again. 'Maybe,' she whispered.

This caused Mae to look back at Canada as well. 'I never realised you had acne. Have you got a bottle of Tazorac?'

My sister snuffled sharply. 'No, but I'll probably buy some from the nearest pharmacy. Is that alright with you?'

I ordered Despoena to slow down as I studied the map. It wouldn't be good if we suddenly realised we'd passed our destination by several miles!

'Gosh, this mountain here,' I observed, pointing at the tallest mountain in the distance, 'is Mount Uropia. It says Mount Uropia here on the map, it's just appeared! I don't know if we'll need it in the future...' I had an idea.

'What shall we do, then?' Mae asked me.

I smiled at the mountain and without answering Mae's question, I pointed at a ledge a fair way up the mountain. 'Stop right there.'

By this point, Canada and Mae were more confused than ever.

* * *

Once Despoena stopped on the ledge, I told the others my idea.

'First of all, we need a clear signal. Despoena obviously can't fly too high up the mountain, so I told her to stop as far as she can get, which is here. We'll trek for twenty minutes up the mountain slope; when we've reached the perfect place, we'll place our signal. This mountain is going to guide our way back home.'

'Of course. There are always mountains in quests,' Mae sighed.

Canada didn't look so keen on the idea. 'You sure this won't waste our time? I mean, we can always use twenty minutes, since we have — what — three days to complete this quest, and the mountain is tall enough to see from a distance. We've got three more days to finish this quest, we won't forget where the tallest mountain around here is. Besides, you're wasting our time.

I stared Canada in the eye. 'You know that gut feeling you had when you said you should come? I think I'm having the same sort of feeling. I feel like this is a part of the quest they forgot to tell us, "Remember to mark the mountain" or something.'

Canada grunted but managed to pull a fake smile. 'Of course, boss!' she moaned through gritted teeth.

'That's the spirit, kid,' I replied, enjoying every moment.

I rummaged around in the hefty backpack I had managed to keep on my back all the way. 'I think there should be something here...'

I pulled out a red flag with a ginormous pole.

'Whoah,' Canada breathed.

Mae gawped at the two-metre-high flag. 'What are you? The male version of Mary Poppins? What else have you got in there, a city?'

I stared at what I'd pulled out. 'I have absolutely no idea what just happened. But it's great. Come on, guys, who knows what other magical stuff this backpack can release?'

'A toothpick?' Canada sarcastically asked.

Once again, she was spoiling all my fun and amazement. 'Are you ever gonna get serious about this quest? Everything's a plain joke to you. I'm telling you now — if you don't get your act together, you might be killed.'

Canada gulped and didn't say a word. Hopefully, (if her brain functioned properly) she'd start acting a bit more concerned.

I heard Mae snort, then it grew into a heap of laughter.

Glaring at her, she stopped. 'Whoops.'

'Let's get reasonably high before the sun goes down.'

I do have to admit, going up wasn't easy, but we managed to climb another half kilometre.

'I — I think this is enough,' I gasped.

Canada nodded. 'Yeah, let's place the flag and start going b — back.' She and Mae were wheezing as much as I was.

The oxygen was getting pretty scarce at the top of Mount Uropia, but we managed not to pass out, which was apparently an accomplishment for Mae.

'W — what, we're gonna embed the pole in rock?' Mae stammered.

I felt around in the bag, and this time brought a roll of duct tape. 'No, we're gonna embed it in this patch of soil and secure it to this small tree with duct tape. Everyone, help me!'

I pushed the flagpole as far as I could into the ground. We unravelled loads of duct tape and started winding it around the flagpole and the nearby tree. In a few minutes, we'd properly secured the pole.

'That's g — good,' Mae puffed.

We walked down the slope back to the ledge so it wouldn't be hard for Despoena to pick us up.

Mae petted her head. 'Thanks, girl, it's so nice of you.' She climbed onto her back and she looked at us.

Despoena was just like the fairy tales: she had a pastel yellow mane, a matching tail and feathered wings. She wasn't a cream white colour like normal. She had dark-stone grey skin and black hooves.

'At least we know where to look for guidance,' Mae remarked. 'Placing the flag marker really was a good idea.'

'Quick, get on!' I urged Canada, ignoring Mae's compliment. 'Despoena might not have enough lung capacity!'

'I — I have a feeling her lungs are twice the size of ours,' Mae pointed out, wheezing as she did.

We sat in the exact same order we'd sat on our way here, Canada at the back, Mae at the front and me in the middle.

'Just get us lower,' I ordered Despoena. 'Then we can find out where we're going.' She actually understood me and headed downwards.

I'd never been so high up. Sure, my family and I had gone hiking in Wales, but simple mountains like Snowdonia National Park were nothing compared to Mount Uropia. It was very tall and very skinny, the worst mountains for hiking but the best for signaling.

When Despoena was not too high off the ground, I told her a location that wasn't written on the map.

'Go to the nearest convenience store.'

Canada and Mae were questioning me the whole way to the store and why I needed to go there in the first place. To be honest, I had no idea. I didn't need to go there; I was in need of a Sprite and maybe a Twix.

'Do you, uh, want sweets or anything?' I asked as we stepped off Despoena.

Canada facepalmed herself. 'You bonehead! This is a serious quest; we can't pop off at a corner shop! We've got three days to complete the whole quest and you want to get sweets? How foolish can you be? Why would you make this guy,' she pointed vigorously at me, 'lead a life-threatening quest?'

I hung my head in shame. She was right. It was absurd to let my cravings drive me to utilise the power I'd been given as lead in such a cheap way.

Trying not to act embarrassed, I brought out the map from the backpack I was still carrying and studied it carefully. 'We have to...'

I stared at the map in shock.

Once again, Mae and Canada tried to see what was on the map. This time, I let them, and they nearly spat out their teeth.

What I saw in front of me was something I hadn't noticed on all the occasions I'd taken a look at the map. In fact, I believe it had just appeared there.

'Despoena, let's go,' I demanded, forgetting about the convenience store. 'Now.'

Thirteen

The (What Mae Calls It) Temsle

'So, where are we actually supposed to go?' Mae asked. I stared back at her. 'Don't ask me! 'Mae scoffed. 'Who else am I supposed to ask? You're the leader!'

True, but the truth is, I had no clue either.

I looked back down at the almost illegible handwriting and shook my head. It was in black splatted ink, it read *"Anywhere"*. 'You must be thinking, how in the world is that shocking considering what Nurogonia could be like? But when you have a quest which is yet to be fully revealed, a map and you have no idea what country or even city you are in, it's the last possible word you'd like to read. And not unusually, the creepiest.

It was weird. I vaguely remembered the writing, but I couldn't grab hold of the memory of it completely. It was as if it were a fish out of water, flopping around for something too far away.

'So... since we're going anywhere...' I said sneakily, 'why don't we go to the convenience store?'

'Or we could go somewhere more practical. Where about are we?' Canada asked.

I turned the map towards her. It was exactly like before, apart from the newly written word.

'Well, we're definitely not in England. I've never heard of Mount Uropia.'

'Me neither,' I confessed. 'I have a feeling we're in a whole new dimension — like maybe we're in a place that's a rival of Nurogonia, or...'

'Don't get your hopes up,' Canada interrupted. 'I know what you're like.'

'I suggest we go to Feldo Forgutt,' Mae suddenly blurted out. 'Ten miles north, eight miles west.'

I didn't wait for a confused silence. 'Who are you?' I shouted.

Mae looked at me, and the weirdest thing happened. She started crying and repeating sorry over and over.

It was all so quick. All I could do was watch her and say "What's wrong?" or "Why are you crying?" Those were my only options since I couldn't really give her a hug, because — you know what, I just couldn't, okay? Having to lean into her on the back of Despoena was more than enough I felt.

'C'mon, Mae, stop being all sappy on us,' Canada moaned. It didn't look as if she wanted to give Mae a cuddle either.

Mae eventually stopped. 'I don't know what's wrong with me. It always happens! I gush out random things without thinking! Like the forgotten souls. You remember that, right?'

Despoena started shaking. We weren't too high up in the sky, but it was still a dangerous move to make. The Pegasus obviously didn't like the words "forgotten souls."

After recovering from the shake, Mae continued. 'Sorry, Dessy. Anyways, I've never heard of the blessed things! It's not me telling you that stuff, it's like there's another person inside me. The odd thing is, that person is always right. Ever since I got to Nurogonia, I've been switching between the two personalities. Trust me, I much prefer the dangerous Mae who loves unicorns and pinkness.'

'Speaking about unicorns, I'm amazed you didn't faint when Torkie summoned Despoena,' Canada pointed out.

'Oh, trust me, I fainted a thousand times inside, but my therapist taught me this way of holding it in.'

Canada snorted. 'You should've told my mum that when Hayden was gone.'

'What? Tell me more!' Mae begged.

'Why don't we listen to Mae's view of the world for a change?' I suggested. 'You were saying?'

Mae looked upset she hadn't heard about what happened to Mum, but she also looked delighted to carry on her story.

'Did any of you notice Nomki called me Bravy at one point? For a second, I thought Bravy was a distant relative of his or something whose name he'd mistaken and accidentally called me, but then my second personality started owning up to the name. I realized Nomki must know something about my second personality and being a second relative of his was actually an option.'

Canada shivered as if Mae's story were giving her the chills.

'Scared yet?' Mae asked.

My sister glared at Mae as if she were a bit mental. 'Of course not! I was — uh — really cold.

233

You know when you get random shivers down your spine?'

'Sure,' I laughed, and Mae started laughing too. Canada joined in and reached forward and gave Mae a soft punch in the side.

'Oww!' Mae wailed. She wasn't hurt, she just wanted to make a big deal of the event. 'Do that to Hayden, not me!'

I scowled but decided not to say anything. 'Where did you say Felpo Ferott was?'

'You mean the Feldo Forgutt? I'm guessing you do. And I already told you, it's ten miles north, eight miles west!'

'Jee, calm down, Bravy!' I joked. Mae being Mae took it seriously.

'Stop it! You're not funny! Why can't anyone leave me alone?'

I tried hard not to laugh at the near fourteen-year-old having a strop. Someone would've thought she was turning eight for goodness sake.

Ignoring Mae, I told Despoena where we were going and she abruptly switched direction. I held onto the lead rope around the Pegasus's neck so hard she leaned over to the side in an attempt to knock me off.

She let out a boisterous neigh and headed north

* * *

'Wake-up!' I heard a distant voice call.

'What — what is it?' I murmured, opening my eyes only to close them again.

I was leaning forward, into Mae's back as I snored away. I didn't realise I was so exhausted.

I heard a groan. Then, suddenly, I and everything around me started vibrating. This time, I opened my eyes and kept them open. A huge, black marble building stood in front of us. It didn't have a moat like a castle, or fancy pillars or a curved roof like a temple, but it felt like a mix of both. It wasn't a fantasy make-believe castle or temple, it was real.

'It's a temsle,' Mae marvelled.

'No, it's a...' Canada took a moment to think. 'A castle! No, a — no fair! The other way doesn't really make sense!'

I chuckled. 'Don't get so worked up about it, those silly names will never outdo the actual name of this place.'

'You mean the Feldo Forgutt?' Canada asked.

Suddenly, a deeper, more mature voice came out of Mae's mouth. 'In English, it is called "The Fields of Forgotten Souls." Many forgotten souls lie in this building, and the person who oversees them all is the person who will be joining you on your quest.'

Mae covered her mouth in shock and let out a muffled scream that was still loud enough to make fish rise to the surface. Her voice echoed through the distance and I could almost see the ripple in the sound wave.

'Shush!' Canada and I simultaneously hushed. But it was too late.

I stared at the temsle and my jaw dropped open. 'What on Earth is that?'

Mae removed her hand from her mouth. 'I don't think we are on Earth.

Fourteen

Zest for Rest

'So, I see you have awakened my souls,' a deep, wispy voice hissed. I had no idea where I was. The last thing I heard from the other two was Mae saying *"I don't think we are on Earth."* Then it all went pitch black.

OK, let me recap for you.

The last thing I had seen was thousands of tiny (they seemed tiny from the height we were at) figures. Some of them pulled open a hefty-looking gate, whilst others stood their ground dressed in black armour with square shields and terrifyingly pointy swords. I was going to open my mouth to scream as well, but that's when I saw nothing. I couldn't smell, touch, see or hear. As for the last sense, tasting... there was nothing much to taste, although I wished there was.

Actually, I could taste that dry feeling in your mouth when you haven't drunk something for a while, even though I was pretty sure I had drunk at least a bottle of mountain water in the last ten hours.

Mae and Canada must've been around somewhere, so I fumbled all over the place in search of them. It's like slicing your hand through thin air — you get nothing out of it.

It reminded me of when Canada and I first entered Nurogonia. We couldn't see a thing. But this time it was much worse. I had no one to grab onto or talk to.

Back to the present.

'What is your purpose?' the voice bellowed. It was definitely a male voice. It sounded like something I had heard in medieval movies. This guy had the same voice a king would.

I stayed silent.

'Answer me, you puny Earthling!'

As soon as he said the word "Earthling" I knew for a fact he was not your average human.

'Are you here to see the soul guarder? Hmm?' His voice got more and more desperate and impatient as he spoke. 'Hmm?'

I shook my head, then realised this was pointless. 'No, sir.'

Apocalypse, where are you? I impatiently thought.

Sir? I had no idea who he was! But when you hear a voice like that, it's kind of the expected name.

I heard a click, and two lanterns came on. I looked around worriedly and saw myself on my knees with my hands tied behind my back. No friends. No bag. No Apocalypse!

In front of me sat a giant throne made out of moving, black mist. On the throne sat my could-be nightmare.

There was a tall, muscly man. His skin was so dark it was nearly black. He had braided, dark ginger hair that reached three-quarters of the way down his back. He had an all-black cloak that reached his ankles, under which I could make out black cowboy boots with many spurs.

'I am Master Sosiri; I will not accept a pathetic "sir." You can call me a god if you want...'

I wouldn't go that far, I thought.

'And answer my question, you fool!'

I didn't know what question to answer, as he had asked me two: what my purpose was and if I was there to see the soul guarder.

'Where are my sister and friend?' I yelled, ripping the rope tying my hands together.

Master Sosiri stood up and brought something out from behind his throne: a long, black staff suited for a devil. On top, it had an oval with devil horns. Around the symbol, a red mist swirled.

'How dare you cross me!' he hollered. Then, he calmed down, put away his staff and sat back down on his throne. Lacing his fingers, he whispered, 'I'll tell you where your friends are on one condition — you take my soul guarder on the rest of your journey.'

I stood there, wheezing from all the shouting I'd recently done. My arms were already ready to strike, but my legs were trembling. For the next thirty seconds, I thought as hard as possible.

'Take your time, boy,' Sosiri hissed.

'I'll take the soul guarder.'

Sosiri's smile expanded. 'Follow me to the "Arsenal of Forgotten Souls."'

Sosiri was waiting at the door, desperate to open it.

'Arsenal? Cool! Will I get to see Aubameyang?' I squealed and got more excited than usual (well, the most excited I'd ever be in this situation).

Sosiri cackled, his voice making my spine tingle. 'Well, I used to support them, but — argh! I'm getting carried away! You look about fourteen; how can you not know what an arsenal is?'

All I was thinking was Sweet! He used to support my favourite team! But at the same time, I needed to find out what arsenal meant (apart from the football team).

'Uh — no, nothing. Sorry,' I mumbled.

'You are more witless than I expected! So much for a quest leader.'

I felt embarrassed someone hadn't come over to admire my talents.

'An arsenal is a weaponry room! But we do not keep weapons there, no. Many people fulfil their quests with obsidian axes or other precious items from an armoury. This is the arsenal... of souls.'

He opened the door and my jaw dropped open.

There were shelves of moving air, all of them a slightly different colour to the rest.

'I will call my assistant. Do not under any circumstances touch anything, boy,' the deep voice urged. 'I'm warning you...'

With a snap of his fingers, he disappeared, just like that. But what turned up instead of him nearly made me faint.

'Hi,' Rodger's voice said.

Fifteen

I Suspect My Best Friend is a Fugitive

❧

odger was dressed exactly like Master Sosiri, but his coat only reached past his knees. His face looked bruised and his legs were purple in places. His hair was spikier and not at all clean.

'Rodger Calendor, is that really you?' I asked, secretly pinching myself.

Rodger walked around me like I was under arrest. 'Hayden Smith, what are you doing here?' 'The same goes for you!' I protested. 'Answer my question first, you foolish boy!' he yelled. Then, his face went paler than it was before. 'I — I'm so sorry, I didn't mean to...'

'So I see you've learned some of your master's ways. He said the exact same thing to me.'

Rodger gulped. 'I've been his sidekick for a while. He calls for me whenever there's a slight problem. He nominated me as his soul guarder over all the other souls, and he...'

'He let souls be an option in crucial safeguarding?' He must've been completely bonkers.

'... and made me protect all of these. If one gets unleashed, bad things can happen. Well, the intensity of what happens is based on what soul you unleash. Cracket got unleashed once. His name isn't really that, it's merely a perfect nickname. Plus, no one really knows his name.'

I wasn't having any of it.

'Apocalypse!' I yelled. Oh boy! He should have been scared. Within a second, my staff appeared in my hand.

'Hayden, you don't have to...'

I ignored him. 'What are you doing here? Are you an enemy of Nurogonia?'

Rodger backed away from me. 'Wait! Let me explain! Please!'

'You're on the run, aren't you? You're an escapee. Don't try to protest, I know what's going on.'

'Stop!' Rodger hollered. Then, he quietened down. 'Just because I help out a bad guy, doesn't mean I am a bad guy. All I do is hang around these souls and make sure they don't escape. It's the most boring job in the worl...'

'So it's a job, now?' I interrupted. 'And Master Sosiri is a bad guy? And what about school? I'm guessing you abandoned that as well?'

Rodger turned red with fury. 'You know I go to a boarding school?'

I was puzzled for a second. Why in the world was that relevant? 'Just answer my question and maybe you'll live.'

I felt bad saying that. We used to be the best of mates, now I was threatening to — I'd rather not repeat it.

'It's going to shut down. There's been a host of problems. My parents were devastated, you know how they were all about my education. So they found another nearby boarding school, St. Carlos' Academic School for Boys. As its almost end of term, I went for the trial week and I absolutely hated it. All the teachers said was "We need to get the boys to achieve the highest academic levels" and "We have some of the smartest in the county" and stuff like that.

'Boy, I'm smart, but I'd never attain their expectations. So I ran away. I'd been alone a few hours, and I had some spare cash, so I caught the bus and went to my aunt and uncles. I told them my parents had sent me there, and as they had no proof to challenge me, they believed me like no one's business.

'So I had my parents thinking I was still at school, and my aunt and uncle thought I was on holiday at theirs. I'd got small recordings of my mum saying stuff. I'd changed her number to redirect to mine on my aunt and uncles contacts, so I played the recording close to the screen when they tried calling. I did the same with Dad. I always had to be in a different room when they wanted to call Mum or Dad. You know the school my parents sent me to?'

I nodded, taking in every word.

'The best thing about it is you only get to see your parents for a couple of weeks a year, so I had plenty of time to find a different place. I called my parents twice that week, saying I loved school.

'You rebel!' I murmured. 'How could you? How could you do that to your parents, your auntie and uncle, even the school!

'Yeah,' Rodger gulped, looking at the floor.

'How did you get here?'

'In my sleep,' Rodger replied sadly.

I laughed. 'Excuse me, I thought you said you got here in your sleep!'

Rodger didn't look too amused. 'Yes, I did come here in my sleep. I dreamed of this place, then, poof, here I was.'

Dreams, I thought. Nurogonia has got a big thing about dreams.

'I think this place is related to Nurogonia,' I thought aloud.

'What in the world is Nurvogonria?' Rodger questioned.

'The Land of Dreams. If Nurogonia is the place of dreams, and this is the place if forgotten souls...'

Rodger muttered something and shook his head. 'We're in Feldo Forgutt, but this building is called Deronca. This is the place of forgotten souls. Somehow...'

I didn't believe any of it. 'How can they be linked?'

Rodger looked up at the racks of jars, then looked back at me. 'There's one way to find out.'

Sixteen

The Story-Teller Soul

Rodger was looking through the shelves to find the right jar. He passed a few shades of orange, said to be the colour of happiness.

I asked him why he didn't take those.

'It's weird back here in Deronca. An orange spirit could actually be one of the deadliest spirits. We're gonna get a dark grey colour; this way we can be sure they're smart and can tell us all the needed information.'

'I thought you said your place could be a bit weird. How come dark grey is the colour of smartness, that seems pretty normal.'

'It's weird, so you don't know what to expect. Sometimes, I bottle the spirits, so I know which ones to let out again. Most times, they switch colours to confuse everyone. Once, Master Sosiri told me to get a rainbow spirit for his daughter, Mania. Turns out, the souls had switched colours and I accidentally released a bad soul.'

'Why on Earth would Master Sosiri give his daughter a spirit or soul? They mean the same, right?'

'Yes, they do. And most spirits you can't see, so Master Sosiri wanted to give his daughter a rainbow spirit so it could read her bedtime stories. Rainbow spirits are the most kind.'

'Aww, that's — I mean, why would you have a soul pantry in the first place?'

Rodger laughed. 'But it let out a mischievous spirit. And guess who got the blame?'

He sounded like an older sibling, always complaining because they have to do everything.

'Fortunately, smart spirits know not to swap colours, since it makes it so hard for the soul guarder. So you can almost always be sure.'

'I still don't think this is a good idea,' I stammered. 'What if...'

But Rodger was already reaching for a dark grey jar. I couldn't help but notice a bold red line going across the jar. Before I knew it, he grabbed it and attempted to open the lid.

Suddenly, there was a clang as the lid flew across the room. I watched the open jar carefully and observed an airy mist float out. It was only visible because of the colouring of the mist. It was a dark grey, just like it was said to be.

'Wait for it...' Rodger murmured.

Next, the strangest thing happened. The mist started taking shape — first, smart Dr Martens boots took form, then, legs suddenly sprouted out of the holes where you insert your feet. Then, the legs grew to waist level, and so on.

It had only been a few seconds before a fully-grown woman had appeared. I couldn't tell what colour skin she had, or hair colour, eye colour or anything else.

'Ooh aye, two for the price of one!' The lady looked around forty-five years old with deep cheekbones, a pair of glasses and her hair laid back in a ponytail. She was wearing a baggy T-shirt and mom jeans, making her look casual.

'Oh, Ms Pinnacle!' Rodger stretched out his hand for the lady to shake.

The so-called Ms Pinnacle ignored Rodger's outstretched hand and looked at me. 'Let's greet the newcomer first! I don't even know his name! Oh, wait. It's Hayden, isn't it?'

I stared at her. 'How did you...'

Ms Pinnacle put a finger to her lips. 'I have my ways. Besides, I never reveal my secrets. We'd have a world of Einsteins if I did.'

Very modest. If I shared my secrets, we'd have a world of Scooby-Doos.

'Look, what did you want me for? Let's get it over with before I fade,' Ms Pinnacle urged.

I stared at her. 'Fade?'

Ms Pinnacle sighed. 'You must've learnt about this at school. If evaporation is kept in an enclosed room for a while, it will become condensation, the stuff you get on windows. You know, the thing little kids write on and kiss on.

'If condensation hits something cold, it will become water, as condensation is really evaporation which really is water. In my case, the floor. It isn't the warmest thing in the world. Once the condensation is cooled, it becomes the form it started with originally. I'm like that, only if you take out the bit where the condensation was originally water.'

'I do not understand any of that — apart from the bit where you said about drawing with the steamy stuff on windows — that was practically a hobby when I was, like, four.'

Rodger sighed. 'Uh-huh.' He turned to look at the lady. 'As for you, the floor isn't cold and you

250

have plenty of time to talk. Speaking about talking, you've done enough of off-topic blabbering. We need to ask you about the "Thing." You know?'

'Oh, Der...' Ms Pinnacle basically shouted.

Rodger hushed her and muttered, 'If Master Sosiri finds out I let you out...' He imitated a slicing head off action, and Ms Pinnacle gulped.

'You mean Dero...'

Rodger hushed her again.

'Oh, c'mon!' Ms Pinnacle whined.

'I thought you were the smartest soul!' Rodger huffed.

Ms Pinnacle probably turned red with anger. She could've turned green for all I know. 'I am the smartest soul!'

You know when you have to keep quiet and someone is fuming, and they let out that sharp whisper? That's what Ms Pinnacle did. She sounded like a librarian chewing on a wasp.

'Then how come you don't understand me? When I say the "Thing," do you not realise I don't want to say its proper name?'

Ms Pinnacle groaned and raised her voice a little bit. 'How was I supposed to know what you meant by the "Thing?" There are approximately 231.36792 padzillion, mactillion, gadzillion, fazillion, quintrillion, quadrillion, trillion and 45.719843824 billion "things" on Earth.'

I was dazed. Fun fact, kids. 'Well, that was a mouthful.'

Rodger paced around the room like a caged tiger or a detective. Then, he stopped again in front of Ms Pinnacle, who was innocently looking at her nails. 'Aargh! There's no point arguing with someone who is barely here, but I'm determined to get the last word. If you didn't know what I was going to say, how did you start saying it in the first place?'

'Because...' Ms Pinnacle started.

'Both of you, shush!' I shout-whispered. 'You look about forty (no offence) and I know for a fact Rodger is fourteen, so why in the world are you two arguing with each other? That could make headlines: "A forty and fourteen-year-old caught bickering over 'things.'" Sounds nice, doesn't it?'

Ms Pinnacle pulled her mouth to the side of her face. 'He's right. There's no point. We could've used this precious time asking and answering questions, but Rodger and I decided to use it badly.'

Rodger scoffed. 'Whatever.' He turned to me. 'Hayden has plenty of questions, don't you?'

'Erm...' I hesitated. Rodger glared at me, and I knew I had no choice. 'Yes, I do. First off, what relationship does Deronca have with Nurogonia?'

A grin spread across Ms Pinnacle's face. 'I thought you'd never ask. Sit down, it's gonna be a long one.'

Rodger frowned and sat on the floor and I did the same. Ms Pinnacle closed her eyes for a few seconds, and before I knew it, her feet had been chopped off. She literally didn't have anything from her knees down.

'Huh?' I thickly blurted.

'Meh, it's normal,' Rodger replied as if he saw people losing their legs every day. He probably did.

Ms Pinnacle chuckled to herself. 'It's only because I'll turn to water if I do touch the floor.'

It wasn't cold, but I guess I sort of understood. At least you couldn't see bones dripping with blood sticking out of her knees.

'So, if there are any other questions that might be relevant to what my answers might be, ask them now,' Ms Pinnacle instructed.

'Where are Mae and Canada?' I blurted out. 'Not that you'll know them, anyway.'

'Aah.' A smile spread across Ms Pinnacle's grey face. 'I know them. The older girl with blonde hair? Yes, Canada. And the younger one with the frizzy ginger hair who likes unicorns and pink? It could only be Mae.'

I gulped down all my emotions — fear, hope, shock, hunger. 'Uh, yeah...' Purely to make sure she had the correct people, I asked more specific questions.

'What hairstyle do they have in now?' I queried.

She tapped her head in thought. 'Um...'

Got 'em, I thought.

'Mae's got hers in a plait, Canada's in a ponytail?'

'S — sure...' I stuttered in utter confusion.

'If I'm right — which always occurs, Rodger can tell you — they should be in the dining hall getting served by the soul waiters and waitresses. Mae changed her hairstyle so it didn't get covered in the chocolate from the chocolate fountain.'

I was pretty sure my ears were screwed on back to front. 'What do you mean "chocolate fountain?" '

Ms Pinnacle gulped. 'I'm sorry to say, Hayden, but they're having the feast of their lives. They were apprehensive at first but I think hunger got the better of them. It's the long trip I suppose. Puts people on the ravenous side. There's this huge medieval dining hall with a twelve-seater table and wooden chairs cushioned with the softest of pillows. They've already had starters and mains. For starters, they had this lovely crispy chicken Caesar salad, for mains, they had a sizzling steak with shallot marinade and for dessert, they're having squishy marshmallows dipped in oozing chocolate as well as brownie sundaes with sprinkles, sauce and a cherry on top.'

I frowned. 'Way to make one happy, eh?'

Ms Pinnacle threw her head back in laughter. 'Sorry, boys. Well, let me answer your original question. Switch your brains into story mode.'

Rodger started getting excited just as he did when we watched a movie together. 'Is there any sweet and salted popcorn?'

Ms Pinnacle glared and replied sarcastically, 'I think I have slate flavour back in my storage compartment behind my jar…'

'Uh — not to be rude, but no thanks.'

Ms Pinnacle ignored Rodger's stupidity and started telling the story.

'There once was a place called Haevan…' she started. 'It was a large, peaceful land where they believed all was one. Legend says "Haevan" originated from the word Heaven. Personally, I think vice versa, but it's not for me to judge. There were no kings, no lords — everyone was equal. The Haevanians, the beings living there, either considered themselves equal, if one was king or queen, they were all kings and queens. Similarly, if one was a commoner, they were all commoners. Until one day… you can imagine how this is going, am I right?'

'Yep,' I sighed.

'Well, one day, a man called Sosiri came, stomping on all of the freshly grown grass, scaring all of the Haevanians and knocking down statues in shrines to the deities they worshipped. He claimed he had ruled Haevan and was back to claim his rights. The Haevanians didn't believe him, so they started a great riot, but little did they know Sosiri had come prepared. He released a whole army but ordered them not to attack. "Show me your oldest and wisest one!" he yelled.

'Many Haevanians were pushing to the front. You would've thought they would be completely terrified of Sosiri, but the deities had apparently taught them to repeat a prayer in their minds when in a bad situation. Seemingly, the prayer was supposed to empower and protect them from anything.

'After much pushing and arguing, a man named Portio stepped to the front. Sosiri examined him and finally made up his mind. Pointing his crooked, dirty finger at Portio, he hollered, "You! Show me your temple and let me rule the land!" Portio, the poor guy, was terrified. He stood there, shivering. Eventually, he gathered the courage to answer. "We — we believe in equality and — and say there is no one higher than us than the deities."

'Sosiri was furious. He raged and yelled at the top of his voice, "I will tear this place down to shreds if I do not get what I demand. You will all become my slaves and will bow and pray to me for an hour every day! You will give me two of your three meals! Now show me where that temple is!"

'Portio looked close to fainting. "B — but sir," he stuttered, "Because we believe in equality, there is no temple or castle. We only have shrines for the deities!" Sosiri wanted to know what deities exactly, and Portio named all three: Corptu, Viabe and Nurogi.'

I gasped. 'Hold on a second. Nurogi? He was alive then?'

'Not the Nurogi you're thinking of. And besides, this was thousands and thousands of years ago. Nurogi III was only born... five hundred years ago? Maybe six hundred.'

And yet the Nurogi I've seen looked around seventy.

'Anyway, that doesn't matter for now. Corptu was the deity of buildings, Viabe was the deity of peace, and Nurogi was the deity of security. By that, I mean watching over Haevan. He was like Zeus in Greek mythology. Most mythological stuff, whether its gods or deities, are very similar. But don't think you're recreating a Roman or Greek quest, because Nurogonia is something totally different.'

'You're getting a bit off track, Ms Pinnacle,' Rodger prompted. 'Knowing you, you'll soon be telling us some story about how Zeus got his lightning bolt or whatever.'

'Oh, sorry.' Ms Pinnacle shook herself silly and got back into the story. 'Superior Greek mythology, though. Back to the story — where was I? Oh yes, Nurogi was like Zeus...'

'And you're back to the start,' I murmured.

Ms Pinnacle nervously chuckled. 'Oh, pardon me. Sosiri demanded all the Haevanians to destroy all the shrines to the three deities. Up above, the deities were watching...'

'With popcorn?' Rodger chipped in, hopefully.

'No, not with popcorn,' Ms Pinnacle replied as if Rodger was a toddler. 'Not with popcorn, but with gasps and gulps and godly screams. The deities conferred amongst themselves on what to do about Sosiri. Nothing went on in Haevan that they didn't know about. From the other side of Haevan, they observed Sosiri's interactions with Portio. Corptu wanted to build a graphene wall around him, caging him in effectively. As we all know graphene is a super-strong building material, but Viabe said the idea was too harsh. She wanted to try to calm him down using a harp, but Nurogi also denied it.

258

In the end, they agreed to wait for some action from Sosiri before taking the next step. Nurogi said he had experienced many encounters like this, but they were purely to threaten people so someone could get their own way. He was sure Sosiri wasn't going to harm a soul.

'Little did he know he was wrong. Sosiri wreaked havoc. There was a forest nearby full of glistening cherry blossom trees and freshly cut summer grass. It was the most beautiful forest in the whole of Haevan. In the middle, there was a stone path that the younger Haevanians used to play hop-to-hop with.

'Sosiri had these horrible boots with short spikes on the bottom, so he created spiky holes wherever he walked. It ruined the whole forest. In the forest, they collected as many destructive weapons as possible from a cobblestone shed. The Haevanians were forced to use long, wooden sticks to pull the shrines off their pedestals. They were also forced to bring the shrines down until they were completely out of sight. This is when the deities reacted.

'Sosiri never left anywhere without putting up a fight. He had an army of black souls armed with shields and black armour. The Haevanians had nothing but their bare hands and feet. They'd never thought to get swords and all that whatnot

259

to approach Sosiri — they were peaceful beings. If I were them, I would have made Viabe the official leader of deities. As the Haevanians were told to be peaceful, it would only have made sense for the deity of peace to lead them... Viabe had the least amount of power of all the deities but the most will power. Sometimes, she managed to persuade the other deities not to compromise the peace of Haevan, but that would only be for a brief time before they prevailed against her with their will. She couldn't coax Nurogi this time. He shouted at the others to follow his lead, and all the deities could soar without needing wings or whatever. So, they took flight for the other side of Haevan.

'From miles away, they could already see hundreds of Haevanians separated by some invisible line. They were ant-sized, and no mortal or anyone without special abilities could see them. Nurogi had abnormally good eyesight. He could spot Sosiri when the other deities could only see a blob of dark ginger. They were confused when they saw all the moving black stuff. It flowed in the wind but stayed in the same place. "Those are souls!" Nurogi cried. His voice sounded funny because of the strong winds buffeting his mouth, which wobbled about like jelly. "Those souls belong to Sosiri, the dark lord. I think he is invading Haevan!"

'The other deities gasped in shock and instantly flew faster. When they were about twenty yards from the ground, they shouted a warrior cry and Sosiri instantly looked up and ordered his army of souls to grab as many Haevanians as possible and run. The souls were incredibly fast, so they ran over to where the Haevanians were and grabbed everyone on the front line. There was such chaos, mothers were grabbing their children and running, children were screaming, it was all chaos. The deities were too late, but they managed to take control of seventy or so souls. How did they do this? They had one of a kind swords. One swipe and the souls dissolved into thin air. Sosiri and the surviving souls fled the area by the same way they had come — a stone pathway surrounded by pine trees.

'Corptu and Viabe were going to go after them, but Nurogi held them back and said it was no use. Sosiri wouldn't be back for a while, at least. Nurogi came down to land with the others and greeted the Haevanians. They looked the same apart from the radiant glow around their bodies. In a flash, Corptu rebuilt the shrines, Viabe calmed down the Haevanians and gave them soup and fish. Nurogi, being the self-appointed leader, told everyone the plan and had a major vote.'

I'd been sitting down and listening to the whole story word for word, not letting out a beep. Until now, at least.

'Wow. That was super long — are you done yet? What was the vote, anyway?'

Ms Pinnacle sighed. 'I was getting to that bit! The vote was either to stay the way they were — in peace and equality — or to get Corptu to build Nurogi a temple and finally have an official leader. The Haevanians couldn't really say no to the idea of having Nurogi as a leader, and they did fancy the idea of having a deity as a master. So it was set. Little did they know what kind of a leader they were getting. Nurogi flipped the whole place upside down. And named the Haevanians after himself. Corptu and Viabe were sent up to the clouds whilst Nurogi ruled.'

I gasped. 'So... the Nurogi that is currently the leader of Nurogi now is the original leader? And Haevan was Nurogonia?' I had too many questions.

'One step at a time, boy,' Ms Pinnacle stated. 'The present Nurogi in Nurogonia right now is Lord Nurogi III, as I said before. Lord Nurogi I wanted to keep his name the same throughout the generations of Nurogonia's lords. So, you'll find a lot of Nurogi's if you live for a few millennia.'

'Pfft. Millennia? Like anyone's gonna live that long!' I huffed.

'Well, Hayden, dear, Mr Mocha, bless his soul, is two millennia old. He lives in the next soul storage room.'

'Oh, yes! I had his jar once. He got out, and cried — and I really mean sobbed his eyes out — because his back needed stretching s'much!'

I laughed at the thought of a guy so old he should've been called wrinkles (no harm meant, elderly).

'Well, he wasn't too good at being a ruler. Haevan would have been better off with Viabe as the main deity. And that is your quest. To find Viabe and release her spirit in Nurogonia. When you do, you will see Nurogonia form back to Haevan piece by piece. The Nurogons will become Haevanians. And all will be well. But be careful, because there is a nasty side effect that might...'

Before she could finish talking, Ms Pinnacle dissolved into a grey puddle.

Seventeen

In Pursuit of the Party Makers

'**M**s Pinnacle!' I yelled, a little too loudly. I felt around in the puddle, getting my hands wet.

'Ssh!' Rodger hushed. 'You'll alert Sosiri! Besides, you'd better get Viabe and leave. My master could've been listening all this time!'

I got rushed by that but also mourned the sight of the puddle. 'She — she was with us for ten minutes, and we already have to say goodbye!'

Rodger complained. 'Trust you to be sad and all. If there's good weather, the floor will heat up and she'll form back, no problem. I'd give you a call when she's reformed... but we're not allowed phones here, plus, you'll most likely be gone by that time.'

I leaned over, looking down at the floor and stared at my reflection in the puddle. My hair was amazing, as usual, but apart from that, I didn't look too good. I had bags under my eyes and I'd started to get stress lines on my forehead. I felt as weak and skinny as ever. My plain, blue T-shirt had gotten baggy on me and my trousers had the pockets sticking out and the zip was undone.

Yeah, all I can say is I didn't look a picture (good job my mum wasn't here to take a million of them).

'I — I have one thing to focus on, and that's getting my friend and sister. Reason A - I can't abandon them like that, and Reason B - I really wanna know if they had a chocolate fountain.'

Rodger understood and produced a circular metal key ring holding multiple dangling black keys. 'The key I use for this door is the one you can't actually feel.' Rodger swept his hands through all of the keys until he stopped at the last one. 'Try to touch it, Hayden. Go on.'

I expected to feel the hard metallic form of a normal key, but I pushed my hand through the one Rodger showed me. There was nothing odd about it, no. Think of the key to your home. It was just like that, but the one I was touching had no apparent substance to it.

'Cool!' I exclaimed. I was waiting for Rodger to unlock the door when I remembered something. Something terrible.

'Rodger,' I muttered.

He raised an eyebrow at me.

'There — there was a line in our quest prediction. It said something like "is the exile, eviction, castaway" — I think it might be...'

Just as I said this I heard a click. I watched the door swing open, creaking eerily as it did. 'Go on, this is your stop.'

I don't think he'd heard me. 'Rodger! Don't you get it? You are the exile! You are the evictee! You are the castaway! You have to come with us. It's the way of the quest. I have no idea what'll happen if you don't pay attention to what the prediction states, but I'm sure it could possibly lead to dea...'

Rodger lowered his head. I know he'd taken it all in because his shoulders were hunched and his fists were balled. 'I — I can't, Hayden. If I don't do what Sosiri says, I could get seriously hurt. I'm not gonna take such a big risk.'

I cursed under my breath. 'See, you said you could get hurt. I have a good chance of...' I didn't want to say the word. 'Let's say — of being a goner.

Would you rather suffer a bit of pain or let your best friend d — or let your best friend "you know what." 'Rodger grunted. 'You could die. See, that's the keyword here, could. I'll one-hundred-per cent get hurt. Or maimed.'

'I wouldn't go that far. But if that's what you desire, you know, for me to die, then...'

'I'm sorry, Hayden. I refuse. I'm risking my life here, don't you understand? You haven't seen the things Sosiri does to traitors. And I'm his number two, his best man. If I ditched him, this whole building would probably be up in flames as soon as he knows! I know that you are so sure about this, but I'm sorry.'

I frowned. 'I feel like you know this place inside out. I know that you know this place inside out. And you would bring so much credit to us, you're with Master Sosiri all the time, you must know everything about him. But, fine, if you want to choose a murderer over your best friend, so be it.'

'This is almost definitely our last words. I hope that you enjoy your time with Sosiri, maybe even grow to learn his ways.' I was about to shut the door, taking my time and waiting to see if he would change his mind.

'OK, OK. You're a real teaser, Hayden. Talking about all the stuff that is at the front of my mind... I hope you're right, though, that you'd most certainly tragically perish if I was not there to your aid.'

I gave him a gentle slap. 'Thanks, mate. Trust me, you'll want me alive. I doubt any of us will get a scratch when you're here. All we have to do is get Mae and Canada, search the area with them for Viabe and release her into Nurogonia! Imagine how sick that would be: seeing Nurogonia slowly transform back into Haevan...'

'It's like evaporation turning back into water!' Rodger piped in, suddenly chirpier.

'Erm, sure.'

At least we'd got him on our side, I thought. To be honest, he probably wouldn't be returning to Deronca anyways. He'll come running back home with Mae, Canada and me like a wonky toy soldier. Let's see him get hurt then.

* * *

'Just down this long hallway,' Rodger instructed, pointing with his bony finger.

I stared at the black walls and black floor and black carpet. The only light was a single (you guessed it) black chandelier in the middle of the hallway.

'You sure this leads to the dining hall?' I questioned.

Rodger gave me a look. 'I know this place inside out,' he snapped. 'I never get a turn wrong. Now come on, you dimwit! If you want to find your pals, that is.'

I breathed in and followed Rodger. He'd been with me the longest. I remember holding my Bam-Bam bear as I strode into Year 1. A few weeks later, Rodger joined. He had the same shaggy, black hair to this day, but he was much chubbier and not so bony around his face. He had the same dark brown freckles, but they had grown to be spotted all over his face from around his nose.

'You scared or something?'

I solemnly shook my head and carried on walking like the Queen's guard. Deronca wasn't my first choice for a luxury getaway. Not with forgotten souls floating about the place, no.

'Thinking about souls...' I pondered aloud, 'How is Ms Pinnacle forgotten?'

Rodger sighed dramatically. 'She was a Haevanian, Hayden. The ones that were captured were brought here and turned into souls depending on their lifestyle. Ms Pinnacle was one of them. I could tell, she tried not to admit it in her story, but she couldn't hide it. Think back to her jar, Hayden. Remember the red mark on it?'

I nodded. 'What's it for?'

Rodger sighed. 'They mark all of the rivals with red, Hayden. It's like how Hitler marked the Jews with stars. Sosiri gets especially mad when one comes out. So happens I know he's got a busy schedule today...'

'What's he up to?'

My friend hesitated. 'I — I shouldn't really be telling you. Sosiri says we can trust no one.'

'Excluding me,' I added. 'I've been your best friend for forever! Only just so happens we're both in different schools.'

'And you've got Laurence as your mate now.'

I facepalmed myself. 'It's Darren. And yes, am I not allowed to have another friend?'

Rodger looked at the floor. 'Let's find them, okay? The whole time we've been talking, we haven't moved an inch.'

I knew he was trying to change the subject. Darren was a touchy subject to Rodger. He thought he could be my only best friend. On the other hand, Darren would let me blabber on about Rodger and he wouldn't care one bit. He'd even ask me questions about him. One time, he asked if he could meet him! And here's Rodger, complaining about his existence.

I followed him down the dark corridor, and at the end, I saw grand, black double doors. They had small slits with glass at the top, but it was all blurry and I had no idea what was going on in there.

'You sure this is the right way?' I asked again, turning to face Rodger. But he had already chosen one of the many keys he had in his pocket.

'Dining Hall, Rodger Calendor,' he shouted.

A keyhole appeared on the right side of the door. I was pretty sure it wasn't there before, but I had seen some pretty bizarre things in the last few weeks, so I wasn't too taken aback.

Rodger slid they key into the hole, and a robot voice spoke, "Opening Dining Hall doors."

The doors swung open. Luckily, I was nowhere near. Unluckily, what I saw in the dining hall wasn't the best sight.

Canada and Mae were sitting on elegant stools with velvet cushioning, munching their way through marshmallows. Between them was a metre-tall chocolate fountain. From the very top, it was oozing out milk chocolate like thick water. There was a stack of empty plates at the other end of the table.

'A meal fit for a king,' Rodger grunted.

Mae looked at Rodger. 'Queen, mind you. Aren't you the vermin that works for Sosiri?'

Rodger stepped forward in defence, but I held him back.

271

'Sorry, Rodger. Mae's the — what should I say? — confident one of the team. She hasn't met you, yet she's calling you a pest!'

Mae rolled her eyes. 'Total idiots. And he is a pest. And I do know him, thank you very much. I met him when you weren't in Nurogonia, Hayden.'

I sort of felt left out. I didn't know about Canada; she was happily chomping away on a coated marshmallow.

'I wish I didn't know him. He's on the side that made Nurogonia miserable. Why would I want him here? And anyway, is he your friend? Oh, Hayden, do tell me you don't know this guy one bit.'

I shrugged. 'Rodger and I have been mates since Year 1. He's going to help us Mae, I've made sure of it.'

Mae did an over-exaggerated performance of her gagging. 'You are so revolting. Take a look at his hair! I could've sworn I saw something moving around in there. Was it head lice? Don't tell me it's nits...'

'If it were nits, I would've already given 'em to you, clod.'

'Why don't you leave each other alone?' Canada moaned, finally looking up from her food. 'Anyways, where were you all this time?'

I shook my head. 'We were doing stuff. Why were you here having the feast of your life?'

272

'When we arrived here, you were knocked out. You were escorted to wherever by a black-silhouetted ghost. On the other hand, Canada and I were taken straight here. To eat.'

What were they thinking? 'Don't you get it?'

'Nope,' Canada said, gulping down another wad of marshmallows.

'They're fattening you up! When you come to a strange place and they give you a gazillion plates of really good food, what else are they gonna do with you? You're like a fly, they let you buzz around for a second, then bam, you're gone.'

Mae shook her head firmly. 'They won't. That's only in fairy tales. Besides, we'll escape before they can get a fig out of us. I've got a rough outline of the place so far. There should be an escape route if we go thirty feet down the hallway and turn right. There was a door there, but it was all blocked up. There's absolutely no chance of us getting in. Unless someone has a key...' She glanced at Rodger. 'You have keys, don't you?'

Rodger put his hands in his pocket, then took them out again. 'Not sure.'

What Mae did next was as funny as it was shocking. She got a palm full of chocolate from the fountain and flung her hand at Rodger, flicking droplets of chocolate all over him.

He flinched, covering his face, but it was too late. Splats of chocolate dotted all around his face. For the first few seconds, he didn't mind having it on his face. Then, when he looked down to see half of his clothes covered in chocolate, he turned red.

'Mae!' he yelled, angrily stomping towards her. He stopped a metre away from her. 'I have one of these! One!' He held up a finger.

Mae backed away. 'S — sorry...'

'Well, "sorry" never helped a soul! In my case, literally! Do you know how mad Sosiri is gonna be if he finds out my black cloak has been splatted in chocolate? He won't give me a spare, and does it look like there's a washing machine here? No, there's not! I have to travel two whole miles to get to the nearest lake, and then my cloak takes five hours to dry. When Sosiri catches me without it, I get put in a spare dungeon for a few hours. He says there was no need for it to be dirty in the first place. Do you know how much effort it takes for me to simply wash a cloak? Think about others before acting up like that!'

The culprit raised her hands in a sorry. 'I know, I know, I'm guilty. I shouldn't have done that and I'm sorry, truly.'

Rodger calmed down a bit and walked back to me. I gently patted his back. 'You still coming with us?'

'As long as she stays a couple of metres out of my reach, yes.'

' "She" has a name,' Mae mumbled.

I shot her a look. 'Mae please. Let's stop this silly nonsense and get outta here.'

Canada stood up and tucked her chair in. 'Despoena is right outside the front doors.'

'That's a bit risky,' Rodger said. 'Who is Despoena anyways?'

'The Pegasus. Our ticket home,' Mae grunted. 'And that ticket could have been dropped down the drain by the looks of it.' She said looking at Rodger

'Well, no-one's reported anything else besides the arrival of you three. We have brilliant security here,' Rodger stated. 'How on earth would they have not noticed?'

I shrugged. 'Lunchbreak?'

No, probably not, I thought. If they did have lunch breaks here, they'd be ten minutes long, maximum.

Rodger was probably thinking the same thing. 'They have sandwiches in their pockets. I've seen them take them out. Instead of sitting down for lunch, they have it on the spot. I believe you got taken in by security, Hayden, and the girls were taken here by an Escorter. However — I do know a place your ride could very well be.'

'Yes?' I asked inquisitively.

'The LDs. "Large Dungeons." Anything bigger than a normal soul or human gets put there.'

Canada gasped. 'Oh, poor Dessy! We have to go right now. Rodger and Mae, be nice to each other or I'll whack you with a stick with hedgehogs on the end.'

Simultaneously, Rodger and Mae glared at each other.

'Whatcha waiting for?' Mae remarked. 'To the dungeons!'

Eighteen

The Slightly Larger-Than-Usual Dungeons

'Where did you say these dungeons were?' Canada asked, walking down the corridor.

Rodger pointed. 'You'll find some main doors; I'll unlock them for you.'

'So you do have keys,' Mae mumbled.

'Yes, I do,' Rodger replied, without looking up.

I remembered what Canada had said. I doubt she would have a stick with hedgehogs on the end, but it would be pretty cool to see. Maybe I could have it as a pet and call it Mr Spikeball or something.

Now that's cool. My hopes became more and more real. Mae and Rodger couldn't last a minute without bickering.

'I don't think it's this way,' Mae declared. 'We've been walking for five minutes and there's no possible chance of us reaching any sort of door!'

On the other hand, Rodger knew exactly where he was going. 'Who's been around this place more? Me, or you?'

'Stop it!' Canada cut in. 'Can you last another thirty seconds, please? I see the doors up ahead.'

Mae pulled a face. 'You see — well, I can't really explain it but — uh.'

'But what?' I asked.

'We really have no choice but to utterly despise each other. We're on completely different sides. It's like Adolf Hitler and Winston Churchill. They wouldn't necessarily skip around arm-in-arm doing the jitterbug, would they?'

I sighed. 'Just get along for a few days, is that too much to ask?'

'Considering we can't for half a minute, yes,' Rodger grumbled.

Canada and I shared a look. I think we both thought they weren't acting their age and needed ignoring for a little bit. We could leave them bickering for a gazillion years, they'd still be in the same place. But I'd rather them arguing with each other than have one of them missing.

I know, I know, I sound a bit like a teacher on a field trip: "You have to stay with the teachers because we have to look out for you more, as you don't belong to us," they'd say in their sappy voices.

Anyway, Canada was right. Ahead were double doors twice the size of the dining hall doors. They were covered from top to bottom in chains and looked incredibly hard to get through.

We arrived at the door and Rodger pulled out a key.

'I call this one the Chain-Maker,' he smirked, picking a key. He chose a black one exactly like the others and brushed it against a chain. 'Rodger.'

The chains (which had been tightly secured over the door) snapped in two and the door opened all on its own.

'Can I take the lead?' Rodger asked.

I looked outside at the dark, misty sky. 'Be my guest.'

* * *

The large dungeons were so huge they had a separate building for it. It was made of stone and looked a bit like the car park you see in towns. The LD looked around three storeys high and could easily fit a thousand people on one floor. There were no windows or anything else around it.

The sky was a dark grey and the clouds looked like they were filled with thunder, ready to shower us with rain at any moment. There was nothing special about Feldo Forgutt, it wasn't like Nurogonia where you had to access a portal to get there. As far as I could recall, we flew in.

I looked back at the Deronca. There was something odd about it — well, there was always something odd about it. Call me crazy, but the "temsle" looked as if it were moving. I looked at it once, then again; it seemed to be shifting each time by a metre or two.

'What's going on with this place?' I questioned.

Rodger shrugged. 'It's always been weird, I guess. Let's keep going, the dungeons are only a few hundred yards away from here.'

'Actually, look at it. It's moving.'

He looked back at the place and made a "meh" sound. 'It's like the souls: they're waving about like that as well. You might not have noticed, but Ms Pinnacle was still stirring the tiniest bit.'

I did sense something unusual about Ms Pinnacle, but I was so intrigued by her story I wasn't bothered about her appearance.

'I'm so sorry for all the questions,' I continued, 'but...'

'But...?'

'Is Deronca the town or the name of this building?'

My friend facepalmed himself and exhaled heavily. 'Deronca is the name of that building and the 25,000 square feet of it. Feldo Forgutt is the name of the town we are in. Have you heard of Wakanda, the magical place in the movie Black Panther? Feldo Forgutt's like that — it has a protective forcefield around the perimeter. If you are outside the forcefield, you will see nothing but fields of summer grass. If you're within the forcefield, you will see all of its content. Deronca's a very secretive place, and to make it harder to access, it doesn't allow any normal person or Nurogon.

'It's either someone who is assigned a quest that specifically includes Deronca, or someone who works here. We'd have too many unwanted visitors. Farmers have tried to walk through to get to some of the crops planted on the fields of grass, but they just get pushed back as if there's heavy wind. They always think: "It's really windy today...

281

Never mind, I'll have to get that wheat another time!" It drives me batty.'

'You could've just said Deronca is the building with the magical forcefield and Feldo Forgutt is the place it's in, you know. You don't have to go into all this special detail nobody needs to hear,' I informed him.

'Good to know,' Rodger mumbled.

It wasn't three minutes before we reached the dungeons. There was a grey metal door two metres high, and through the glass slits, I could already see ugly walls, floors and a receptionist's desk in a small corner. These dungeons made a prison cell look welcoming, and I'd only seen a snippet of the building so far.

'One question,' Canada said, as we examined the structure. 'Why on earth would they put an animal in a dungeon?'

Mae looked heartbroken. 'I thought the same! Just imagine her... the poor thing! I can picture her neighing in anger as she's trying to headbutt the bars. It's so sad how people are so cruel in life.'

'Wooooah, that's so not hypocritical at all!' Rodger sarcastically grunted. 'Look, the plan is, I use the key card I have somewhere in my pocket and we bust whatever it is out.'

'Whatever she is, you mean!' Mae retorted.

Rodger rolled his eyes. 'Yeah, sure. Since I'm really well known around Deronca, I can simply ask the receptionists to free Despoena and explain the incident.'

I frowned. 'So you lied about busting her out?'

My sister nudged me. 'Grow up Hayden.'

I stared at her piercing ice-blue eyes. Boy, they were scary. She could drive off a lion with those. Her tatty hair was tied up in a deformed ponytail. I was surprised she hadn't demanded a hairbrush. She didn't seem to notice very much. Nor the fact her grey NASA T-shirt was fading tremendously. Lucky for her, though, she had purposely worn oversized ripped jeans for the journey. I could've sworn there were fewer rips before...

'Once we've got Despoena, can we change?' Mae questioned. 'I've got this really babyish kitten top underneath this hoodie, so there's no way I'm taking it off, but it's boiling! And I'd rather boil than die of embarrassment.'

The thought of Mae wearing a pink kitten top made my brain throw up. It was probably the same with Rodger.

'There's bound to be a toilet somewhere in the dungeons. Where did you put your backpack? Doesn't it have all your supplies in there?'

Canada turned around to reveal the black rucksack that had been on her back the whole time. I hadn't really noticed it, but it was a good job we hadn't left it anywhere.

Mae sighed with relief, simultaneously pulling her hoodie in and out to blow air towards her as proof she'd be barbecued if she didn't get the hoodie off soon. I'd never seen her without that lime green hoodie. It made the statement: I AM MAE! And she took awesome care of it as well. Not once had I seen a splash of mud or a juice stain on it. It had two small white strings coming out of two holes at the top. Sometimes, I'd see her pull them and nearly get strangled, as they tighten the hood.

'Follow me,' Rodger eventually ordered. We accepted his command and stopped with him at a numeric keypad with a slot in it.

'It needs a password, Rodger. You can't use a key card,' Canada pointed out.

Despite the protest, Rodger pulled out a key card from a pocket in his black cloak.

'That's what they want you to think...' He placed it against the numbers and the metal door slid open.

'Umm...' I mumbled. 'Okaaaay?'

He chuckled to himself. 'If you press a button a siren goes off and this really annoying voice booms "INTRUDER, INTRUDER." They catch you before you can escape.'

I gulped, happy I hadn't attempted to open the door. 'What happens to you then?'

My friend shook his head sadly. 'You wouldn't want to know.'

I did want to know. Why would I ask in the first place if I didn't want to know?

Once again, we followed Rodger. This time, we went forward a few metres before turning right. Black desks were positioned in the corners of a reception area. Dark purple souls were sitting on the office chair next to them, punching away on their computers. They had thick-rimmed, round glasses, smart shirts, trousers and stripy ties. They looked more like office workers than dungeon clerks.

They were too busy typing away on their computers to notice us patiently waiting in front of them.

'Uh-huh,' Rodger coughed.

The man we were in front of looked up. 'Oh, hello, Rodger!' He had a jolly American accent and sounded like a cartoon. 'I'm Mr McChear for all of you who don't know. Whatcha doing here?'

'There's been a mistake,' Rodger started. 'I think...'

'We think you've mistakenly locked up a Pegasus in one of your cells that happens to belong to us,' Mae interrupted. 'By the way, it looks quite

285

modern in here. Aren't dungeons supposed to be old-timey and what not?'

Mr McChear chuckled. 'We call it that to scare people...' He made a supposedly creepy face and Mae glanced at the door.

We all laughed at her, and she went pink.

'I'm just joking with ya, lovey,' the receptionist beamed. 'What really happened is this place used to be a dungeon, but since things come and go, we had it renovated a bit to suit this generation. But Sosiri wants us to call it a dungeon, the poor man.'

'The poor man?' I shrieked. 'He took many lives and stored them in jars! How can he be a poor man?'

The man behind the desk tutted. 'He doesn't know what to do with himself anymore. He's given up. So when someone like you comes in, he has to make the most of visitors. And I think we all have entirely different definitions when we say "make the most." '

He sounded like the old chap you had living next door. Not once had he frowned or kept a straight face. Even when he was typing on his computer and didn't see us, he was grinning wider than the Cheshire cat in Alice's Adventures in Wonderland. It was sort of creepy.

'So, what's the issue? Got someone in the cells you want to visit? I'll book you in now! The times are half four, quarter past...'

'No, no. We're not visiting, are we? I'm pretty sure our friend Mae here said we think you've accidentally locked up a Pegasus of ours,' Canada explained.

Mr McChear spent a while clicking the keys on his computer and every so often moving his mouse around. Eventually, he made social contact by turning his computer screen to face us and pointing at a load of squares.

'From my research, your Pegasus should be in one of these cells,' he said, pointing at three squares on the screen.

Canada shrugged. 'That was easy! We just ask for her and leave! Simple math.'

Mr McChear chuckled. 'Nuh-uh-uh!' He waggled his airy finger from side to side. 'It's not that easy, m'dear. If we let a prisoner out every time someone asked us to, we'd be empty! The thousands of requests we get asked every week: "Get my wife outta here!" or "Can I have me son?" Yeah, there's loads. But what I can do is ask the Cell Breakers why they locked the Pegasus up in the first place. If they don't have a suitable reason, we will free the prisoner.' He rubbed his hands together.

'Simple with an e! Let me get someone to escort you to the Cell Breaker Department!'

He reached for something next to his computer.

'Hallo? Can I have someone to escort guests to the Cell Breaker Department, please? We're on the first floor, desk B2,' he inquired into a walkie-talkie. It was a few seconds of nodding and an 'OK' or two before he finished off with 'Ta!'

Ten minutes later, a brown soul came from around a curtain. She looked like one of those shy high school nerds who wander around clutching their books to their chests.

Her shoulder-length hair was secured by a hair grip at the front. She had rectangular glasses with a tiny butterfly in the left corner, and a short-sleeved shirt tucked into a tight skirt, finished off with tights and stubby high-heels.

'H — hello,' she mumbled. 'Wh — what can I help you with?'

Mr McChear sighed. 'Oh, dearie me! Could they not get professional staff, eh?'

The lady looked highly embarrassed. 'Uh, um, sorry sir. Most of them are booking visiting times for other days. Is — is there a problem with me being here? I could leave if...'

'No, no,' Mr McChear exhaled. 'Since you're here now, we might as well. All they need is to be led to a Cell Breaker cell. Shouldn't be too much to ask for. Also, could I have a chat with you afterwards, lovey?'

The lady slowly nodded. 'Affirmative sir. And yes, I would l — love a chat!'

She was obviously new to the job and didn't want to get into any sort of trouble, but she was also looked innocent but terrible at her job.

'This way, guys,' she sighed, walking towards a large lift.

We did as we were told and followed her until we reached the lift. Just as Rodger had done, she swiped a key card against the buttons that summoned the lift. It did just that, but with a totally different control system. It was as if everything had been wired to something else.

'Come on in, guys,' she ordered bashfully.

There was nothing odd about the inside of the lift. Well, until the lady slid her key card down over a built-in red button.

'Hold on, folks. Grab onto the...'

Before she could finish speaking, we were whooshed straight downwards. Everyone was screaming and rushing to grab hold of the rails in the lift. Unfortunately, everything was such a blur, not one of us managed to calm down.

All of this ended as quickly as it had started.

Everyone in the lift — apart from the nerdy soul — was clutching their chest and trying to establish what had just happened.

'You creep!' Mae yelled, moving as far away from the lady as possible. 'You did that on purpose, didn't you?' She turned to Canada and me, as we were standing casually next to her. Mae's face looked shocked as well as angry. 'Why are you not running? You should be trying to get as far away as you can from her, not still be standing next to her!'

'My name is Rachael, dear.'

'Don't give me "dear!" ' Mae shrieked. 'You look flamin' sixteen!'

Rachael turned bright pink, but pushed out a muffled, 'Nineteen and counting.'

Mae let out a sharp sigh. 'Ugh! Do you not understand? My heart was about to burst! Do you want me to have a heart attack?'

Rachael shook her head.

'Do you want me to whack you round the head?' Mae said to Canada and me.

We both shook our heads.

Mae took a deep breath. 'I suggest we get moving, then,' she said. She was somewhat near calmer now, and Rachael looked so relieved — she probably didn't want to get into any sort of trouble with her job.

I was just as relieved as she was, being only seconds away from getting walloped. It was a bit of a random thing to say, that was. But if I'm conscious and breathing, the world won't end.

Once again, a button was pressed, but this time, it was yellow and made the doors open. Rachael stood aside for us to exit the lift, but instead of saying thank you, Mae gave Rachael a dirty look.

'So,' Rachael started. 'My name's Rachael, as I told you, and I'm your Escorter for the day!' She sounded one hundred times happier than she probably was; as people say, what you see on the outside doesn't always reflect what's on the inside. 'I know, I know, you might think I'm stupid, but yes, Escorter is a word around here. But please, don't go back to school and ask if you could be an Escorter, it won't go down well.'

Mae huffed. 'Like I'd do that anyway.'

You could tell she was hurt. But being a staff member, she tried not to show it; she ignored Mae's comment and carried on doing her job. 'If I take you down this corridor, we'll turn right to the biggest Cell Breaker Department in this building. It's so big we have to go underground to get there, hence the awful lift trip. You would've thought this place was big enough, eh?'

'You're kidding me,' Canada said. 'I mean — that's a bit selfish, claiming all of this land to yourself. There could be diamonds below us, and you'd be doing your job, totally oblivious you have a fortune beneath your feet.'

Rachael let out a soft chuckle. 'Well, you never know! But as you can't dig to the Earth's core, there will always be the possibility there's a diamond or two under your feet.'

Canada shrugged. 'True, but you could go that extra mile and find what you're looking for. You could build this whole building out of diamonds!'

I rolled my eyes. 'Let's take her to the clinic, shall we? I think she's got some serious problem.'

'I'm sorry, but you'll have to take the lift for that,' Rachael stated.

Rodger tutted. 'He was joking. Whatever — tell us where you've come from.'

'Well... it's a long story. Do you really wanna hear it?'

We all agreed, and I hoped it wasn't as long as Ms Pinnacle's story. That was more yarn than a story.

'Okay, here goes! I'll try to be quick — it's a three to five-minute walk to get to where we're going. Anyway, enough rambling. It all started off in a cosy little meadow house. I lived in a farmhouse with my mother, but it was the best little place you could ever imagine. It had little brown Tudor designs on exterior walls, and my mother had planted daisies and buttercups and cornflowers in a neat row outside.

'We also had pens upon pens of cows and sheep and pigs and these cute, fluffy rabbits that we used to breed in the springtime. Oh, and you won't believe the beautiful white stallion in our fenced-off field. Her name was Uggy, and don't tell any of the other horses, but she was my favourite. I fed her extra carrots and rode her more than the others. I constructed little wooden boards for her to jump over! And I was so proud I'd learned to ride a horse all by myself. Until the day. I was riding Uggy so much that one day she tripped and landed on her leg. It was so sore for days, she wouldn't stand up! So we fetched a vet, and they took her away. And — sorry, it's hard to say this. Sadly, she got put down.'

Mae gasped, and without thinking, gave Rachael a tight squeeze and repeatedly said, 'Oh, I'm so sorry to hear!'

Then she realised what she was doing and stepped away from her in disgust. 'I mean, if the horse is yours, you don't deserve to have it. Don't act all sappy on us when it was your fault it got put down in the first place.'

Rachael lowered her head. 'I know, and I'm terribly sorry.'

The remaining three of us glared at Mae.

'Shut up!' Rodger mouthed.

'You moron!' I whispered.

'Who do you think you are?' Canada yelled. She gave Rachael a look of apology. 'She's a right idiot, Mae is. Carry on, your story was lovely! You were getting to the good bit as well. Well, since we stopped arguing, we need to get moving. I believe we're nearly there. C'mon, let's get back to the story please! You're the best employee in this place!'

I could tell Canada was trying to get Rachael to cheer up.

It worked.

She told us she had another handsome, brown stallion with a white stripe down his nose whose name was Sebstan. He was apparently ever so kind and would know when Rachael wanted to ride him because he'd lower down a bit for her to mount him, as he was so tall. But it turned out Rachael had dropped out of secondary school and spent all of her time on the farm since that's what she wanted to do.

Her mother had promised her she'd be home-schooled, but it looked like that wasn't going to happen. So when she needed to go to college, her mother had to send her hundreds of miles away from her home to a college for not-so-intelligent people. In university, it was far worse since she was so shy, so she had to study and have a part-time job that helped her to interact with people. That's when she went to work at the "dungeons."

At the time, everyone and everything about the dungeons was humane and normal. Then her mother died and she instantly got forgotten. There wasn't anyone else around to remember her or think about her since she was so introverted, and she got instantly teleported to Deronca.

'Unusually,' she finished off, 'I was so good at this job when I was studying. Must have been why they took me away early. A bit too early, don't you think?'

Rodger nodded. 'Shouldn't you go back to Soul School and train or something?'

Rachael sighed. 'Yes, I should really. That would allow people to call me Miss Sebstan, not just silly old Rachael. And yes, my horse was named after me.'

'Is that true, Miss Sebstan?' I rather kindly replied.

Rachael went pink in the face. 'Actually, don't. I was just joking about the Miss Sebstan thing and whatnot. I'm only a bit older than you and still have my braces in, so I'll stick with Rachael.'

'No, no, I insist. You're five years older than me and deserve to be called a la-di-da name.'

'La-di-da? Oh, don't think I'm haughty or anything. Rachael will do me just fine.'

Rodger nudged me. 'Oh, well done, then!' He quietly and sarcastically gave me a clap, and I pushed his hands away.

Rachael turned to face Rodger for a second. 'Hey... have I seen you before?'

Rodger gulped. 'Erm... yeah, you've been leading us to the department all this time!' He added a nervous laugh.

'No, you're — you're that kid! The Soul Keeper, right? I've got to ring the intruder alarm; you're not supposed to be here! Intruder! Intru...'

'Oh, Miss Sebstan, you're got yourself all muddled up!' I reassured. 'Look, the cloak he's wearing is his, you know.' I whispered this bit — 'He's one of those teens who enjoy rock music and the colour black and skulls.'

'Ah, I'm sorry,' Rachael whispered. 'Of course. I thought for a second...'

'You thought wrong,' I beamed, glad she'd fallen for it.

It wasn't thirty seconds before we reached huge blacked-out double doors with a long, horizontal sign above it reading,

CELL BREAKER DEPARTMENT

DO NOT ENTER WITHOUT AUTHORISED ASSISTANCE

'I'm your assistance,' Miss Sebstan said triumphantly. She repeated it slowly and unsurely. 'I'm... your assistance? I'm your assistance! I am! Your,' she pointed at us, 'assistance! Would you believe that! I've come so far, haven't I?'

'From sorting out horse muck, yes,' Mae mumbled.

Miss Sebstan grabbed Canada's shoulders and looked into her eyes.

'Thank you, thank you, thank you! Oh, you guys are the best practice customers ever — oops.'

Mae's eyes grew open. 'Practice customers?' She stepped closer to Miss Sebstan. 'Does this mean we're not gonna get served? You better sort this out and get us home, lady!'

Miss Sebstan backed away. 'I — I didn't mean it that way. You will get served, you're just one of my first practice customers in this job!'

Canada looked grumpy. 'Admit it. You only got us into this to advance in your job, didn't you? I can't believe I actually encouraged you to do your job. If you are gonna use your customers to convince the managers of this place you're some super-star employee, I'd leave. Maybe — maybe — go back to cleaning up the horse poop.'

Rachael looked angry more than embarrassed.

'Could we please get a different Escorter?' Rodger moaned clearly and louder than usual. 'I don't care if we're five steps away from the place we're supposed to be, I'd rather someone different. Someone who's actually done this before.'

I tutted and shook my head at her.

'Argh!' she abruptly yelled.

We all stopped and turned to her.

'I take it back! You aren't the best practice customers, and I don't want to be your assistance! You, Canada, you really made me think I was good at this job, but now I should go back to cleaning up mucky horse poo? And for you, Mae.'

She made an obviously frustrated noise that sounded like a trumpeting elephant mixed with a croaking, dying frog.

'You are the worst! Can't you have a bit of belief in me for once? We've only known each other for less than ten minutes, and I don't have these arguments with friends I've known for years! It was all your fault! You know what? You can go into that place all by yourself! You don't need assistance, because your too good for it, aren't you?'

Tears were streaming down her cheeks and her glasses had gone steamy. Rachael's cheeks looked like they were burning, and strands of her hair had fallen out. She looked more like the victim of abuse than a simple worker.

'What have we done?' I moaned.

Meanwhile, Mae had stormed into the Cell Breaker Department and we were forced to follow her.

In an enormous room, there were dozens and dozens of desks lined up behind each other. They weren't cluttered or junk-food filled; there was a simple work laptop, papers, pen pots and books. Most seats were empty, but on the odd few seats were sat unsatisfied-looking souls. I could see why they wouldn't be so cheery, they're forgotten souls after all, but at least Rachael had managed to carry a smile. It was heartbreaking knowing everyone here had once been alive in some living form or another.

'We've got an important task,' Mae firmly declared.

Everyone at the desks looked up at her.

One shouted, 'Come to me!'

The other stated, 'I give the best service!'

And a third, fourth, fifth, until every worker was bickering to help us out.

'I did ask first,' a soul pointed out, nodding at the others. 'Come over here, you lot.'

Everyone else moaned and went back to their computers.

We inched closer and closer until we were standing at the desk.

Once again, it was a young lady, but there was something extremely odd. I could see her in full colour. She had light blonde hair tied up in a small ponytail, a navy cardigan with a white shirt underneath and a black pair of trousers. She didn't look any older than Canada.

'Wait, what?' I asked. 'But how...'

'How what?' she asked, flashing us her shiny, white teeth.

I breathed in and out and pinched myself hard, just to make sure I wasn't some sort of nutcase who saw everything in reverse.

Good. I wasn't.

'Why can't I see a plain colour throughout? Aren't you supposed to be one colour?'

Everyone else agreed with me.

The girl looked down at herself and pulled a face. 'Wait, what — oh, I know! I'm only seventeen years, two weeks, four days, four minutes and thirty-seven seconds old. Thirty-eight now. Thirty-nine... you get the memo. You get a full colour when you're eighteen years old upwards. That's why so many people stay up on their eighteenth birthday here. I think I'll be pink, because I'm extremely enthusiastic, chatty and bubbly, am I right?'

I slowly nodded. 'And why were you guys so eager to assist us? Don't we need authorised assistance?'

'Yes, you do,' the girl said slowly, realising what was going on. 'But we haven't had a visitor in days! Anyway, for the time being, my name's Khloe Hillman, how may I help?'

Mae hesitated. 'Well... a friend of ours has accidentally been locked up in a dungeon... we think.'

Khloe gasped. 'Oh, my word! We'd better sort it out right away! Male or female?'

'Female,' I replied.

'Age?'

Mae looked at me for help.

'Well, the thing is... by judgement, ten years old?' I gulped worriedly.

Khloe was punching this all down on her computer keyboard. 'Micro-sized, extra extra small, extra small, small, average, a bit above average, a bit smaller than big, big, bigger than big, extra big, extra extra big or humongous?'

'Extra big,' Canada chimed in.

'Describe this person.'

'Smooth fur, dark grey fur, light-yellow mane, four legs, black hooves,' Mae stated.

Khloe was typing like mad. At last, she looked up from her computer. 'Is it this young fella?'

We all huddled up to examine the picture.

'Yes!' Everyone but Rodger cheered.

Phew! We were one step closer to finishing this quest.

'Of course,' Khloe tutted. 'They almost always take animals in like this. You know what, I'll grab her from the cell, let me just locate it now.' She started humming a little tune as we waited to free our winged companion. 'Doo-doo-doo,' she sang. 'Oh! Cell 246. This should be an easy one to locate. Let me find the key in the drawers, chaps!'

She strolled along to a door at the side of the room. I hadn't noticed it before, but when she pushed it open, I could see lots of cupboards with lots of drawers. She left the door wide ajar, so I could see her tracing her finger along each drawer, trying to find something.

At last, she stopped at a drawer and pulled something out from it.

She came strolling back with a key dangling from her fingers.

'This is like the magic wand,' she chimed. 'But first, is there a reason as to why you'd like to release your friend? It said the reason she was locked in was N/A — not available. That's what usually happens when they lock someone up for a reason that cannot be shared with mere forgotten souls or for no reason whatsoever.'

When we all looked blankly back at her, she chuckled.

'Oh, you kids are so clueless, you don't even know!'

Mae nodded awkwardly. 'Yes, that's what we think anyways! She's a Pegasus, what could she do wrong? I bet she was just having a nibble on the grass.'

Khloe shook her head. 'Well, well, what can I say? Since I'm nice, I'll set her free for you. It's not like she'll... it's a she, right?'

'Yep,' Rodger sighed.

'... It's not like she'll get a criminal record or anything like that. Because it'll be quicker, I'll go and get her. Be back in a jiffy!'

She excitedly ran through the back door and it swung shut after her.

'We're dead,' Rodger griped.

I was confused. 'How?'

'We were supposed to release Viabe into Nurogonia to make it peaceful again! She's locked up in a jar somewhere, but it will take hours and hours to find her. Even if we could, I am not risking going back there to certain death if Sosiri returns and finds I have defected. We might as well take our chances, go home and accept our fate.'

He had a point. It didn't bear thinking how little progress we would have made without Rodger giving us access to the rest of Deronca, Feldo Forgutt and the dungeons. It had already taken us ages just to get back our ticket home, so how were we supposed to finish the whole quest when we had left Deronca so far behind, the place where Viabe could possibly be?

Nineteen

Just Our Luck

Khloe came back through the door she had gone through a few minutes earlier. This time, she wasn't alone.

In her left hand were the keys, and in her right hand was a piece of rope leading to...

'Despoena!' Mae screeched, running up to the Pegasus. She took the piece of rope out of her mouth and gave her a tight squeeze. 'Oh boy, I'm glad you're alive!'

Despoena whinnied and nuzzled into Mae in return. The Pegasus looked back at Rodger, Canada and me. She took a few cautious steps over to us and opened one of her wings.

Underneath it was a jar full of a moving light-green wind.

Rodger gawped. 'Oh. My. Gosh.'

Mae, my sister and I were oblivious of what was happening for the first few seconds. We hadn't a clue as to what was going on. And then Rodger told us.

'Why are you guys looking so confused?' he grinned, astonished. 'Do you not realise what's going on? Despoena took...'

He caught himself and shut his mouth tight.

'What?' Khloe innocently questioned. 'Is there a problem? Or would you like to take your pal and go to wherever you're going? You're on a quest, huh? Nobody else visits unless they live or work here.'

An awkward silence struck us all. Were we to let Khloe know for sure we were on a quest? What if she became suspicious and tried to stop us? We couldn't obviously say we were here for a tropical vacay or something.

'Erm...' Rodger murmured. He nudged me and I beckoned him to break the news. 'Yes, we're so sorry. Go on. Do whatever it takes to destroy us. Get it over with' he bluffed.

Khloe slowly nodded, and for a second I thought she was serious. 'We can use the incinerator?'

Rodger went pale. 'Uhh...'

'Bahahaha!' Khloe spat. 'You thought I was serious? I'm actually over the moon you're on a quest! Well, you better — wait for it — trot on! Badum-ching!'

I heard a forehead slap as well as a tut.

'No? Okay — good luck, fellas! I wish you could stay, but unfortunately, you canter!'

'Actually, stop now,' I implored.

Khloe shrugged awkwardly. 'For the last time, b'bye!'

It was easy going up in the lift, as we knew to hold onto the handrails this time. At least no one screamed or screeched — just a few groans (cough, Mae, cough).

In a flash, we were out of the dungeons, ready to mount Despoena. Then we noticed a problem. A big problem.

'Um, guys?' Rodger said, once Canada, Mae and I had already climbed onto Despoena. 'There's no space for me.'

'Uh-oh,' Canada mumbled.

However, Mae looked delighted. 'You can hang onto her tail! It'll be fun seeing you swing and maybe fall — swoosh, swoosh, aaah!'

Annoyed, I rolled my eyes. 'Let's be serious. Who's the slimmest here?'

'We've done this before,' Mae grumbled.

There were a few arguments and weight swapping, but in the end, we decided Canada was the thinnest.

'Then me,' I proudly declared. 'Then Rodger, then…'

'Me,' Mae grumbled. 'I knew it would end like this. "Ooh, Mae's the fattest!" and "Look how big she is!" I'm used to people picking on me, though. It's — it's fine.'

'Oh, Mae, we didn't mean it that way!' Rodger offered, surprisingly.

We were all taken aback a bit, thinking no way had he just said that. Until Rodger said…

'It's Despoena, then you, silly!' he chuckled.

Oh. It was too good to be true. Rodger comforting Mae. It was so impossible to imagine, dreams would refuse to make it happen.

Mae, the victim, slowly clapped her hands. 'Ha-ha-ha. Very funny. Now let's go, OK? Come on, Dessy!'

* * *

But Despoena remained glued to the ground. Her wings were stuck to her body as if someone had superglued them together.

308

'Erm…' Canada murmured. 'Despoena? Yoo-hoo!' She waved her hand in front of Despoena.

Suddenly, she started whinnying and stamping her hooves on the ground. It was like she was being abused, like a rope was tied around her neck, strangling her.

'This is not normal,' Mae whispered, her look anxious.

Rodger gulped. 'We figured.'

I frantically looked around, determined to find what was spooking Despoena so much.

'I don't have a clue about what's going on, but it can't be good,' I whispered. Holding Despoena by the snout, I said, 'Please, Dessy, stop. C'mon, quick, get us outta here.'

Mae stepped forwards. 'Quick, move, let me tr — oh, no, no, no!'

Despoena's knees had buckled and she had collapsed on the ground.

'What — did — you — do?' Rodger growled through gritted teeth.

'It wasn't me, I swear!' Mae gasped, raising her hands. Then her face brightened and her hands fell. 'I have an idea!'

Before anyone could ask, she had whipped open the backpack full of potions and was looking through it.

After a few seconds, she stood back up, holding a glass bottle full of purple, bubbling liquid.

'#012 - Regeneration/Healing Potion! It must work on animals!'

Canada raised her eyebrows. 'And if it doesn't?'

'Then we're all stuck here for eternity.' Mae looked definite about this life-threatening choice, despite her statement. 'Guys, it's worth a try. This is our ticket...' Mae looked up from Despoena. 'out...'

Once we'd all followed her gaze, we knew why she was so surprised.

All the time we'd been hurriedly watching Mae's attempt to cure the Pegasus, we didn't realise a silent and near-invisible army was building up directly in front of us.

Hundreds upon hundreds of souls were lined up, the strongest looking at the front. They were all armed with transparent shields in their right hand, some spotless, some stained. I couldn't detect the colour of the stains, but there was no denying what it was.

In their right hands were the deadliest objects of all. Swords, spears, daggers, pole arms — name any weapon and you'd find it in the hands of a soul.

'Look, there's Rachael!' Rodger whispered, pointing left.

He was right. Rachael, our Escorter, was near the front, even though she was as mighty as a chipmunk. She was holding a pitchfork, and what was most highly disturbing was that a gloopy substance was leaking from one of the prongs.

'Don't tell me that's...'

'Horse dung,' we all said simultaneously.

At the front of all the souls was the one and only, the man himself, Master Sosiri, holding nothing but his staff and a murderous look on his face.

What is going on? I thought, my heart racing.

'Mae, give Despoena the potion,' I said out of the corner of my mouth. 'We'll distract them...'

Mae quickly spun around to nurse Despoena.

'Aww, little horsey need a bandage?' Master Sosiri mocked, imitating a baby voice. Which was impossible, by the way, seeing as his voice was as deep as a full-grown lion's. 'You foolish children have no idea what you walked right in on.'

'Oh yeah?' I said, trying to sound as casual as possible. 'Apocalypse!'

Everyone stared as my staff zoomed towards me. I smiled and tilted my head.

'Not so reassured now, eh?' It was my time to mimic him. 'Masterw Sosirwi thinks he's a superhewo?'

311

I observed his mouth twitch a bit, but he resisted frowning. 'There are no superheroes, you foolish child! I heard that you weak little humans read storybooks about them? No, I am much more than a superhero. You see, I am an ex-deity.'

I couldn't stop my mouth from dropping open. 'You? You were a deity?'

'Hm, quite astounding news, I see. Well, there we are then.'

'But...' Rodger's voice muttered. 'But Ms Pinnacle never told us th...'

I shot him a furious look.

'Uh, Ms Pinnacle never told us anything. Like, who is Ms Pinnacle?'

Rodger had drawn attention to himself. I didn't think Master Sosiri had noticed that his Soul Keeper had turned sides, but he was bound to now.

'Ah, Rodger,' Master Sosiri hissed softly. 'My one and only man... I see you have turned on me?'

Rodger gulped. 'Erm...'

'Do not waste your breath,' he continued, wagging a dismissive finger. 'Your loyalty is still with me, I see, as you have just handed me the purest of information. Puyew Ms Pinnacle johac.'

Ms Pinnacle appeared abruptly at Master Sosiri's side. Her expression changed from relieved to horror-struck in a matter of seconds.

'I see you have managed to hide your jar so you would not be brought out to war,' Master Sosiri hissed. 'Is this true?'

Ms Pinnacle trembled, before saying, 'No, Lord.'

Master Sosiri smiled. 'The only way to move your jar somewhere else is for someone to have let you out. Which, conveniently, we have proof of.'

Ms Pinnacle shot us all a dangerous look. Mae pretended to still be nursing Despoena, even though we all knew the potion had been used; I could sense her rising.

'H — h — how is that so?' Ms Pinnacle murmured. 'Lord,' she added.

'Your friends here,' Master Sosiri waved a vague hand at the lot of us, 'have kindly lent me that information.'

Ms Pinnacle let out a gasp. 'They — they wouldn't...'

'So you do know them?' Master Sosiri, stated triumphantly. 'My dear, you are supposed to be the smartest of all souls.'

This riled Ms Pinnacle. 'I stand by that. Lord.'

'If you were so smart,' the man whispered, leaning forward, 'then why didn't you see... this.'

With one thud of his staff, Ms Pinnacle began turning to ash, her legs first.

'Argh!' she cried, obviously in agonising pain.

Rodger ran forward, but I held him back.

313

'Fourth on the right!' she screamed. 'Fourth on the right...'

Ash. All that was left of Ms Pinnacle was grey, lifeless ash.

Looking up from the dust, I shouted. 'You filthy...'

I lifted my staff and bashed it on the ground, as Master Sosiri had done, simultaneously yelling, 'Evicto!'

The whole area pulsed and vibrated. You could see the air.

Then, out of the blue, the forgotten souls and Master Sosiri were pushed back; many fell onto their backs, some collapsed to their knees. Only the front line and Master Sosiri stayed standing.

'You want to play it that way, then?' he whispered. 'For Feldo Forgott!'

Ah, he had a battle cry. Wonderful. If I had a phone, I would've quickly pulled it out to say my last goodbyes.

'FOR FELDO FORGOTT!' everyone else yelled, "charging" towards us — although they weren't running at full speed, but doing some sort of marching routine. We had time to think.

Fourth on the right, I thought. What could that have meant? The fourth door on the right? I mean, there was one, don't laugh at me.

314

'Of course!' Canada whispered. 'It's a body part! The fourth on the right!'

But I didn't have any time to properly process this, as the forgotten souls were raising their weapons.

'How do we...?'

'Think!' I urged myself. 'Nurogonia is the place of dreams, you can get there by thoughts. Think — it'll come to you!'

'Katropolis!' Canada cried. Her white staff came zooming towards her.

'Dreamatizer!' Mae screamed, and her staff came floating to her as well.

Canada yelled. 'Hayden, I see something! My staff — it's the eye, the Future! I see Rachael — she's going to stab you with her pitchfork if you don't...'

'Oblivitot Rachael!' I hollered, thrashing my staff on the ground. I heard her yell as she was knocked down, clearly unconscious.

'Nice one!' Mae said.

'No time for compliments!' I retorted, concentrating on my surroundings. 'Give us a shout if you see anything, Canada!'

I dodged out of the way as a nunchaku missed my ear by inches.

'Rodger, watch out!' Canada shouted.

Oh no, I thought. Rodger has no —

But my thoughts were promptly interrupted as Rodger cried, 'Hollostius!'

A smaller version of Master Sosiri's staff found its way to Rodger's outstretched arm.

'Craterok!'

I watched, awestruck, as small holes appeared at random. The holes appeared underneath a few souls, causing them to fall through into deep craters.

This caused Master Sosiri to start a murderous rampage. He looked mad.

'Cloudito!' Mae yelled, bashing her staff twice.

The cloud on top of her staff detached itself, expanded and hovered over many souls.

'Lightnos!'

This incant made the cloud above the souls strike with lightning. Many of them fell, their eyes rolled and they didn't get back up.

'I don't believe it,' Mae whispered, astonished.

'What I do believe is that there's a spear heading straight for us all!' Canada cried. 'Duck!'

Once we had all resurfaced, I took a step forward, in front of everybody else.

Fourth on the right... Canada had said it was a body part. I was thinking fingers or toes.

'It's his fourth toe on the right!' I yelled. He's got those boots to cover it up! Aim for his fourth toe on the right!'

A blast of light was speeding towards us. It looked like a spark from a distance, but the closer it got, the clearer it became. Fire. If that hit us, we'd all be toast!

'Obstrupt!' I said, hammering Apocalypse down three times.

A forcefield wound its way around us. It was yellow, glittering and purposeful — it seemed as though the line of fire merely rebounded off it — straight for Sosiri...

With a tap of his staff, the fire stopped and fell to nothing but ash.

Master Sosiri looked at his nails with a look of disinterest. 'Oh, sorry, are we still fighting?'

I grunted. 'This forcefield won't last long. I doubt he can hear us in here, but we need to be quiet just in case. Rodger and Canada, you aim for his toes. I'm pretty sure that when Ms Pinnacle said "fourth on the right" she meant a body part, and it can only be fingers or toes. Mae and I will go for his fingers. You guys are doing really well; I don't know how this is all coming to me. When he's down, we jump on Despoena. She's up to full health now, Mae?'

'Y — yes, she is,' Mae said, not looking me in the eye. She was shaking from head to toe.

'Quick, the forcefield is faltering. Remember what I've said.'

As the circle around us died away, we all leapt into action at once.

'Destructo!' Rodger yelled. One thrash of his staff and the front of Master Sosiri's shoe was blown off.

'Oblivitot fourth toe, right foot!' Canada shouted.

Weird thing to say, but it worked. Master Sosiri's fourth toe on his right foot was sliced off. Blood was dripping out of the hole at the front of his boot.

'Agh!' he cried. But other than that, he showed no more evidence of pain.

'Not it!' Rodger whimpered. 'Not it!'

'Obstrupt right hand!' Master Sosiri yelled — an obvious giveaway.

A mini-forcefield came to shape, wrapping itself around his right hand. Master Sosiri quickly swapped his staff to his left hand.

The forcefield was black, and it looked stronger than ever. I could see the power it held.

'The stronger the force, the harder to repel,' a woman's voice said. I turned around. Mae was looking straight ahead, a malicious glint in her eye. The voice was deep, calm and correct as it spoke again. 'It is me — Bravy.'

Mae looked at us all. 'I have temporarily possessed the spirit of Mae Amber Greens, a young girl with a fruitful mind and an adventurous temper. She does not know this, but I hope I am correct in assuming that you will inform her. I am a former warrior of Nurogonia — the best, they say. I am human too but have been graciously gifted with the powers of a deity, although I am not officially one. Hayden, you were born with a true talent that needs to be used. I am not permitted to tell you how to do this, but delve into your deepest thoughts — the most sorrowful — and you will save all of your friends.'

Mae shook her head and stared blankly at us all. 'What? Wait, did I...'

'No time to explain,' I said breathlessly.

'Hayden, quick!' Canada said with anxiety etched into every syllable.

I tried to think of something deep, something meaningful, but nothing came to me.

'I — I can't do it,' I told them.

'Do what?' Mae persisted, looking irate.

Rodger sighed. 'Later!'

Master Sosiri was advancing on us, his staff raised.

'Distract him!' I whispered. 'Put him off me for a bit!'

'Eyeosok!' Canada said, thrashing her staff down again.

The eye on top of her staff blinked. It looked ugly, blank and pointless until its pupil popped out. I mean, it was still mega ugly, but what happened next wasn't.

The pupil rose into the sky and flipped like a coin; when it faced the correct way again, it was the sun. It came tumbling down, landing right in the middle of the soul army as a ball of fire. Many immediately turned to ash, but some managed to escape with a lost leg or arm at most.

'Yes, you're the Katropolis,' Master Sosiri hissed. 'I sensed one in my midst.'

'Well, oh greatest-most-powerful-Lord-of-dung-beetles, I did scream it out loud at one point, didn't I?'

Despite the circumstances, Canada's sarcasm still managed to squeeze its way in.

'Respect your elders, you foolish child,' Master Sosiri hissed through gritted teeth.

Canada shrugged. 'If setting them on fire counts as "respecting your elders," job done, innit?'

'Argh! Crate...'

I thought of an image of Mum, thin and blotchy with tears, fainting every so often. I imagined her holding Canada for support, crying endlessly.

I thought of Dad, chugging a beer, his eyes bloodshot and his appearance drowsy.

I imagined Canada, at school, leaning against a locker as she always does, skipping meals and her classes.

Just as Master Sosiri was about to use the same incant that Rodger had, I yelled back, 'Demonisho!'

The air went stiff. You could almost see the tension etched in it. Everything was silent. Everything was still.

There was a crack. It took me a second to notice that the forcefield around Master Sosiri's right hand was breaking into shards on the ground.

He tried frantically to repair it. He tried using incants that I believed were not real. But nothing worked. Soon, every shard of the forcefield was gone.

I knew what to do. Gripping my staff tightly, I lifted it and gave it a soft tap on the ground.

Master Sosiri looked down at his finger. It was splitting, a zigzagging cut was making its way vertically down it. The fourth finger on the right hand.

'No, NO, NO!' he cried. 'Healoptis! Curekulos! Mendoptus!'

'I'm sorry,' I said softly. 'There's no stopping it.'

Master Sosiri gave me one last, killer look. 'You, Hayden, will meet me again. And next time, you will not live to tell the tale...'

With a dazzling and sparkling white light, he was gone.

The remaining souls all looked at each other.

'M — Master did not give us a "Plan B" in case this happened,' one trembled.

'I have a sugge... a suggestion,' another muttered. 'Run!'

All the souls headed for the castle or the dungeons.

This left Mae, Canada, Rodger and me.

No one spoke for a while.

Then Mae muttered, 'Yay,' and collapsed.

We bundled Mae and ourselves onto Despoena in what felt like the first time in forever and shot upward.

Twenty

Nurogonia, Sweet Nurogonia

*A*fter a while, we swooped below the clouds as none of us wanted to lose our lungs. There was just enough room for us to squeeze into. I was happy with my space since I could clutch onto my sister. The way Despoena flew wasn't going to make anyone fall off anyway: she either went straight, left, right and backwards; no abrupt turns or loop-the-loops, fortunately.

'I'm so tired, I hope it's a long journey,' Canada muttered, yawning. 'I don't want to go over what's just happened, please let me sleep. 'I've got it, Rodger murmured as if someone was lurking behind us. Everyone was so shocked about the recent events that they couldn't fall asleep, or so exhausted that they wanted to sleep. Well, Mae already was. And, on top of that, we hadn't retrieved the soul we were supposed to retrieve — Viabe. She was still inside one of those jars, enclosed. Plus, Despoena had picked up a stray soul on the way.

'I've got it' Rodger piped up, but no-one bothered to respond.

'I said I've got it!' he repeated a little louder.

We all looked back at him, annoyed.

Mae sat up and rubbed her eyes. 'W — what's going on?'

Finally, Canada (obviously irritated) grumbled, 'What do you mean?'

Slowly but surely, Rodger raised a jar containing a green cloud — similar to the one Despoena had stolen.

Great. Now we have two thieves.

Unnervingly, Mae squealed with delight and nearly gave Rodger a hug.

Quickly, she retracted her hands. 'I was getting a bit ahead of myself there! Um — well, thanks a bunch, you saved our butts.'

Canada and I were trying to figure out what was occurring. My brain kept telling me the same thing: Mae overexcited, green jar equals ERROR!

'So you...' I took a pause. 'You stole it?'

Mae and Rodger fell into hysterics while I and Canada sat looking like a deer caught in headlights.

'Do you not understand?' Rodger spluttered breathlessly. 'Th — that is the last puzzle piece! We've finished the quest! Viabe — the one and only Viabe — is in this jar!'

At first, we didn't believe him and told them to stop messing around. But they were one-hundred-and-one per cent sure the two of them were right.

'Just wait till Nurogonia becomes magical all over again!' Mae childishly screamed.

Rodger was also eagerly nodding his head. 'I can't wait! Oh, how satisfying will that be? Watching Nurogonia ripple back to its old days. Aaah...'

'Aaah...' Mae echoed dreamily.

'And all that time you let us think we'd failed the quest?' I was livid. 'And you made us think we had to go through a whole showdown for nothing?'

'How on earth did you manage that?' Canada insisted. 'We were with you the whole time!'

'I do have my ways and uses,' Rodger replied, mischievously. 'I couldn't risk you lot knowing whilst we were in Feldo Forgutt.'

'But you work for The Almighty Master Terrorist of Nurogonia's Attacks!' Canada exclaimed. 'Why are you celebrating?'

'You don't know an itsy-bitsy thing about Nurogonia yourself!' Mae smirked. 'So why are you complaining about history you know nothing about?'

Canada turned red. 'I — I...'

Rolling my eyes, I ordered everyone to shush until we got to our destination.

Thankfully, everyone did.

* * *

'Are you ready Wembley?' Rodger shouted.

We looked a sight: four teenagers striding up a wooden bridge talking to about four people who were listening. The others either screamed and ran for the hills, or tutted and cursed under their breath.

'Say "thanks" to your saviours!' Rodger boastfully cried. 'Ring the bells! And most importantly... can one of you get me a cup of tea, please?'

'Rodger!' We all grunted in embarrassment.

The air was cold. Our surroundings were silent.

326

'Woohoo,' someone half-heartedly called.

And then, out of the blue, there was a single clap. Then another. Six Nurogons turned the corner and walked onto the bridge we were standing on.

The bridge became full with them, rows and rows of Nurogons excitedly trying to get to the front.

I looked at Rodger, who looked at Mae, who looked at Canada, who looked at the crowd and coughed. The rest of us urged her to say something whilst we tried to brush ourselves down or tidy up our uncombed hair.

'Uh...' Canada started.

She looked at me for advice. I smiled and gave her the thumbs-up to continue.

'Hello, all!' she shouted.

Multiple "hoorays" came from the assembled Nurogons. That's probably what encouraged Canada to speak up, keep her head high and carry on.

'My name is Canada. This is Mae... whom you probably know?'

Mae gave a little wave.

'... and Rodger...'

Rodger gave a funny salute.

'And, again, someone you also probably know — last but least,' she said cheekily. 'Well, I say that, but if it wasn't for my brother, we wouldn't be here right now. Yeah, he sure is pretty annoying, but I'm proud to say... my brother Hayden!'

I gave a nervous laugh and bowed grandly.

My sister nodded to me to take her place, and I was more than happy to.

'Hello! Um, as my sister told you, I'm Hayden! We will get to the point soon, but first I'm gonna tell you one of those extremely long sappy stories.'

An exaggerated sigh came from the crowd.

'Yeah, sorry. Nah, I'm kidding. I'll make this short and straight to the point, because I know I'm excited about what's gonna happen next, even though I'm not so sure about it. Anyways, these past few days have been — weird, there's no denying it. We weren't prepared for anything that happened at all, but we got through it. And, yes, in case you're wondering, we did put our staffs to good use.'

'Can I have one?' a smaller Nurogon giggled. I was reminded painfully of Botilda.

'Aw, sorry, chap, but I'm sure there will be more to come from us and our staffs. This is our first quest, but I'm certain it's not the last!'

Energised cheering emerged from the Nurogons. Some were even repeating prayers in their language as if their tongue was on fire.

'And, if I do say so myself, we're getting quite good at the whole quest thing. And I am sure you will all be delighted to hear that I, Hayden Smith, conquered Master Sosiri.'

A few seconds of silence echoed around the area. Then Nurogons started cheering and whistling and clapping and high-fouring. More were shouting praises to all of us and some bowed. Whatever they were doing, they were happy.

'But now, this is why we started are quest. Rodger here — also known as my brother from another mother — has a jar. Not just any jar, but — well, why don't we see for ourselves?'

Rodger rummaged around in a backpack planted next to his feet, and after a few awkward seconds of coughing and apologising for the wait, he brought out the jackpot.

'I present to you,' I said slowly and grandly, 'the token of peace!'

This was it. The moment of truth. Rodger held the jar, breathed three times and turned the lid cautiously.

Immense tension filled the air. Was it going to work? Had we come all this way for nothing?

Boom!

An incredibly strong wind threw everyone off their feet and the ground shook.

'Take cover!' Mae screamed.

329

It all happened so quickly.

Everyone was screaming and yelling and trying to find shelter as if it was an air raid.

The shaking lasted for half a minute — or expressed more accurately, half a minute of everyone crying out loud and grabbing onto whoever or whatever they could!

Once it stopped, everyone looked around. The place was a wreck. Bits of the huts had broken away to reveal small families huddling inside. Some of the huts were perfectly fine, but pieces of the wood used to build the bridge had come apart to reveal the rock-filled water that lay beneath. The bridge was well constructed and thick, so, fortunately, no Nurogons had ever been killed crossing it, but now many of the Nurogons were hopping from side to side, frantically trying to make it back to their families.

'What — what have we done?' Canada shrieked in shock.

We saw one Nurogon looking to the sky and gasping, then another, and soon dozens were shouting at the sky.

We all looked up.

'Is that...' I gawped.

A green silhouette floated high above. It was a lady — a pretty one too — with long, tousled hair. A flower crown was planted on top of her head. It had pink cornflowers surrounding it, as well as daisies and mint.

Then I realised, the lady's full colour was coming into view. She had dark brown hair with the same coloured freckles. She appeared to be in her twenties, yet her presence made me feel like I'd seen her in my history book. Her light-green dress passed her knees, embroidered with real flowers of many kinds. And to top it off, she had sandals decorated with pink alyssums. I knew they weren't artificial because I saw plenty of bees hopping on and off of them.

'At last, the quest-comers,' she whispered gracefully.

Every Nurogon bowed or curtseyed, so we did the same.

'Your majesty!' someone gasped. 'Your presence is apprecia...'

'Thank you kindly, sir. But can I ask one thing of you?'

Everyone cheered in delight and nodded in awe. Some shouted words of praise, others bowed their heads once again.

Viabe grinned smugly, and for a second, I wondered what was behind that beautiful, flowery facade.

'Here are my terms,' she started. 'I will repair your world. You will make me your queen and call me Lady Viabe. Nurogi and Corptu will assume subordinate positions. If you do not agree, I will continually destroy your lands, no matter how many times you rebuild them.'

Character Descriptions

𝓗ayden Smith – A thirteen-year-old teenage boy with dark brown hair styled in a regular cut, brown eyes and light freckles. His go-to colour is black, including his favourite pair of black trainers.

Canada Smith – Hayden's Sister. A sharp-tongued fifteen-year-old with beige-blond hair which she normally ties up in a loose ponytail. Like most teenage girls, she seems not to be able to stand Hayden until crunch time. She has light blue eyes. Canada's go to look is girly tops, blue jeans and white Converse.

𝓜ae – A girl Hayden meets in Nurogonia. She has a mop of curly, ginger hair that falls down most of her back, green eyes and lots of freckles. Mae and

Canada barely get along which makes for a lot more "fun" on the quests. Mae loves the colour green and normally wears a vibrant purple T-shirt covered by a lime green fleece. You can just about see the T-shirt through the unzipped top of her fleece.

Rodger – Hayden's best mate has shaggy hair that's a deep shade of black. He has dark brown eyes and likes to wear black, like Hayden. His character presents a surprise on the quest.

Nurogons: Are strong four-fingered, two-toed, freckled muddy green creatures about the size of a toddler. They have long dark green nails, green eyes, sloping noses, big white teeth, hunched backs, and large chins under which are several folds of skin! Clusters of hair can be seen on the top of their heads, the tips of their large Pinnochio-Esque ears and the tip of their tails, and they have shaggy sideburns. They are often seen wearing a white toga with a red sash and sporting a weird smile! Tuck in and you will find some very interesting Nurogon characters

Lord Nurogi – He lives in a fabulous temple made of gold and had once looked like a regular Nurogon, but following his coronation to become 'Lord' of all of Nurogonia, he has since worn a small crown and a gold-lined toga. He has also gone grey.

Nurogonia – The land of Nurogonia used to be a magical place, with cherry blossom trees, clear walkways, and beautiful wildlife - but a turn of events caused it to become a horrible place. There is now a shallow but rocky pool of water across the entire bottom of Nurogonia, over which bridges have been built to get about. The bridges are shaped like a cross with four separate bridges running out from the centre to go north, south, east, and west. Alongside the bridges on stilts are huts in which the Nurogons live, work, and shop.

About the Author

Aiyven Mbawa is a ten-year-old Year 6 pupil, and one half of the famed Mbawa Book Reviewers duo. A keenly avid reader and book reviewer, *Land of the Nurogons* is her debut fantasy adventure novel. Will it become a series — who knows? Aiyven lives in Northamptonshire in the United Kingdom where she was born. She lives with her parents, two other sisters and pet cat Zaki. In her spare time, Aiyven attends drama lessons, learns Mandarin, participates in gymnastics, and plays tennis and the piano!

Connect with the Mbawa Book Reviewers by following the social media links below, or search Mbawa Book Reviewers on YouTube YouTube—Don't forget to subscribe!

You can connect with me on:

🌐 http//mbawabooks.co.uk

📘 https//www.facebook.com/mbawabookreviewers

📷 https//www.instagram.com/mbawabookreviewers

🐦 https//twitter.com/mbawabookreview

Subscribe to my newsletter:

✉ http://mbawabooks.co.uk